MICHAEL CONNOLLY

GUNSHOTS

Fidelis ad Mortem series: Book 1

A New Vision Books paperback

First published in the USA in 2013
By New Vision Books
This paperback edition published in 2013
By New Vision Books Ltd.

Reissued 2013
Copyright@ 2013 New Vision Books Inc.

If you would like to be added onto the mailing list for future releases
then email:

newvisionbooks@hotmail.com

Contents

Chapter 1

Johnson sweated beside his wife, tossing and turning, reliving the nightmare of 9/11. As always he was in the stairwell of the South Tower when the building collapsed. Dust engulfed his dreams, choking him, making him gasp for breath. Then, his phone rang. A distant echo trying to waken him. He clutched at the sound like a drowning man and rose to the surface. Drenched in sweat, he lay there, panicked, thinking he was trapped underneath the rubble. After a couple of seconds he realized where he was. At home. In bed. Safe. Relief flooding through him, he snatched up his cell before it could waken his wife Jane.

"Hello," he said, a slight tremor in his voice.

"Detective Johnson?"

Johnson recognized the voice. It was the aging Desk Sergeant from his Precinct. William Clark. Or Gums as he was better known because of the way he ate his food minus his false teeth. Those he left on the counter.

"What's up Gums?" he asked.

"A body's been found on 10th Avenue," he said. "Yourself and Detective Abramo have the lead."

"Did you ring him yet?"

"No, I was just about to."

"Then tell him I'll pick him up in twenty minutes."

"Okay, will do," said Gums.

Johnson knocked his phone off and checked his watch. 2.32am. Rolling onto his side he looked at his wife. Even in the gloom he could tell that her eyes were open.

"You going?" she asked.

"Yeah," he said.

"I hate this," she replied then to emphasize her dislike she turned away from him.

Johnson laid his hand on her upper arm and gave it a gentle squeeze.

"Sorry love," he said.

"Just go."

Used to his wife's moods Johnson climbed out of bed and dressed quickly. Strapping on his shoulder holster he pulled on his jacket then opened the top drawer of his bedside cabinet. Inside was his gun. A Glock 19. Standard issue for the NYPD. He picked it up and slipped it into place underneath his left armpit then lifted out his handcuffs and shoved them into his pocket. Now fully dressed he tiptoed across the wooden floor lest he wake any of his daughters: Rachel, Amy or Rebecca: His three angels. Outside the bedroom he relaxed as the floor was carpeted and muffled the sound of his shoes. He walked down the stairs into the kitchen and switched on the light. When his eyes re-adjusted to the sudden glare he stepped over to the fridge and grabbed out an apple. After three big bites he threw it in the bin and left the house.

Outside he got into the unmarked police car that sat in his driveway. An old Ford Fusion with plenty of miles on the clock it had seen better days. For that reason Johnson had been pestering his Lieutenant for a newer model but with the recession in full throttle she'd repeatedly told him "No". He had to "make do". He turned the key in the ignition then because a light rain had begun to fall he switched on the wipers. Using his rear view mirrors he reversed out on to the street then straightened up and tuned the radio in to WBAI, his favorite station. Adele's 'Someone like you' was playing. As he liked it he turned it up then pressed his foot down on the accelerator and drove out of the street.

Within minutes he was on 11th Avenue heading towards the remnants of Little Italy to pick up Abramo. Impatient, he sped past the Ardesia Wine bar, the lampposts on either side casting giant, black fingers across the road. As he drove along he wondered who tonight's victim would be. A male? A female? Someone young? Someone old? In his mind he prayed for anything other than a child. After ten years as a homicide Detective he still got affected when a young innocent was killed. Always imagined what it would be like to lose one of his own children. Even now, thinking about it sent a shiver down his spine so he pushed the thoughts away and concentrated on listening to the music.

When he reached Little Italy he was amazed at how much the area had changed over the years. Once a thriving hotbed of Italian culture the area was now predominantly Chinese with 'Little Italy' now an Italian restaurant area down Mulberry and Grand. But even there Chinese advertisements peppered the sidewalk. Gone were the days of the Gambino crime family and people speaking Italian in the narrow streets. Now, 'Little Italy' was no more than a nostalgic memory in the minds of tourists who still had it as a must-see on their itinerary list. As he drove along Johnson glanced at a poster announcing celebrations for the Lunar New Year.

"Littler Italy," he said to himself as he pulled up outside Abramo's apartment. He checked his watch. Far too late to honk the horn. 2.51am. Instead, he prized his cell phone off the hands free bracket and gave his partner a ring. Abramo answered immediately. When he spoke he kept his voice low so as not to waken his wife and son.

"Be out now Joe," he said.

A minute later Abramo exited the apartment pulling on his jacket. After he closed the front door he hunched his wide shoulders to ward off the drizzle and crept up the pathway. At the top he opened the gate

6

as slowly and silently as he could then tiptoed across and got into the car.

"Have to be quiet," he explained. "Little Angelo's asleep."

Johnson nodded. The last time he'd seen Angelo had been at his fifth birthday party three months before in the Mulberry. At the time Abramo had performed as a magician with the children at the party loving his act, especially when Abramo escaped from a set of handcuffs Johnson had clamped onto his wrists. Later, Abramo explained it was accomplished with the use of a real handcuff key that he'd curled into a ring before slipping onto his finger.

Abramo rolled his window down then opened the glove compartment. Inside was the siren. He pulled it out, connected the lead to the lighter socket and stuck it on the roof. When his partner pulled his arm back in Johnson pressed his foot down hard on the accelerator.

"You still moonlighting doing security Sal?" he asked as they raced along.

"Have to Joe if I want my kids to go to college. Twenty thousand dollars to get into Columbia which'll be forty thousand for Angelo and Teresa."

"Teresa?"

"My little girl that's on the way."

"You know already?"

"Curiosity was killing us. We had to find out," said Abramo.

"A gentleman's family," said Johnson.

"What's that?" asked Abramo. "I've never heard that before."

"A son and a daughter. It's called a gentleman's family."

Abramo beamed at this.

"Yeah," he said. "That's me. A gentleman."

Johnson smiled himself. Abramo might only be joking but as far as he was concerned his partner truly was a gentleman. From the hairs on his head to the soles of his feet. Abramo turned to him, all seriousness now.

"We want you to be Godfather Joe," he said.

Johnson was taken aback.

"Serious?" he asked swiveling to look at his partner.

"Of course I'm serious Joe," said Abramo. "You're practically family."

"But sure I'm a Mick, is that allowed?"

"Course it's allowed."

"Then I accept," said Johnson. "Thanks Sal...I'm blown away buddy."

"No Joe, thank you. I'm honored that you'll do it."

Chapter 2

Johnson drove along delighted that he'd been asked. On the radio Bon Jovi's 'You give love a bad name' started playing. As the song brought back memories for Johnson he turned it up.

"Didn't know you liked Bon Jovi Joe," said Abramo.

Johnson glanced at the horizontal scar on the palm of his right hand.

"Grew up on him," he said. "Used to have the perm and everything."

As they raced along icy crosswinds battered angrily at the car, making the two detectives glad to be ensconced in the confines of the Ford Fusion where it was hot and dry. As the rain had stopped Johnson knocked the wipers off.

Thanks to the late hour and the near empty roads they made it to 10th Avenue inside fifteen minutes. At the police cordon a Patrolman raised the yellow crime scene tape and they drove under.

Inside the perimeter Johnson looked around for somewhere to park. Spotting a space behind a police cruiser he bumped up onto the pavement behind it then got out and looked around. Already, ten uniforms were present at the crime scene. Johnson locked the car then stepped over to Hank Halbrook, a Sergeant from his Precinct. Hank, an older man in his mid fifties, was busy reciting his shield number to a Patrolman with the duty of listing those present at the crime scene. After Johnson had his own presence recorded he turned to Hank.

"The Medical Examiner here yet?" he asked.

"No, but he's on his way," Hank replied.

It was standard procedure to wait on the Medical Examiner to declare the victim deceased. Only when he was pronounced dead and a time of death given could the investigation begin. Johnson glanced around taking in his surroundings. Houses on either side of the road had windows directly above where the body had been found.

"Has anyone started canvassing the area?" he asked.

Hank shook his head.

"No Joe," he said. "We were waiting for you to arrive."

"Okay, at seven o'clock Hank I want you and two other officers rapping the doors of these houses backing onto the crime scene. With a bit of luck someone might have seen something. When you're finished just leave the Canvass Sheets with the Desk Sergeant at the Precinct. I'll get them at eleven when I'm on my way back in."

"Will do Joe."

"Who got here first?" Johnson asked.

"Kelly."

Johnson scanned the vicinity searching for Kelly. He was standing at the crime scene tape with his arms folded staring up at the sky. Johnson crossed over to him.

"Who called it in?" he asked.

"A girl called Kathleen Rice. She's in the back of the Impala," said Kelly hooking a thumb over his shoulder.

"Okay, thanks," said Johnson already beginning to turn.

When he opened the back door and peered in, a pair of frightened eyes stared back at him.

"Don't be alarmed Ma'am," he said. "I'm Detective Johnson, the investigating officer."

When the woman continued to look scared Johnson gave her a friendly smile.

"I'm just letting you know Ma'am that I'll be with you shortly," he said.

"I just want to get a quick look at the crime scene so that I know what I'm dealing with first. Is that okay?"

The woman nodded but didn't answer so Johnson shut the door and went back to his partner.

"Time to suit up," he said.

Understanding what he meant Abramo pulled a pair of white latex gloves out of his pocket. Simultaneously they slipped them on. As Johnson adjusted his, a wine stain on his right sleeve reminded him that a visit to the drycleaners was necessary.

Together they crossed the road to the corpse lying amongst the bushes. It was a man with his arms flung out behind him and his head tilted sideways. The first thing Johnson noticed were the eyes. Dark brown they stared vacantly at some distant point whilst the man's tongue, a mottled purple, protruded like a rotted plum. Next, Johnson noticed that the man's shirt was bunched up around his chest revealing a hairy, toned midriff. If nothing else he thought, the victim had kept himself in shape before he'd been murdered. At first glance he judged the man to be in his early thirties. Taking a small notebook out of his jacket pocket he poked out the tiny pen that was stuck through the spiral then crouched down on his haunches.

"He was definitely dumped here," he said.

Abramo, who'd also squatted down, nodded in agreement.

"Looks like he was dragged along by the feet," he said. "Look at how the arms are flung out behind him."

"Yeah, shirt's up around his chest, another indicator," said Johnson then he peered closer at the dead man's skin.

Whitish-grey it had a translucent quality caused by the rain that had fallen earlier. He moved his eyes upward to study the entry wound on the left side of the head just above the ear. Small and dark it looked innocuous compared to the gaping exit wound on the opposite side. He

9

leant in close. This time he noticed that the hairs around the entry wound had been burnt away, caused by the close up contact of the gun barrel being pressed directly against the head. There was also stippling on the skin caused by the explosion of the gunpowder.

"Entry wound above the left ear," he said. "Execution style."

Then he moved around and examined the exit wound. Whilst he'd seen numerous gunshot wounds during his time in Iraq and in the police it never ceased to amaze him the damage a single bullet could do.

"Took half his head away," he said.

Abramo nodded solemnly.

"Probably a soft nosed bullet."

Johnson bent forward staring at the man's neck. Vivid red welts were visible.

"Looks like whoever killed him tried to strangle him as well," he said.

Abramo gave a somber nod then pointed at the man's hands.

"There's marks on his wrists," he said.

Johnson studied the abrasions then examined the man's face. There was swelling down the left side around the eye indicating the man had been beaten before he'd been killed. Johnson tilted forwards for a closer inspection.

"Can you see that?" he asked Abramo pointing at the man's temple.

Abramo narrowed his eyes to focus. There were numerous impressions in the man's skin in the shape of tiny circles about the size of a thumbnail.

"It's like someone's repeatedly pressed a marble into his face," he said.

Johnson nodded.

"Strange isn't it."

"You any ideas?" Abramo asked.

"No," said Johnson shaking his head. "Not at the minute."

Next, he studied the dead man's clothes then jotted down what he was wearing: A grey shirt, faded jeans, black socks and brown shoes. Again, he looked at the eyes. Brown without focus they were the one thing that always threw him. The one thing that he could never get used to no matter how many dead people he encountered: The glazed, fixed stare of death. The futility of the murder got to him. Pointless. Senseless. Barbaric. As always he vowed to himself that he'd find the killer. Whoever did this had to be held accountable. Would be held accountable. He glanced at the left hand searching for a wedding ring. It was there on the smaller middle finger, a circle of gold that in the near future would be returned to the widow. Another life ruined. Another reason to find the person responsible.

He stood up and glanced around. Kelly was holding the crime scene tape up for the M.E's van to get through. A minute later, Charles B.

Firth, the Medical Examiner, walked up with his two assistants from the main office on 1st Avenue. A lean man with a cannon ball head, Firth had intelligent green eyes in a pale face. As usual, perched on his nose were his trademark iron-rimmed glasses. He glanced around as he approached, his tiny eyes taking in everything. Johnson didn't like him and vice versa but because they both respected each other's ability their mutual antipathy never interfered with their working relationship.

"Not a good night for it Detective," said Firth, his cultured tone contrasting sharply with the corpse at his feet.

"No," Johnson replied. "Is there ever?"

"No, I suppose there's not," said Firth then he knelt down and checked the victim's pulse.

When he stood up he took out a silver Dictaphone from his inside pocket.

"I'm pronouncing John Doe 23541 deceased at 3.20am," he said then he turned to his two assistants.

"Start snapping gentlemen."

Immediately, the two men with him set to work, quickly and expertly photographing the body in situ. When they'd finished Firth looked at Johnson.

"I am officially turning the death of this man over to you Detective as a homicide."

Johnson nodded. It was standard procedure.

Behind them a screech of tires alerted them that someone new had just arrived. When they turned around they realized it was the CSU van. As they stared at it the driver's door flung open and the charismatic leader of the Crime Scene Unit, Francis Donato, climbed out. As his team opened the back doors of the van and began unpacking their equipment he strode up to them with a wide smile on his face.

"Now why are you all looking so unhappy," he said. "It's at a time like this you should rejoice that you're alive."

"Maybe it's because we have a little bit of decorum," said Firth.

"Over-rated Charles. Far better to enjoy life instead of submitting to etiquette. That's just boring."

"Well, he's all yours," said Firth.

"Thanks Charley boy, I'll give you a ring when we're finished so you can get the body," said Donato.

"Okay, I'll see you then," said Firth then he signaled to his two co-workers and they returned to their van.

As they drove away Johnson studied Donato. Vain and humorous, he had Elvis-style hair that was swept back over his head with a generous amount of gel. At the minute however, his quiff was hidden underneath the hood of his white Crime Scene coveralls making him

11

look like the abominable snowman. As always he smelt of expensive aftershave whilst his face, deeply tanned due to his love of sun beds, looked like polished leather.

"You smell lovely Francis," said Johnson.

"You like it? Just bought it yesterday...Davidoff...Hot Water."

"Haven't you been in enough of that already?"

Donato laughed at this. Known as an infamous philanderer throughout the department he had the reputation of an alley cat and was rumored to have three illegitimate children by three different women, none of which he paid alimony for. Only a few months prior an irate husband had tried to decapitate him with an axe after he'd caught him in bed with his wife.

"It's not my fault I'm so handsome and irresistible," he said, "women just throw themselves at me."

"But why do they always have to be married?" Johnson asked.

"Not always Joe. Get your facts straight because I don't discriminate. Married, unmarried, makes little odds to me because I'm an equal opportunity Lothario. Trust me, I'll sleep with anything...up to a certain standard of course. Well, that's not exactly true as sleeping is the last thing I do...but you know what I mean."

Johnson shook his head. Despite his intelligence Donato was one of the sleaziest men on the planet with everything in his life, outside of his work, revolving around the pursuit of women.

"You the Primary Investigator on this Joe?" Donato asked.

"I am."

"Then lead the way because I've two sisters waiting for me in a Jacuzzi. Don't want to be keeping them waiting."

Again Johnson shook his head. Sometimes it was difficult to tell the difference between truth and fiction where Donato was concerned but at least his stories were always colorful. Together, they began the 'walk through' which was carried out to determine the strategy for documentation of the entire crime scene. This was the third step at a crime scene, the first being the establishment of a perimeter, the second being the Medical Examiner's pronouncement of death. Fifty yards from the body, in the middle of the road, they came across a trail of blood and skid marks from a vehicle that came to a halt on the far pathway. Donato knelt down and placed a yellow marker at them both. This was to alert people that entered the crime scene later that they were nearing evidence and to tread carefully lest they contaminate or destroy it by accident.

"We're lucky," said Donato when he stood up. "If the rain had have stayed on any longer we'd have lost the blood and possibly the skid marks."

"What do you reckon?" Johnson asked him.

"On first appearances," he said. "It looks like our doer shot him here then dragged him over to the bushes."

"But the trail of blood stops after ten yards in the middle of the road," said Johnson. "It's nowhere near where the body is."

"He could've lifted the body into the vehicle at that point then drove over."

"Suppose but what about the skid marks on the sidewalk? Why over there?"

"Don't know, the killer might be a bad driver Joe or those skid marks could have nothing to do with the murder."

"Well, make sure to get an impression anyway."

"Don't worry, I was intending to," said Donato, slightly annoyed.

For the next few seconds they continued the walk through in silence. However, when they circled back towards the body Johnson noticed something small and red tight up against the curb.

"Over there Francis," he said pointing.

When they walked over Donato knelt down and placed a yellow marker two inches from the object as Johnson and Abramo squatted beside him. Together, they scrutinized what they now realized was a small piece of red metal.

"Looks like a steel clip or hook of some kind," said Abramo.

It was around an inch long. Johnson leaned in close.

"Looks to have broken away from something," he said.

Abramo nodded.

"Yeah but from what?"

"At the minute, no idea," said Johnson. "You Francis?"

"Sorry Joe, no."

Finished examining the object they stood up and resumed the walk through. In all it took them ten minutes to complete. When they stopped they were back where they'd started having completed a full one hundred meter circumference of the body. The best clue they'd found had been a footprint in the mud beside the body.

Now it was step four: Photographing the crime scene followed by step five, the collection of evidence.

"How long do you think you'll be Francis?" Johnson asked.

"An hour Joe to take the photographs then I'll give you a shout to help with evidence collection."

As a crime scene analyst it was Donato's job to take both photographs and collect evidence from the scene. The procedure for photographing the crime scene was simple: Overview photographs first then medium sized ones followed by macro photographs that were extreme close-ups. Videotaping was then carried out in the exact same manner. After that the evidence was bagged and tagged.

Chapter 3

"Ok, let us know when you're finished snapping," said Johnson.

"Will do."

Johnson turned to Abramo.

"Sal, you set up the command post. I'll go talk to the girl that called it in."

Abramo nodded then turned and walked back to the car. Johnson crossed over to the cruiser and opened the door. Again, frightened eyes peered out at him.

"You don't mind if I get in?" he asked. "It's cold out here."

"No, no, please do," said the woman.

Johnson waited until she'd scooted across the back seat then he climbed in beside her. Because it was dark he reached up and switched on the interior light on the ceiling. Immediately, light flooded the inside of the car. Now able to see, Johnson realized the woman inside the car was very young, perhaps around eighteen or nineteen.

"Your name's Kathleen, isn't that right?" he asked.

"Yes," she replied.

Johnson extended his hand. After a moment's hesitation the girl accepted it and they shook.

"I'm Detective Joseph Johnson of the Midtown North Precinct," said Johnson before releasing her hand.

The girl nodded quickly but didn't say anything, her eyes still filled with fear.

"Look Kathleen, I know this is difficult for you," said Johnson. "But I need to ask you a few questions."

"Ok," she said, her voice and body shaking with fear.

Despite this Johnson knew he had to plough on.

"At what time did you discover the body?" he asked.

Although he hadn't thought it possible, the distraught woman's face paled even further when he used the word 'body'.

"I...I...," she stammered and then she burst out crying.

Johnson sat where he was, prepared to wait her out. After a couple of seconds sobbing she lifted her head and looked at him with beseeching eyes.

"I'm sorry," she said. "You must think I'm a complete idiot."

"Not at all," he said. "It's a perfectly natural reaction."

"Thank you," she murmured under her breath then she bent down and lifted a black handbag off the floor. When she opened it and rummaged around her hand came out holding a packet of handkerchiefs. After opening them she extracted one then wiped her eyes and blew her nose.

"I'm not usually this emotional," she said.

"I understand," said Johnson. "It must have been quite a shock for you."

She nodded then sniffed a couple of times trying to compose herself. Knowing she was still on the brink of tears Johnson gave her a bit more time. After a few more seconds she sat up straight and looked him in the eye with renewed determination and purpose.

"I'm ready," she said.

"I was asking what time you came across the..." Johnson racked his mind for a better word than body. He settled on "...man."

"It was just before two thirty," the young woman said, her words tumbling out. "I was walking home from a friend's house and there he was lying there. At first I thought he was drunk but then when I got closer I saw his eyes and the way he was lying. I knew then he was dead."

After saying this she blessed herself.

"How close did you get to him?" Johnson asked.

"As close as I am to you now," she replied.

"Was there anyone around when you made the discovery?"

"No, only me."

"What about vehicles? Any cars or vans around?"

"Not that I seen."

"Ok Miss Rice, thank you," said Johnson. "We've got your name and address so if we need you again we'll give you a call but for now you can go on home and put this terrible night behind you."

"Thank you," she said then without saying anything further she exited the car and hurried away.

Behind her Johnson climbed out of the car and watched her leave.

"Pretty, isn't she," said Kelly.

His sudden appearance made Johnson jump. The Patrolman had moved real quiet.

"She's a witness," said Johnson.

"Yeah right," Kelly replied, a lopsided grin on his face. "Sure you're a saint."

After saying this he sauntered away without waiting on Johnson's reply. Johnson watched him leave. For a second he was tempted to go after him but he changed his mind and decided he wasn't worth it.

To kill the hour until Donato finished photographing the crime scene Johnson went back to Abramo who was standing outside the Fusion talking on the phone to his wife.

"Honey, I have to go," he said seeing Johnson approach.

When his wife told him she loved him he repeated the endearment back to her and then hung up.

"You hungry?" Johnson asked as his big partner slid his cell phone into his pocket.

"Now that's a silly question. You buying Joe?"

"That I am, jump in."

Five minutes later they were at Gergio's Country Grill on 9th Avenue. Famished, Johnson ordered fried Mozzarella Sticks with chicken fingers and Buffalo wings whilst Abramo got the arm in with fried calamari, grilled portabello mushrooms and shrimp scampi. Afterwards, as Johnson paid the bill Donato rang him.

"We're ready Joe," he said.

"Okay, on our way Francis."

When they arrived back Johnson took out his notebook and made a quick sketch of the crime scene. After that, satisfied that he'd captured a good likeness, he pulled on his gloves and walked over to the body. Kneeling down he pushed his hand into the dead man's pockets and pulled out a key-ring with the smiling face of a young toddler on one side. The youngster looked to be around one year old but the key-ring was worn and damaged with a crack across the middle making Johnson think the child would be older now. He turned it over. On the back in red letters was printed 'I love Dad' the picture of a heart substituting for the word 'love'. A single key was attached to the key-ring. Memories of his own father flooded in on Johnson. Like himself, his Dad had been in the army, only Vietnam not Iraq, and then the NYPD. A big man with a barrel chest and unruly red hair he'd been gunned down on 11th Avenue during a liqour store robbery back in 1985. Joe had been fifteen at the time. The killer, never caught, had run into the liquor store brandishing a huge Magnum revolver, the type made famous by Clint Eastwood in the film 'Dirty Harry'. Joe's father who had been off duty at the time had been paying for a six pack of bud. The store owner, a Chinese man by the name of Wei Sun, said in his statement afterwards that Joe's father, Rocky, had tried to wrestle the Magnum out of the thief's hands but that the robber, at point blank range, had pulled the trigger. His father's heart, a big generous one, was blown out the rear of his back. Johnson stared at the word 'Dad' on the key-ring and made a promise to himself. Whoever did this was not going to get away. They would pay for leaving this young boy without a father.

"Can I see that?" Abramo asked.

Johnson passed the keys across to his partner. After looking at the key ring Abramo shook his head.

"I have one of these," he said.

Johnson nodded. He had one too. Shaking his head at being sentimental he told himself to concentrate and checked the man's other pocket. Inside, his fingers curled around what felt like a phone which proved to be true when he extracted his hand. It was an Iphone 5 with

15% of its battery left. When he tried to open it he realized it was pass code protected. Holding it firmly in one hand he tapped in obvious sequences of four numbers in an effort to open it: 1234. 0000. 2011. None of them worked and the phone knocked off after the third attempt. Johnson shrugged. It would be easy enough to get into. The NYPD's Forensic Department at One Police Plaza had a handheld device called the Cellebrite UFED that could bypass the password and extract all the information in less than two minutes. Johnson dropped it into an evidence bag then slipped it into the pocket of his raincoat.

When he returned his gaze to the corpse he decided to search the man's shirt pockets this time. The first one was empty but in the second there was a small bag of white powder. He opened it then licked the end of his index finger and dipped it into the bag. When he pulled it out some of the white powder had stuck to the tip of his finger. He rubbed it onto the flat of his tongue then rolled it around the inside of his mouth.

"Coke," he said to Abramo.

"That shit's everywhere," his partner replied.

Johnson placed the bag of white powder in a separate evidence bag. With the front finished the two Detectives rolled the body over onto its side. In the back pocket Johnson found what he'd hoped for: The man's wallet. He opened it. Inside was a driving license and credit cards. He took the license out and looked at the photograph. It was the dead man. He read the name and address:

Richard Wright, 28 West 50th Street.

"Bingo," he said then he handed the license across to his partner.

After opening it Abramo looked at the photograph then popped it into an evidence bag of his own.

Half an hour later Johnson and Abramo handed the evidence they'd collected over to Donato. After it was safely stored in his van Donato took out his cell and rang Firth.

"That's us finished Charles," he said.

Five minutes later the Medical Examiner and his two assistants arrived back.

"You get much?" Firth asked Donato.

"Enough to get us started."

"They always leave something," said Firth.

"They do at that," said Donato then he took out his cell phone and walked away with it stuck to his ear. Behind him, Firth turned to his two assistants.

"Right lads, now it's our turn," he said.

The two assistants nodded in unison then walked to the back of the Medical Examiner's van. After opening the doors they reached in together and slid out a stretcher. Within seconds they had Richard Wright rolled onto it and in the back of the van on top of a trolley.

"When will you be doing the autopsy?" Johnson asked Firth as he was about to climb into the front of the van.

"Later today at 1pm."

"Any chance you could give me a time of death now?"

Firth frowned.

"Right this minute?" he asked.

Johnson nodded.

"It'll help us get started."

"Okay, if that's what you want, then that's what you'll get," said Firth and he stepped back down.

"Charlie, Dennis, I'll need your help," he said.

His two assistants got out then together all three of them walked to the rear of the van with Johnson and Abramo following in their wake. After the back doors were open Firth and his two colleagues climbed in beside the body. As they stood around it Firth took a square, cardboard box off a shelf in the back. It was filled with latex gloves, one glove protruding like a paper handkerchief. Firth plucked two out and tugged them on then leant over the corpse that was lying face up on the trolley. The first thing he did was unbuckle the dead man's belt then afterwards he unbuttoned and unzipped his jeans. Johnson and Abramo, who were outside the van looking in, had seen this done a thousand times so they both knew what was to come and stared stoically.

"Help me turn him," Firth said to his two assistants.

Together they rolled the body onto its front.

"Avert your eyes boys if you're homophobic," Firth said as he gripped the back of the man's jeans and boxers.

"One, two, three," he said then he yanked the man's jeans and underwear down to thigh level exposing the man's buttocks which Johnson noticed were quite hairy. There was also some writing tattooed on the man's left butt cheek. Johnson stood on his tip toes to read it: *Carpe Diem*. A Latin phrase meaning 'Seize the day' that had become famous after the Robin William's film "Dead Poets Society" back in 1989.

Now that the man's rear was on display Firth plucked a ten inch forensic thermometer out of the top pocket of his lab coat. It was brand new and still had protective cellophane covering it. He ripped the cellophane off then dutifully placed it in his pocket.

"Don't want you fining me for littering, eh Detective," he said.

Johnson gave him a weak smile. Firth smirked back then continued with the job at hand. Using the thumb and index finger of his left hand he separated the man's buttocks so that the anus was exposed. Next, he positioned the thermometer at the entrance of the rectum.

"Now you see it," he said then he pushed the thermometer up into the anal cavity until it was the whole way in.

"Now you don't," he finished then he started to count out loud as he took the man's core temperature to help verify the time of death.

"It's a shitty job but someone's gotta do it," he quipped in mid count.

Firth's flippancy annoyed Johnson but he kept his mouth shut. The procedure was undignified enough he thought without the wisecracks but as he was the one that had asked for the impromptu time of death he remained quiet. When Firth reached thirty he withdrew the thermometer and took the reading.

"Well?" Johnson asked.

Firth did the computation in his head calculating the rate of cooling after death. Dividing the difference between the outside temperature and the body's core temperature by 1.5 he estimated the number of hours the victim had been dead.

"Approximately two hours," he said.

"Approximately?"

"It's the best I can do at such short notice Joe. I'm not a miracle worker but once Rigor Mortis has set in and I've examined his stomach contents I'll have a better idea."

"Okay, fair enough. Thanks Charles."

"The pleasure was all mine," he said then he hauled the man's boxers and jeans up around his waist again before nodding at his two assistants. Together they flipped the body back over so that it was face up. When they got out and closed the doors the three of them once more got back into the front. As they drove away towards the hospital Donato came sauntering back with his phone in his hand and tapped Johnson on the shoulder.

"Right Joe, I'll love you and leave you," he said. "I've an important date with two of Hugh Heffner's bunny girls."

"Thought you said they were sisters?"

"They are. Twins!"

"I wish I lived in the virtual reality you inhabit Francis."

"You dare to doubt me Joe? Think I'm lying? Then come on back and meet the girls."

"No, you're alright Francis. I'll take a pass."

"Lightweight," said Donato then he gave a cheerful wave and strode across to his van.

"He's certainly a character, isn't he," said Abramo.

Johnson nodded in agreement then his face turned serious.

"Now the part I don't like," he said.

"Yeah," Abramo replied, knowing full well what his partner was referring to: It was time to notify the next of kin.

Chapter 4

28 West 50th Street was ten minutes away. When they pulled up outside it Johnson realized it was a large three-storey brick townhouse with grey steps leading up to a door behind a white decorative grill. But despite this embellishment it didn't fool Johnson for a second. The grill was there for security reasons. Above the door was a pink and white awning. Johnson lifted the letterbox and rapped the door but after a minute there was still no sign of life inside.

"It's 5.20am," said Abramo. "She's most likely in bed."

"You reckon?" said Johnson. "You must be a detective."

"Ha ha very funny Joe...but remember...sarcasm is the lowest form of wit."

"But the highest form of intelligence."

Abramo laughed at this.

"You've an answer for everything," he said.

Johnson smiled then turned and rapped the door again, louder this time. After a few seconds lights came on inside the house.

"When we get in make sure to look around," said Johnson. "For all we know the wife could be the one that killed him."

Abramo nodded. It was normal practice to always look closely at relatives, especially spouses when it came to murder. A few seconds later a blurred figure appeared behind the front door.

"Who is it?" a female voice enquired but it was so low the two detectives could barely make her out.

As planned Johnson took the lead. Abramo would be the one taking notes.

"It's the police Ma'am. Can we talk to you please?" he asked.

The woman opened the door then unlocked the grill and pushed it wide. With the hallway light behind her she was silhouetted in the doorway.

"Mrs. Wright?" Johnson asked.

"Keep your voice down," she said, her voice a sharp whisper. "My son's in bed asleep."

Johnson instantly lowered his voice.

"Mrs. Wright, I'm Detective Joseph Johnson with the NYPD. This is my partner Detective Salvatore Abramo."

"What is it? What's wrong?" she asked, panic now creeping into her voice.

"Can we speak to you inside Ma'am?"

Involuntarily, her right hand rose to her throat where it fluttered nervously. Already she knew what was coming. They all did. Why else would the police be at your door at five in the morning. There was only one possible explanation. The dreaded nightmare had finally come true. She stood aside and allowed the two Detectives to enter. Once they were in the hallway she pulled the grill over and closed the door behind them. When she turned around her eyes were filled with fear.

"Is it Richard?" she asked.

"I think it's better if we speak in the living room Ma'am," said Johnson.

Again her hand scrabbled at the side of her neck, her fingers dancing an anxious tattoo on her clavicle. It was heartbreaking to watch yet at the same time Johnson had to treat her as a suspect. Nevertheless, he didn't think she was faking it.

"This way," she said walking in front of them.

Halfway up the hall she cast a single worried glance back over her shoulder. Heavy and overweight with big bags underneath her eyes she looked exhausted. As he walked through the house Johnson scanned his surroundings taking in everything he could see. There was nothing in the hallway besides a phone and a long rectangular mirror that ran along the length of the wall. Once they were in the living room Johnson asked Mrs. Wright to sit down. She did so immediately, her hands clasped tightly on her lap, her fingers pressing into the skin on the back of her hand. When the two detectives sat on the two-seater facing her, Abramo took out his notebook whilst Johnson, his face a solemn mask, leant forward.

"Ma'am, there's no other way to say this," he said, "but your husband was murdered tonight. Shot dead."

Immediately, the woman raised her hands and cupped them around her mouth. For a full ten seconds she stared in absolute horror as the import of what Johnson had just told her started to sink in. Then, her face crumpled with pain, caving in on itself and her chin trembled. Johnson got up.

"I'll get you a glass of water," he said.

When he walked into the kitchen he took his time searching for a glass. It gave him the excuse he needed to glance around the room looking for clues. On the windowsill above the sink was a red, wooden sculpture of the word 'love'. As the kitchen was predominantly a woman's domain Johnson guessed the wife had been the one that had bought and placed it there. On top of the microwave sat a silver framed photograph. Johnson crossed the tiles, picked it up and examined it. It showed Richard Wright with his wife and a young boy, an older version of the toddler Johnson had seen on the key ring. Johnson took this to be the couple's son. He noted the expressions on their faces. All three looked extremely happy, each wearing a mile long smile. Johnson found a glass in a wall cupboard above the microwave. He filled it with tap water then walked back into the living room.

"Thank you," Mrs. Wright said when he handed it to her.

After three large gulps she sat the glass on the floor at her feet.

"I knew this would happen," she said, tears in her eyes. "I always told him he'd end up dead."

Johnson nodded to encourage her.

"And why's that Mrs. Wright?" he asked.

"Please, call me Elizabeth."

"Sorry, Elizabeth. Why did you think this would happen?"

"Because of his gambling and all that money he kept borrowing. I knew he wouldn't be able to pay it back."

"Pay who back?"

"That gangster...Yerzov."

"Vitaly Yerzov...the Russian bookmaker?"

"Yes, yes, him."

Nicknamed "Hatchet" Vitaly Yerzov owned numerous businesses including a bookmakers on 9th Avenue as well as a strip club called Flawless that was situated on West 44th Street. A barrel-chested brute with a cannon ball head he was renowned for his cruelty and viciousness. Infamous for supposedly chopping people up Yerzov had spent a year on Riker's Island in 2003 awaiting trial on a charge of rape and murder. However, one month before he was due to step into court the charges were dropped after the sole witness in the case was shot dead at a cinema in the Bronx. Since then Yerzov had avoided arrest and built up his criminal empire through racketeering, loan-sharking, extortion and prostitution.

"How do you know that your husband owed Yerzov money Mrs. Wright?" Johnson asked.

"Because a thug with a broken nose and a scar on his cheek called here to the house about three weeks ago."

Johnson knew who she was talking about. Dimitry Garin, a vicious thug, who when he wasn't cage fighting, was breaking arms and backs for Yerzov.

"Did you hear what he happened to say to your husband?"

Elizabeth looked embarrassed and averted her eyes.

"Mrs. Wright?" Johnson prompted.

She looked at him again.

"Richard told me to go into the kitchen...which I did...but I kept the door open and listened to what they were saying."

"Which was what?"

"Richard had missed five payments. That brute told him that if he didn't start paying back what he owed immediately then Yerzov had ordered him to take it out of his flesh."

"What did Richard say?"

"He said he'd start paying."

"How much were the payments?"

"I think Richard owed fifty thousand dollars."

Johnson whistled out loud.

"That's a lot of money," he said.

"I know."

"How much had he to pay back a week?"

"I don't know. I asked Richard after that terrible man left but he wouldn't tell me."

"If he owed fifty grand he was probably paying back about two grand a week," said Abramo.

"Yeah, that'd be about right," Johnson said.

"Would your husband have been able to pay that amount back?" Abramo asked.

"Richard owns..." She shook her head at using the wrong tense. "...owned...Vanity Hotel."

"On 9th Avenue?"

"Yes, that's my husband's," she said then again she corrected herself. "Was my husband's."

Johnson sat back. Nine months prior Vanity had been a non-entity hotel slowly sliding into oblivion. Then, suddenly, out of the blue, builders, painters, decorators, plumbers and joiners had descended on the place like a swarm of locusts. Working non-stop over a three month period they'd transformed what had previously been a hovel into what was now one of the most striking hotels in New York. Before the grand opening a fortune had been spent on publicity. Overnight the hotel became an up market retreat for the rich and famous. Classy and decadent it now had the reputation of being the 'hotel-to-stay-at' in New York never mind Manhattan. Johnson exchanged glances with his partner. If Richard Wright had been in debt to Yerzov and had failed to pay back the fifty grand then it was a definite motive for murder. Taken along with the welts on the victim's neck it looked like the Russian gangster known as Hatchet was shaping up to be their prime suspect.

"What about friends Mrs. Wright. Who would be your husband's friends?"

"His best friend would be George Taylor...he's Richard's partner in the hotel."

"You have an address or a contact number for this George?"

"No, but he's easily found."

"Where?" Johnson asked.

"He drinks at the hotel every night," she said, her voice laced with scorn.

Johnson interpreted her disdain as George having a drink problem.

"George is an alcoholic?" he asked.

"Yes...although he'll never admit it."

"You don't like him, do you?"

"Is it that obvious?"

Johnson shrugged.

"I'm a Detective."

"You have to know George," she said. "He's irritating...annoying...gets under your skin."

"What about his relationship with your husband? You said they were best friends. Did they ever argue?"

"Yes, eleven months ago...on my birthday."

"Which was when?"

"19th June."

"What happened?"

"George called here drunk. Rapped the door so hard it nearly came off its hinges."

"What time did he call?"

"Eleven o'clock at night. Myself and Richard had just returned from a night out and were about to go to bed."

"Who answered the door?"

"Richard. He went out to him...pushed him down the path. They started fighting in the garden."

"Physically fighting or verbal?"

"Physical. I had to run out and separate them. George was screaming 'You want me to tell her? You want me to tell her?'"

"Tell you what?"

"I don't know. Richard punched him then. Knocked George out."

"What about when George woke up? Did he say anything then?"

"No. Richard dragged him over to his car, threw him into the back and drove him home."

"Could you hazard a guess at what George wanted to tell you?"

Her face contorted then out of the blue she burst out crying again. This time it took her a couple of minutes to recover. Johnson plucked a paper handkerchief from a box on the coffee table and handed it to her.

"I'm sorry," she said, dabbing her tears with the hankie.

"It's okay Elizabeth. Just take your time."

She composed herself then started speaking.

"Look at me Detective. I'm a fat, middle-aged woman that isn't ever going to fit into a size six dress again."

Johnson didn't know how to respond and felt slightly uncomfortable. But he was there to do a job. In order to keep her talking he nodded. Active listening the technique was called. For good measure he threw in a sympathetic smile. It worked and she opened up again.

"Richard always liked sex," she said. "He was a very sexual man. But a year ago he stopped sleeping with me. When I asked him why he said I'd let myself go. That's when I knew he was sleeping with other people."

"You've proof of this?"

"A wife knows Detective. I mightn't know exactly which bimbo was flavor of the week at what time but I do know he was cheating on me.

And the reason? That phone of his. It used to be I could lift it and use it like my own...but last year...if I even dared touch it...he went into a temper. Then he starts carrying it about with him. Everywhere he went he'd take his cell with him. Afraid I'd lift it you see...find out all his sordid secrets. Then...when his contract is up for renewal he gets this new Iphone 5 and there's a pass code on it. Four numbers. Locks on its own after a minute. So now...instead of having to carry it around everywhere, he can leave it sitting wherever he wants."

"We have his Iphone."

"Then when you get into it I'm sure you'll find out who all the dirty little sluts are that he was fuckin' behind my back."

Her goat was up and the anger was evident in both her eyes and her voice.

"You've no idea of the pass code?" Johnson asked.

She shook her head quickly then started speaking.

"Every chance I got I lifted that phone Detective. Tried every number I could think of. Our wedding date, his date of birth, our son's date of birth, my date of birth, a combination of them all. Nothing ever worked."

"Did you ever confront him? Tell him you suspected him of cheating?"

"Of course I did but he always denied it. Then...the bastard started staying out."

"What excuse did he give?"

"More lies. Always told me he'd stayed out and had a drink with George...but my husband wasn't a drinker Detective. A reprobate and a shitty husband who liked to chase younger women but not a drinker."

"Then why didn't you leave him?"

Her face slackened and lost its anger.

"Because I loved him," she said, her voice breaking with emotion.

Johnson stood up, lifted her glass off the ground then walked into the kitchen. Once he had it filled he came back into the living room and handed her the glass. After a few sips she looked better so he waded in again.

"When was the last time you seen your husband Elizabeth?"

"Last night before he left for the hotel."

"What time exactly did he leave?"

"Eight o'clock."

"Was that his usual time for going to work?"

"No, it varied, he never kept regular hours."

"When your husband went to work what did you do?"

"I watched TV with my son then at nine o'clock I sent him to bed."

"And you stayed up?"

"Yes. I always watch Nurse Jackie on a Saturday night."

"What channel?"

"Showtime."

"What time did it start at?"

"Nine thirty."

"So you'd half an hour to kill before it started?"

"I always make a cup of coffee and a sandwich for watching it. That's why I send Josh to bed at nine."

Johnson decided to switch direction.

"Does your husband have an office here in the house?"

"No," she said. "But he does have a laptop."

"May I see it?"

Elizabeth got up, disappeared for thirty seconds then came back carrying a black laptop bag. She handed it to Johnson who subsequently laid it across his knees.

"May I open this and turn it on?" he asked.

"Of course."

Johnson unzipped the bag, undid the Velcro straps then lifted the lid of the laptop. It was a Hewlett Packard. He pressed the silver 'on' button then waited patiently as the computer loaded up. When it did there was a single entry portal titled RICHARD. A white space below signified that a password was needed. Johnson looked across at Elizabeth.

"Do you know the password?" he asked.

"No. I wasn't allowed to touch Richard's precious laptop."

Again her contempt was palpable.

"What about when he was out?"

"Same as with the phone. I tried to get into it but I couldn't."

Johnson wasn't unduly worried. He knew the Forensics Department could get into the computer and its contents within minutes using a 'password bypassing disk'.

"May I take this?" he asked.

Elizabeth nodded.

"By all means," she said.

"Mrs. Wright, as this is a murder investigation we're going to get a search warrant then come back here later today at a more reasonable hour to go through the house searching for clues," Johnson said. "It's standard procedure."

"Ok," she said tentatively.

"What about at Vanity? Did your husband have an office there?"

"Yes, on the second floor."

"Okay, that's all for now," said Johnson turning off the lap top. "Thank you for your help Elizabeth. You've been extremely helpful."

After the computer knocked off, Johnson closed the lid, pulled across the Velcro straps and zipped up the case. He stood up with the laptop in his hand and nodded at his partner. Interview terminated his nod said. Abramo climbed to his feet but he kept his notebook out.

"Ma'am, may I have your home and cell number," he asked, "So that we can phone in advance when we're coming back later?"

"Yes, of course," Elizabeth replied.

"Thank you Ma'am."

Abramo held his pen over the page then started writing as soon as Mrs. Wright began calling out her numbers. When she'd finished Abramo slipped the notebook back into his pocket.

"Thank you Ma'am," he said. "I know how difficult this has been for you. But if you need anything and I mean anything...please...don't hesitate to call me. Anytime...day or night."

After saying this Abramo pulled out his wallet and extracted a business card. He handed it to Mrs. Wright.

"Just ring the number on this card."

"Thank you," she said, a little nonplussed, her eyes now vacant.

Johnson recognized the symptoms. Her mind was spiraling inwards with the idea that the man she'd loved, married and had a son to was never coming back. Never. The finality of death was sinking home. Her bottom lip trembled as the full impact hit her.

"Do you have anyone you can contact?" Johnson asked.

She didn't hear him.

"Mrs. Wright?"

She looked up. Fear, bewilderment and sorrow were blended together on her upturned face.

"Yes?" she asked.

Johnson's heart went out to her. It was obvious she was lost.

"Do you have anyone you can contact? A friend? A relative? Someone that could come over?"

"I...I've a sister," she said. "Mary."

"Is she close by?"

"Yes. Twenty minutes away. She lives on the Upper West Side, Amsterdam Avenue."

"Do you want me to ring her?" Johnson asked.

"Yes please. That would be very kind."

Johnson watched her as she picked up her handbag and took out her phone. Her face was blank. On autopilot. When she looked back on this day she'd find it strange that she couldn't remember a thing. Johnson knew this from experience. It was something he'd went through himself when his father had died. Mrs. Wright scrolled through the contacts in her phone to her sister's number. When she reached it she hit the green call button then handed the phone to Johnson.

"Hello, Elizabeth," a voice on the other end said.

Johnson introduced himself then quickly explained the predicament, only hanging up once Mary had assured him she was on her way.

"Is she coming?" Elizabeth asked when Johnson handed her back the phone.

"Yes, she's leaving immediately."

"Thank you Detective. You've been so kind. Both of you."

"Just doing our job Ma'am," said Abramo then he turned and motioned for Johnson to follow him out into the hallway.

"We should stay," he said, keeping his voice low so that Mrs. Wright couldn't hear him. "Until the sister arrives."

Johnson nodded in agreement.

"Of course," he said.

Nineteen minutes later Mary arrived. When Johnson opened the front door to her she brushed past him in a frantic hurry. Upon seeing her enter Mrs. Wright burst into a fresh flood of tears then raced into her sister's arms. Johnson signaled to Abramo.

"That's our cue," he said.

Abramo nodded then as quietly as they could the two detectives left the house.

Chapter 5

"Well, what you think?" Johnson asked when they were back in the car and safely out of earshot.

"She seemed genuine to me," said Abramo.

"Yeah, me too but we do this by the book. She admitted her husband was sleeping around outside the marriage...or at least that she suspected it."

"A wife would know."

"Well, mine definitely would," said Johnson.

Abramo nodded in agreement.

"I even try to tell Gabriella a lie and she knows," he said.

"Same with me and Jane. She's got a sixth sense when it comes to me."

"I wouldn't even like to think what Gabriella would do if she caught me cheating."

"I know what she'd do," said Johnson. "She'd cut your Italian balls off with a rusty knife."

Abramo scrunched up his face.

"Jesus, that doesn't even bear thinking about," he said.

"Then don't cheat on her."

"Don't worry, I wasn't intending to. Now can we get back to the case?"

"Of course," said Johnson.

"Thank you."

"Right, Richard's sleeping around outside his marriage...so we've got a definite motive for murder...centuries old. Jealous wife kills husband...plus... remember...she has no alibi."

"Yeah...but I still don't think she did it."

"Me neither but we'd be stupid to rule her out."

"True."

"Plus, did you hear the venom in her voice when she called him a "bastard". Real hatred there."

"Still don't see it."

"No. Me neither."

"She was inconsolable at the end," said Abramo. "That wasn't put on. She loved the guy."

"Maybe that's why she killed him. She loved him too much."

"No, the welt marks round the neck...wouldn't have been her."

"Yeah, agreed...but we cover our asses just the same. Canvass the area quietly...discretely. Come back in the afternoon and ask around...see if anyone seen her leaving the house last night. Also ask the neighbors what they were like as a couple. Did they ever hear them fighting, arguing, that sort of thing.   And slip it in about her temperament. If she had a temper then she might well have done this."

"What about a criminal background check?"

"Yes, do that too. Get a court order."

Abramo jotted down a reminder in his notebook then looked up.

"Yerzov's a good lead," he said. "I think that's the direction we should be going in."

"Yeah, agreed. We'll check him out later today."

"Plus there's the partner George.   The argument...getting hit...knocked out. There's something going on there."

"Yeah, we'll definitely be speaking to him."

"Okay, now what?" Abramo asked.

"Up to you. We can either go back to the station and write this up or leave it until later today."

Abramo checked his watch. It was one minute away from 6am.

"Now but I don't want to come in until late today."

"11am good?"

"Perfect."

The Midtown North Precinct was a large, rectangular building on West 54th Street with twenty six windows at the front that even on the sunniest day didn't receive enough light because of the larger buildings surrounding it. Bleak and desolate looking its one saving grace and bit of color was the Star Spangled Banner fluttering outside on a flagpole. Sitting squat like an unappreciated guardian the Precinct watched over the area of Midtown Manhattan that included famous tourist sites like St. Patrick's Cathedral and the Rockefeller Plaza. The large, square doorways on either side lent a grandness to the building that the police officers inside sometimes didn't feel. For the last number of years, due to the recession and slashed budgets, they'd been battling wage cuts and pension reductions leading some officers to leave for higher paid jobs with other police agencies that paid over a hundred grand a year. Large numbers had also jumped ship to the New York Fire Department, which although comparable in pay, had far more attractive work schedules. To combat this deluge the Police hierarchy at One Police Plaza in Lower Manhattan had created new contracts forbidding police officers to transfer their seniority for compensation purposes. This alone, had effectively stopped the flood.

When the two Detectives stepped through the big glass paneled doors into the station old Gums was at the front desk munching away happily on a giant hotdog. As they passed him Johnson couldn't help but take a quick look to see if the false teeth were on the counter. They were. Catching him looking Gums gave him the bird. Johnson pretended not to see it and hid a smile. Secretly, he liked the old man. He'd had a tough time of it. Not only was he a widower but he'd also lost his only son, a National Guard, to a roadside bomb in Afghanistan. Abramo, however, couldn't help himself and marched over to the desk.

"Put your bloody teeth in, will you!"

Gums kept chewing and stared back at him, a wide grin on his face. It was common knowledge he only did it to get a rise out of people but Johnson thought he understood why. After the death of his son and then his wife a year later the old man was lonely. Johnson turned back and grabbed Abramo by the shoulder.

"Leave him alone," he said.

"But that's disgusting," said Abramo.

Grabbing him by an elbow Johnson steered Abramo away.

"He's earned the right," he said.

"How?" Abramo asked, his face snarling up in confusion.

Johnson quickly explained about the old man's wife and son. When he'd finished Abramo glanced back.

"Sorry," he said, "I didn't know."

As they walked away Johnson looked back at the Desk Sergeant. Their eyes met and an understanding passed between them. Johnson gave him a curt nod then turned and continued walking towards the elevator with Abramo. When it arrived they got in and Abramo pressed the button for the third floor. As the elevator made its ascent Abramo shook his head, annoyed at himself for having jumped the gun.

"Me and my big mouth," he said.

"Sure you didn't know," said Johnson.

"Sometimes I'm just a complete asshole. I swear, I need my head examined."

When the elevator stopped it shuddered then made them wait thirty seconds before the doors slid open.

"This thing must be ancient," said Abramo. "Every time I get into it I'm ready to have a heart attack."

Johnson nodded in agreement then together they stepped into the Bull pen.

"Right, you type up the search warrants," said Johnson. "I'll do the report."

Abramo nodded and crossed to his desk. As he switched on his computer Johnson did the same. After logging in Johnson opened his Case Folder then created a new folder within it called "Richard Wright". Inside this he opened up a Word Document then typed up his notes from that night. At the end of the hour he printed out two copies of what he'd written then looked over at Abramo.

"You near finished?" he asked.

"Printing now Joe."

Five seconds later the printer kicked into life and ejected two copies of the search warrant, one to be signed, the other to go into the murder file.

"You want a cup of coffee Sal?" Johnson asked.

"Does a bear shit in the proverbial?"

Johnson got up and made two coffees, his without milk, Abramo's with, including two sugars. When Johnson returned Abramo had pulled his chair over to Johnson's desk and was sitting waiting. Johnson handed him his coffee and sat down. As they drank them Johnson read his report out loud.

"Anything I missed?" he asked when he'd finished.

"No, it's all there," said Abramo.

"Ok, I'll pick you up at quarter to eleven then we'll get started on the murder board."

Chapter 6

When Johnson got home and climbed into bed it was half six but because his mind was doing somersaults he couldn't sleep. He wrestled with the duvet for half an hour then when the alarm started ringing at the side of the bed he reached over and knocked it off. As usual Jane was still fast asleep so he rolled over and kissed her on the cheek.

"Wakey, wakey love."

Still in the depths of slumber she mumbled incoherently then lapsed into a deep sleep again. Johnson shook her shoulder.

"Time to get up sleepy head," he said.

When there was no response he shook her again.

"Jane, the house is on fire!"

Her eyes shot open and she stared at him, her eyes at first frightened then slowly filling with anger.

"You're not funny," she said.

"I know but it's time to get up love."

She sat up and swivelled her legs over the edge of the bed. For thirty seconds she perched like that collecting her thoughts then stood up. As she pushed her feet into her slippers she looked over her shoulder at her husband.

"Next time you're on call, sleep in the spare room," she said.

"Okay," Johnson replied, not wanting to get drawn into an argument.

She turned and walked out of the bedroom. Johnson watched her leave then heard her enter the bathroom and lock the door. Five seconds later the shower came on. Johnson lay there thinking about his wife. Married for almost seventeen years now it was hard to believe that he was still madly in love with her. They'd first met in 1991 at a fundraising event for the widows of the first Gulf War. Jane had been attending with her sister-in-law Joanne Montgomery, whose husband, Jane's brother, had been killed at the Battle of Khafji. Shy and demure Jane had been twenty years old at the time and a recently graduated Secondary School teacher. From the moment Johnson laid eyes on her he knew he wanted to marry her. The hard part of course proved to be convincing her of that fact but after a two year courtship he'd finally succeeded and they got married in St. Patrick's Cathedral. But now, a wedding, three daughters and over two decades later, a widening rift had opened between them. At first it was the little things: Him throwing his clothes on the floor and not picking them up; him leaving dishes in the sink for her to clean; him biting his fingernails and leaving them on the arm of the couch. Now, it seemed that he only had to open his mouth and he was in the wrong. Everything he did caused Jane to get angry until now he could actually feel the resentment coming off her in waves. Johnson thought about their sex life. In that department he was persona non grata. Every time he so much as tried to kiss Jane she turned away from him or feigned illness.

Pushing the thoughts away he got up, dressed quickly then gently rapped his daughter Rachel's bedroom door. At fifteen she was the eldest in the house and therefore had a room of her own.

"Yes?" she shouted out.

Johnson opened the door and popped his head in. A proliferation of Rhianna posters were plastered haphazardly around the walls. Above the headboard was a portrait of Rachel that Johnson had painted himself using acrylics.

"Rachel, time to get up love."

"Ok Daddy," she said, sitting up and stretching.

Johnson turned and exited then crossed the hallway to Amy and Rebecca's room. He gave their door a gentle rap.

"We're up Daddy," Rebecca shouted out.

Johnson opened the door and poked his head in. Rebecca, the youngest in the house at eleven, bounced out of the bottom bunk. A fierce little lady she had the swagger of a wrestler in her pink and black Justin Beiber pajamas.

"Move," she ordered and Johnson had to step aside. Never a morning person, something she took after her mother, Rebecca hammered at the bathroom door.

"Mom, let me in, I need to go," she shouted.

Amy, a little more lady-like at fourteen, climbed down from the top bunk. Her large blue eyes, identical to his own, stared up at him.

"I dreamt about you last night Daddy," she said.

"Yeah?" Johnson said, strangely pleased to hear this. "What was I doing?"

"It wasn't a nice dream Daddy, it scared me."

"Why's that sweetheart? Because I was in it?" Johnson said trying to make light of things.

"A big monster...like a Tyrannosaurus Rex...had you in its mouth and it was trying to eat you."

Johnson laughed out loud at this and ruffled his daughter's hair.

"I think he'd have gotten indigestion honey if he'd have eaten me," he said then he bent forward and kissed her on the cheek.

Leaving her to get dressed he strode across to the bathroom and waited patiently for Rebecca to emerge. When she did she jumped back, not having seen him.

"Ahh...you scared me Daddy," she yelled then she kicked him on the shin and sprinted past.

Johnson clutched his leg and hopped around as Rebecca slammed her bedroom door. Behind it he could hear her regaling Amy with the details of her attack.

"Rebecca! That wasn't funny!" he shouted.

"You shouldn't have frightened me then," she replied.

Johnson shook his head at his irascible daughter. Smart and tenacious she was the headstrong one amongst his children and the one that always made him laugh. Recently diagnosed with psoriasis she was an avid reader and was currently devouring the "Lord of the Rings" trilogy. Only yesterday she'd tried to decapitate him with a brush-pole from the kitchen as she pretended to be Aragorn. He, of course, had been an Orc.

Now, Johnson limped into the bathroom then shaved quickly and brushed his teeth before going downstairs. After hobbling into the kitchen he put the kettle on, only filling it a third of the way so that it would boil quicker. When it clicked he poured himself a cup of coffee then went into the living room, turned the TV on and had a seat.

Within minutes the bottom of the house was alive with the sounds made by his three young daughters and his wife so Johnson decided to go to the gym to do some training. Packing his kitbag he said goodbye to Jane and his daughters then headed out and got into his car.

At Crunch Fitness, on West 42nd Street between 9th and 10th Avenue, Johnson started with five three minute rounds on the punch bag. It was a good warm up routine and as he went through his combinations he felt the stress flow out of his body as his shoulders loosened and his hand speed picked up. After the bag Johnson switched over to the bench press. Because he had no spotter he erred on the side of caution and kept the weight down lifting two hundred pound for ten reps. When he sat up after his third set he felt someone staring at him so he turned around. It was Kelly, the Patrolman. Dressed in baggy New York Giant shorts with a blue Venice Beach muscle top it was obvious from the thickness of Kelly's biceps that he worked out regularly. He walked over and looked down at Johnson.

"Mind if I jump in with you?" he asked.

"It's okay, I'm finished," said Johnson.

"What's wrong?" Kelly asked, a big smirk on his face. "You afraid I'll show you up?"

Johnson stood up.

"No," he said. "I know you'd show me up."

"Damn straight Detective," said Kelly filling the word "Detective" with as much contempt as he could muster. Johnson looked at him for a second wondering where the animosity was coming from. Kelly stared back and for a second Johnson thought he was about to swing a punch but then the Patrolman smiled.

"It's a beautiful day, isn't it?!" he said.

"Yes it is," said Johnson then when nothing else was said he turned and walked away.

Chapter 7

When Johnson reached Abramo's apartment in Little Italy he gave the horn a gentle beep. Ten seconds later Abramo opened his front door with Angelo in his arms.

"Coming now Joe," he shouted across then he disappeared back inside to offload his son.

When he re-emerged he got in beside Johnson and they drove to the station. When they entered Sergeant Michael "Mousey" McDonald was covering the front desk, having taken over from Gums two hours previous. A tall lanky man with a laidback attitude and a pallid face he constantly stank of weed and looked high. Twice he'd been reprimanded because of it. When he spotted Johnson he called him over.

"Yes Mousey, what's up buddy?"

McDonald lifted three green sheets off the counter and held them out.

"Hank left these Canvass Sheets for you," he said.

"Right, thanks," Johnson said accepting the forms.

When he walked back to his partner Abramo recognized the Canvass Sheets by their color.

"Anything on them?" he asked.

Johnson scanned the first sheet quickly. It was a pro forma with spaces left for the names, addresses and telephone numbers of those questioned as well as a tick box indicating whether or not a follow up was needed and if there were any notes on the back. There was nothing on the first two sheets but on the last one a name in the middle had been ticked.

"Looks like we got a bite," said Johnson then he flicked the sheet over and read what was written on the back:

Mr. Washington said that he heard screaming and so got up to look out his bedroom window. When he did he saw a girl being dragged over to a van which then drove off. He was unable to provide the model of the van or the license plate.

Abramo raised his eyebrows.

"A girl?"

"Don't ask me. First I heard of it," said Johnson then he flipped the page back over and took out his phone.

Looking at the sheet he typed in the contact number for Mr. A. Washington then hit the green call button. As he was about to hang up and try again someone answered.

"Hello?" the voice said.

"Mr. Washington?" Johnson asked.

"Yes?"

"Sir, I'm Detective Joseph Johnson from the Midtown North Precinct. You were talking to one of our Patrolmen earlier this morning."

"Yes, that nice young man with the hawk nose...though don't tell him I said that."

"Don't worry Sir, I won't say a thing. The reason I'm phoning is that I'd like to come over and talk to you if I may with my partner Detective Salvatore Abramo."

"But I already told that young Patrolman everything I know."

"This is just a follow up Sir. Procedure."

"Okay, I suppose. When do you want to call?"

"Now Sir if that's okay."

"That's fine Detective. Do you have my address?"

Johnson read it off the Canvass Sheet.

"210 10th Avenue."

"Yes, that's it Detective."

"Okay, we're on our way."

210 10th Avenue was a small, two story townhouse. When Johnson rapped the front door it was opened immediately by an old black man with intelligent eyes and a shaved head. The most noticeable thing about him however was that he was missing his right arm.

"Mr. Washington?" Johnson asked.

"Yes, yes, that's me. You must be the Detectives."

"We are Sir."

The old man waved them into the house.

"Then come in," he said. "Come in."

"Thank you Sir."

Johnson stepped into the hallway in front of Abramo.

"This way," said Washington.

As they followed him into the house Johnson scanned his surroundings out of force of habit. A huge poster of Abraham Lincoln was displayed behind a glass frame in the hallway. Underneath the imposing countenance of the 16th President of the United States was Lincoln's "Emancipation Proclamation" that had freed the slaves during the American Civil War. It was dated 1863. Washington glanced back over his shoulder and saw Johnson admiring it.

"I used to be a History Teacher," he said.

Johnson smiled at him.

"I like history myself."

"Then we'll get along famously," said the old man then he ushered them into the dining room.

"Take a seat," he said.

The two Detectives obliged and sat down but Washington remained on his feet.

"Would you like a cup of tea or coffee?" he asked.

Johnson shook his head.

"No thank you Sir. We're pushed for time."

"Of course," said Washington then he too sat down.

When he did Johnson dipped his hand into his jacket and pulled out his notebook. There was a small pen through the spiral at the top so he pushed it out with his finger. When he looked up the old man was waiting expectantly.

"Mr. Washington..." Johnson began but the old man interrupted him.

"Please," he said. "Call me Abayomi."

"Abayomi, you told our Officer this morning that you heard a scream so you went to your bedroom window and witnessed a girl being dragged backwards to a minivan by a man, is that correct?"

"Yes Detective, that is exactly what I saw."

"Could you give me a description of this man?"

"No, I'm sorry. I've been wrecking my mind all morning trying to get an image of him in my head but for the life of me all I see is a dark figure."

"Was he white? Black? Asian? Indian?"

"He was white."

"What about height?"

"No, I'm sorry Detective. I've no idea."

"What color was the minivan?"

"That I do know,' said the old man. "It was also white."

"Do you know what type of minivan?"

"No, I'm sorry."

"Describe for me in detail exactly what happened and what you saw?"

"I was in bed...but because I have asthma I always leave the window open...otherwise I can't breathe. I was fast asleep then suddenly I heard a vehicle braking followed by a crash and a scream...really horrible...full of pain...so I got up and went over to the window. When I looked out there was a man walking towards a girl that was lying on the road. She was the one that had been screaming. At first I thought he was going to help her but instead he just grabbed her by the feet and dragged her back towards the minivan...then when he got there he lifted her up and dumped her into the back."

"When you say "girl"," Johnson asked. "What age would you say she was?"

"Anywhere from eighteen to twenty five but no older."

Johnson nodded.

"What color was her hair? Can you remember?"

"Blonde."

"Can you remember what she was wearing?"

"A green coat over black pants. Black boots."

"What type of coat?"

"All I can tell you is that it was green."

"Shade of green?"

Washington thought about this for a second.

"Forest green," he finally said.

"What about the man? What was he wearing?"

"All black...like a ninja."

"What about his legs?" Johnson asked.

"Black."

"You said the man dragged the girl back to the minivan and put her in. Where was the door he put her in?"

"At the side."

"You're sure?"

"Yes, I'm positive. Then after that the man jumped into the front."

"What about the license plate? Can you remember that?"

"No, I'm sorry. That's one thing I didn't get."

"Lettering on the van? Slogans? The name of a company?"

"I think there was something on the back door," said Washington, "but I can't remember what."

"Could you try to remember now. It's important," said Johnson.

The old man nodded then tilted his head back and closed his eyes. When his brow furrowed it was obvious he was having difficulty.

"Just relax," said Johnson. "It'll come to you if you let it."

But Washington's face kept its tense look so Johnson intervened again.

"Breathe in through your nose and out your nose," he said. "It'll help you to relax."

Washington followed Johnson's advice and sucked air up into his nostrils before blowing it out in a forceful rush

"No, do it slower," said Johnson. "Nice and easy."

This time Washington followed the Detective's counsel. As slowly and deliberately as he could he sucked air up in through his nose then ever so gently expelled it in a steady, measured fashion.

"That's it. Again," said Johnson.

Washington took four more breaths and gradually his face began to relax.

"I think I can see it," he said.

"Just let it come," said Johnson."

"Yes, yes, I can see it, I can see it," said Washington.

"Just keep breathing," said Johnson. "When it's clear tell me what it is you see."

"It's a bumper sticker on the back door," said the old man, his voice filled with excitement.

"Describe it for me?" Johnson asked.

"It's orange, blue and white."

"What's it off?"

"It's still out of focus. I can't make it out clearly."

"Concentrate," urged Johnson. "This is important."

The old man tried for a few more seconds then opened his eyes, a bright gleam of victory sparkling from his retina.

"It's a New York Knicks bumper sticker," he said. "With a large basketball underneath the writing."

"Well done Abayomi, that'll be a great help," Johnson said.

Washington grinned.

"It just came to me."

"I don't mean to intrude Sir," said Abramo, "but could we see the window you looked through to see the minivan?"

"Yes certainly, this way," said the old man.

Washington led them through into his bedroom. It was a small room with pale blue walls dominated by a large double bed that was far too big for the size of the room. A large framed photograph of a young Washington with an aging Ella Fitzgerald hung on the wall. In it Washington still had his two arms, both of them raised excitedly as he stood with the jazz star. Washington noticed the two Detectives staring at it.

"Three days later I lost my arm," he said.

Neither of the two Detectives said anything not wanting to pry but the curiosity must have showed on their faces.

"I lost it during the Harlem riots," said Washington. "18th July 1964. A Patrol cop with a mean streak and a night stick. Turned my arm to pulp, had to get it amputated."

With the two partners deciding to stay quiet the old man motioned them over to the window.

"I heard a screech of brakes," he said when they stopped beside him. "At first I thought I was dreaming then I heard the screams...those I'll never forget."

He shook his head.

"Poor girl."

"So you came over to this window?" Johnson asked.

"Yes, I got up out of bed and looked out...watched the man walk up to the girl then pull her backwards by the feet."

"Why didn't you dial 911?"

"I did but nobody came to see me until hours later."

Johnson stared out the window trying to imagine what Washington had just described. In his mind's eye he envisioned a young girl being dragged back to the minivan leaving a trail of blood in her wake. Even from this distance Johnson could still see the skid marks the tires had left.

Chapter 8

Back at the station Johnson crossed over to the front desk whilst Abramo continued on to the elevator.

"Has anyone phoned in about a missing girl?" he asked.

"Yes, about two hours ago," said the Desk Sergeant.

"Did they leave a name and address or a phone number?"

"Yes, it was the sister. Hold on, I'll get you the details now."

As Mousey checked the log book Johnson pulled out his notebook and pen.

"Here it is," Mousey said stopping his finger halfway down the page. "Ruby Crilly...Apartment 16B West 48th Street. She reported her sister, Kimberly Crilly, as missing. Her number is (917) 555-5432."

Johnson jotted down the information then thanked Mousey and went up to the Bullpen. When he sat down at his desk he lifted up the phone and rang Ruby Crilly's number.

"Hello?" a voice answered.

"Is that Ruby Crilly?" Johnson asked.

"Yes, it is. Who's this?"

"My name is Detective Johnson from the Midtown North Precinct. You phoned a couple of hours ago to report your sister Kimberly missing. Is that correct?"

"Have you found her?" Ruby asked, her voice desperate with hope.

"No, I'm afraid not Miss Crilly. What I'm actually ringing for is to get an idea of why you think your sister is missing."

"Because she said she'd phone me when she got in and she didn't. She always phones Detective. That's how I know something's happened."

"So where exactly was she last night?"

"She was here in my apartment. It was my birthday yesterday so I was having a party but at the end of the night Kimberly decided to walk home instead of getting a cab."

"And why was that?"

"Because she lives with my Mom on West 47th Street. She said it wasn't worth the cab fare."

"What time did she leave your apartment?"

"At 2.30am."

"And she never phoned when she got home?"

"No, she never got home. I checked with my Mom so I phoned her."

"Did the phone ring?"

"Six times then after that it went dead."

Johnson tried to piece it together in his head. The killer must have been dumping Richard Wright's body when Kimberly appeared on 10th

Avenue walking home. Seeing her he knocks her down then throws her into the back of the minivan and drives away only for Kimberly's phone to ring. Therefore he stops, gets into the back and searches her. When he does he finds her phone and turns it off. Now the pertinent question was whether or not he'd held onto the phone or dumped it.

"What color hair has your sister?" Johnson asked seeking further confirmation that Kimberly was the girl Washington had seen being dragged to the van.

"Blonde."

"What age is she?"

"Twenty four."

"Can you tell me what she was wearing?"

"An emerald green jacket with black buttons down the front...it was a Christmas present from my mother."

"Okay, thank you Miss Crilly. If anything comes up we'll get back to you immediately. In the meantime I'm going to send over a Patrol Officer to take your statement. Is that okay?"

"Yes, that's fine."

"Okay, thank you for your time."

"Please find my sister."

"We'll do our best Ma'am."

When Johnson hung up he walked over to Abramo.

"The girl's name is Kimberly Crilly."

"So what do you think happened?"

"What I think is she got unlucky...was walking home down 10th Avenue at the same time the killer was dumping the body."

"So he sees her and decides to silence her."

"Yeah, drives straight at her...knocks her down...then takes her away in his van."

"She could still be alive Joe. We'll have to find her."

"The sister rang her cell phone but it was turned off."

"A dead end then."

"Not necessarily."

"You know something I don't?"

"You know my friend Daniel?"

"Yeah, the big CIA guy that you were in the Marines with."

"He was telling me that the CIA have new technology now that allows them to track a phone using satellite signals and electromagnetic radiation."

"You'll have to speak English Joe...I never understood a word you said there."

"Okay, in layman's terms it means they've a way of tracking a phone even when it's turned off."

"But will the CIA let us use this technology?"

"No...not officially...but Daniel will."

"Then it's worth a shot...try him."

Johnson turned and walked back to his desk then sat down and rang Daniel. When Daniel answered he was his usual upbeat self.

"What's up Joe? What are you looking?"

"What has you thinking I'm looking something?"

"Because that's the only time you call me."

"Sure what are old friends for?"

Daniel laughed.

"Exactly, so go ahead Joe, hit me."

"I need you to track the location of a phone for me."

"Okay, give me the number."

That's what Johnson liked about Daniel. He never huffed or puffed or made excuses. Instead, he got right down to it with a minimum of fuss. Johnson gave him the number.

"I'll run it now Joe. Get back to you in half an hour."

"Okay, great."

After he hung up Johnson crossed back to Abramo's desk and filled him in. Abramo nodded.

"Well, fingers crossed," he said. "While you're waiting on Daniel I'll track down a Judge for the search warrant."

"Okay, I'll make a start on the murder board," Johnson said then he turned and returned to his desk.

When he sat down he logged onto his computer then scanned the photograph from Richard Wright's Driving License onto his desktop. Happy with the resolution he enlarged it then printed it out. This was his first step in preparing a murder board which he always assembled on the large whiteboard that was behind his desk bolted to the wall. Johnson grabbed blue tack out of a drawer then pressed the print out of Richard into the centre of the board. Above it he wrote "Murder Victim: Richard Wright." After this he phoned the Coroner. Firth answered after two short rings.

"Charles, just checking. Is the autopsy for Richard Wright still at one today?"

"Yes Detective it is."

"Ok, I'll see you then."

Johnson stepped over to the whiteboard and lifted a black marker. Above the photograph of Richard Wright he drew a timeline that ran from 8am the day before to 3.30am when Richard's body was found. Next he marked an arrow down from 8pm. Underneath he wrote "Wife said Richard left house." Abramo glanced up from his desk and saw him writing this.

"It's definitely not the wife," he shouted across.

Johnson shrugged.

"Anything's possible."

"Yeah, I agree but my gut tells me it isn't her."

"Did you write down about financial records in the search warrant?" Johnson asked.

"Yes, for his home and for the hotel."

"What about his car, did you put that in?"

"Yes Joe, I know how to write out a search warrant."

"Sorry Sal, I'm just making sure."

"Judge Bartolli is free in an hour. She's going to sign it for me."

"Ok, I'll go with you then we'll go to the M.E's office."

To kill the half hour before Daniel rang back Johnson filled in other details on the Murder Board adding in photographs of Yerzov and Wright's best friend George Corbett. When the half hour was up Daniel phoned back.

"The cell phone's outside an apartment building on 11th Avenue Joe. According to the satellite images it's in a trash can."

"Can you send me a print out?" Johnson asked.

"One step ahead of you Joe, already have."

Armed with the map that Daniel had emailed to him Johnson was able to find the trash can easily enough. When he opened it and sifted through the rubbish he found the phone sitting in an empty KFC box.

"Looks like he wasn't stupid after all," he said.

"Now what?" Abramo asked.

"Now we go see the Judge for that warrant."

The Appellate Division Courthouse of New York State, First Department, also known as Appellate Division of the Supreme Court of the State of New York, was a historic court house located at 27 Madison Avenue at East 25th Street, across from Madison Square Park in Manhattan. Designed by James Brown Lord and finished in 1899 the building was a perfect example of the "City Beautiful Movement" of that era that had been dedicated to beautification and monumental grandeur in cities. As always, when Johnson walked up the steps leading into the Courthouse he was overawed by the magnificence of the building's exterior. Three stories high the outside was dominated by an imposing triangular portico supported by six Corinthian columns. On the outside thirty statues by sixteen different sculptors made for a structure that took the breath away. Two impressive marble statues by Frederick Ruckstuhl flanked the entrance: Wisdom and Force. On the left, Wisdom was depicted by a bearded man in robes reading a law book whilst the allegorical figure of Force on the right was personified by a fierce eyed Roman Centurion with a Gladius across his knees.

"Extraordinary, aren't they?" Johnson said as they passed between the two stone guardians.

"That one on the right looks like he's about to jump up and cleave somebody's head off," said Abramo.

Inside was as equally impressive with painted murals, a stained glass dome and a bronze and glass chandelier that hung from the ceiling. As befitted such a grand structure the walls were marble and divided by Corinthian pilasters and massive, original Herter Brothers furniture.

"Gabriella loves this place," said Abramo.

"It's hard not to like."

Bartolli's chambers were on the third floor so they got the elevator up then waited patiently to be shown in by her clerk. When they were ushered in Bartolli was reading something on her laptop but she logged off when she heard them enter then got up and walked over.

"Joseph, it's been too long," she said extending her hand.

Johnson nodded and accepted her handshake.

"Absence makes the heart grow fonder Judge," he said.

She laughed at this then released his hand and switched to Abramo. After she'd shaken his hand she walked back and sat behind her desk.

"Would either of you like a drink?" she asked. "Tea? Coffee?"

Johnson shook his head.

"Sorry Judge, we can't, we're in a hurry. We've an autopsy to get to."

"In that case, let me see the search warrant."

Abramo took it out of his pocket and handed it across to her. She scanned it quickly.

"Looks to be in order," she said then she lifted a pen and quickly signed the search warrant.

"Thanks Judge," Johnson said.

Back outside Johnson got behind the wheel then drove out of the car park back onto 1st Avenue. As usual the traffic was heavily congested. All around the two partners irate commuters pressed down hard on their car horns creating a mutilated symphony that whilst painful to the ears was all too familiar on the streets of New York. On top of this strident noise, adding an extra layer to the din, were the voices of furious drivers shouting back and forth across the lanes.

"Nobody has any patience anymore," said Johnson.

"Me included," said Abramo. "I hate getting stuck in traffic and it's always their fault."

When he said this Abramo pointed at the three yellow taxi cabs that were boxing them in.

"Tourists love them though," said Johnson.

"Well I don't. They're a pain in the ass. I mean, look! There's five of them for every other car on the road. And do you ever hear the shouting they do? Like fingernails down glass."

"Stop complaining, a yellow taxi cab is as much a part of New York as the skyscrapers."

Abramo rolled the passenger side window down. Immediately, the smell of gasoline fumes assaulted his nostrils. He wrinkled his nose then stared upwards at the towering buildings hemming them in on both sides.

"Would you believe I've lived in New York my entire life," he said. "And not once have I been to the top of the Empire State building."

Johnson glanced at him.

"Never?"

"Not once."

"Jesus Sal, you should definitely go. Take Angelo up, he'd love it."

"Have you been?"

"Yeah, quite a few times but not in a while."

"Why not?"

"Just haven't had the time lately, too busy."

"Right, that's what I'll do next week. A trip up the Empire State building. Me, Gabriella and Angelo."

"Good for you. Angelo will have a ball."

"Why don't you come with us? Take Jane and the girls."

"No, they've been up already. They probably wouldn't go again."

"After 9/11 it's back being the tallest building in the city, isn't it?" asked Abramo.

"I'm not sure but I do know it's one of the seven wonders of the modern world," said Johnson. "I remember that from the last time I was there."

"Jesus! Compared to these monsters," said Abramo. "We're just pin pricks down here."

Johnson nodded.

"Yeah, but you have to admit there's something magnificent about them."

"The concrete jungle."

"You ever think of moving?" Johnson asked.

"No, grew up here, it's home, love it too much," said Abramo. "You?"

"We've talked about it but no decision's been made yet."

"Yet? You trying to tell me you're leaving me Joe?"

"No, I'm not saying that Sal. I'll be around for a while longer."

"I certainly hope so buddy, I don't want to lose you."

"Stop it, you're gonna make me cry."

"Yeah, that'll be the day. Big, bad Joe Johnson crying. Never gonna happen."

As they drove along Abramo stared out the window. On the sidewalk he noticed two Patrol cops, a male and a female, stopping a teenage boy. Even from his position across two lanes of traffic Abramo could tell the adolescent was highly agitated. As he watched, the boy raised his arms sideways into the air for a "Stop and Frisk", the controversial policy aimed at reducing crime but when the male officer placed his hands on him the boy shoved him backwards then burst into a sprint. Cool as a cucumber the female officer unhooked her night stick and threw it at the teenager's legs. It clattered against his ankles and tripped him to the pavement. Jubilant at her success the female cop gave a whoop of delight then raced over and planted her foot on the kid's back. Abramo swung around on his seat.

"You see that Joe?" he asked, his voice excited.

"Yeah, good throw," said Johnson still attempting to edge through the traffic.

Back on the sidewalk the female cop took out her cuffs then used them to manacle her prey. Throughout, the youngster, who was still trying to break free, spat a string of expletives over his shoulder. Hearing this Abramo cupped his hands around his mouth and shouted across.

"Wash that kid's mouth out with soap," he shouted.

Hearing him, the female Officer lifted her head.

"I'll make him put money in the swear box," she yelled back.

Abramo unclipped his Detective's shield from his belt then held it up to show he was on the job.

"That was one hell of an arrest Officer," he shouted.

The female officer gave him a good-natured salute in return.

"Thanks Detective."

As Abramo continued to watch, she turned back to the kid and started to search him. Within seconds she found a gun which she handed up to her partner out of harm's way.

"They got a gun," Abramo shouted then, because they'd now passed the incident, he slumped back into his seat.

"You ever miss being out on patrol Joe?" he asked.

Johnson shook his head.

"No, not with my knee Sal. Glad to be behind the wheel now."

"I miss it. I really enjoyed walking the neighborhoods."

"You have a favorite memory?" Johnson asked.

Abramo's eyes darkened immediately.

"Not exactly a favorite but one I'm proud of," he said.

"What happened?"

"I caught a pedophile before he had time to hurt a little girl."

Johnson's jaw clenched in anger as he imagined one of his own daughters being attacked.

"What happened?" he asked.

"A call came through about 2pm about a possible abduction...so me and Gerry Wright...do you know him?"

"No."

"Great fella, sharp as a razor. He was my partner at the time. Anyway, the call comes through and because me and Gerry are the closest...only the next block away...we tell dispatch that we'll take a look. But when we get to the street I spot this man dragging a trash can towards a van that has its back doors open. Now because I know an abduction has just taken place five minutes beforehand I'm extremely interested in what that man has in his trash can...but when we start walking towards him and I shout for him to stop...lo and behold...that sonofabitch pulls a Berretta and starts shooting.   Me, I'm body swerving all over the place but poor Gerry, who's as slow as a tortoise on crutches gets shot."

"Where'd he get hit?"

"Top of the right shoulder...minor flesh wound....so he drops screaming to the high heavens that he's dying. Meanwhile, I'm running straight at this motherfucker expecting to be shot dead...but when the perp pulls the trigger...misfire Joe...Halleluiah...God on my side.   I body slam that bastard so hard into the ground that the road shakes. Next thing I'm on top of him...swinging punching like there's no tomorrow. He goes out cold. Just to be sure I hit him a few extra."

"You were lucky Sal."

"Not as lucky as that little girl Joe...because when I opened that trash can there she was staring up at me with these terrified blue eyes and a gag in her mouth. And see to this day Joe...that happened eight years ago...I still get a card every Christmas from that little girl. Seventeen she is now...only nine back then."

"What's her name?"

"Catherine Barnes. And do you know who the man was that was taking her Joe?"

"No idea. Who?"

"The mailman that delivered their letters every day. Ends up when they get him into questioning he confesses to three other abductions and murders."

"Jesus Sal, I'm proud of you. That's a great arrest."

"Yeah...got a commendation for it an' all. My old man even bought me a present when he heard...and he's the tightest, stingiest man on the planet."

"What he buy you?"

Sal shot his hands forward to reveal the cuffs of his shirt.

"Italian flag cufflinks."

Johnson looked at the miniature green, white and red flags attached to the bottom of Sal's shirt sleeves.

"The mother land."

"Yeah, my father's always going on about the old country. Swear to God Joe, he thinks he's Don Corleone."

"You're from Sicily?"

"No, Calabria."

"The toe of the boot that's kicking Sicily."

Abramo was surprised that Johnson knew this.

"How'd you know that?" he asked.

Johnson shrugged.

"I'm good at Geography," he said.

"Me and Gabriella actually went to Calabria for our honeymoon," said Sal.

"Nice?"

"Beautiful. Really stunning."

"Me and Jane toured Ireland for three weeks for our honeymoon. Landed in Dublin then went through every county. Ended up in Belfast staying with a distant cousin of mine called Declan and his wife Aoife. Crazy couple."

"Did they like to drink and fight?"

"Only with each other."

"What about you?" Abramo asked.

"What?"

"Your most memorable moment on parole?"

Johnson hesitated.

"Come on Joe...spill."

"I was in the South Tower at 9/11."

"Jesus, sorry Joe, you never told me."

"It's not something I usually talk about."

"Yeah, I've heard quite a few say that."

"I was giving first aid to injured civilians after the North Tower was hit but when the second plane hit we were ordered into the South Tower to help the Fire Department evacuate the building. I'd actually helped three people down the stairwells and was about to go in again when the whole thing collapsed. Others weren't so lucky."

"Sorry Joe, I didn't know."

Johnson wondered whether to tell Abramo about the people that had jumped that day. About how the sound of their bodies exploding on impact still haunted him. His therapist had told him it was healthy to talk about these things. Bottling it up she said led to mental stress. Johnson decided against it, not wanting to burden his friend with the horror.

Twenty minutes later they arrived at the Office of the Chief Medical Examiner on First Avenue. A tall, rectangular building like the other soaring structures that created the jagged Manhattan skyline it was different in that it only had a single row of windows running vertically up its length. On the front of the building was a purple circular plaque with "NYU Medical Center" emblazoned across the front. Underneath in three dimensional letters were the words "Arnold and Marie Schwartz Health Care Center." At the base, attached to the side, was a small square building whose entrance acted as a gateway to the underground car park. Taken altogether as a whole, the entire edifice looked like a large grey "L". Johnson took a right down into the underground car park. A barrier had been installed since the last time he'd been there. He stopped before it and wound his window down.

"You'd easy know we're in a recession," he said as he pressed the button and got his ticket.

"It's ridiculous," said Abramo. "The banker's roll the dice with our money, lose, and it's us, the working suckers that have to pay."

Johnson drove down into the car park. An elderly couple driving an old Mustang were in the middle of reversing so he pulled over and waited patiently. When they drove away Johnson took their space then together, he and Sal got out and walked over to the elevator that sat at the bottom of the building.

"I hate this place," said Abramo as he pressed the button for the tenth floor.

"Why?" Johnson asked.

"Why do you think why?"

"No idea."

"Dead bodies ring a bell?"

"You're a Homicide Detective."

"Doesn't mean I have to like dead bodies or the fact that I'm gonna be one someday."

"We all got to go Sal. God doesn't play favorites."

"Yeah, well, I want to die in my bed aged a hundred with my great grandchildren standing around me crying."

Johnson laughed. Since he'd known him Sal had always had a fear of dying even though he was forever diving into dangerous situations.

"If you don't want to die young and leave a good looking corpse Sal then I suggest that the next time we come across some bad guys you take a deep breath and remember those grandchildren you want to see."

"Great grandchildren."

"Sorry, my apologies. Great grandchildren."

"Okay, I will."

"Yeah, I'll believe it when I see it."

After the elevator doors opened they walked out into a narrow corridor leading up to a receptionist. When they stopped in front of her she stopped typing on her computer and looked up. Johnson was taken aback by the size of her smile. It was one of the widest he'd ever seen.

"Hello, may I help you?" she asked.

"You must be new," said Johnson.

"Yes, I started last week."

"I'm Detective Joseph Johnson and this is my partner Detective Salvatore Abramo. We're from the Midtown North Precinct...here to see Dr. Firth."

"Yes, he's expecting you but may I see some I.D first please?"

"Of course," said Johnson then he flipped open his wallet and showed the receptionist his shield. Satisfied, she then switched her attention to Abramo.

"And yours?" she asked, a polite smile on her face.

Abramo returned her smile then also flashed his shield.

"Can't be too careful," said the receptionist.

"No, you certainly cannot," Abramo replied.

"Doctor Firth is in Autopsy Room 3," she said pointing.

"It's okay,' said Johnson. "We know where it is."

When they opened the door to Autopsy Room Three and walked in Firth was still making verbal notes into a microphone that dangled from the ceiling. The reason for this was so that he could operate and talk at the same time. Meanwhile, his two assistants were busy washing some of the implements Firth had just used to cleave open the chest, neck and skull of Richard Wright. Firth motioned for them to give him a minute with an upheld finger then continued talking after Johnson gave him a corresponding nod. Johnson and Abramo walked across to examine the corpse that had once been the living and breathing Richard Wright. Now, the cadaver lay face up on a gleaming, stainless steel autopsy table that Johnson knew from previous visits had a drain in the centre to run off blood and bodily fluids. A steel trolley sat at the foot of the table. Lying on top of it was a large sewing needle and a bone saw. Behind the table, attached to the wall was a whiteboard with examination data written on it. It included a quick sketch of the human body with red arrows leading to jotted notes. Johnson stared down at what had once been a person with a real life and people that had loved him. Underneath the glare of the overhead spotlights the body was ghostly white with a horrible tint of blue and livid pink. A large stitched "Y" dissected the dead man's chest in a grotesque fashion that made Johnson wonder if he'd one day be lying on a table like this. The odds, considering his line of work, were good. He shivered at the thought and immediately pushed it away. Then Firth came over peeling off his gloves which he dropped into a bin that he opened with his foot.

"You okay Joe?" he asked. "You look a bit pale."

"Just wondering if I'll end up on one of these someday."

"That's a certainty," said Firth. "Everyone does."

"This place gives me the heebie jeebies," said Abramo.

"Brings you down to earth with a bump doesn't it," said Firth. "Makes you realize you're not immortal."

"Exactly, which is why I don't like it."

"You got anything for us?" Johnson asked.

Firth nodded.

"The first thing you need to know is that it wasn't the gunshot to the head that killed this man," he said. "That was after. This poor soul was either strangled or hung then afterwards shot. Given the coup de grace."

"Strangled or hung, we'll need better than that," said Johnson. "One or the other Doc."

"I'm sorry Joe. If he was hung from a low suspension point then those horizontal marks he has on his neck are the same that would occur with manual strangulation."

"No other signs?"

"Similar for both scenarios. Facial congestion, purple protruding tongue, petechial hemorrhages caused by blood leaking from capillaries in the eyes...typical of hanging and strangulation. And because the body was dumped and lying horizontal there's no lividity due to pooling of blood in the legs, forearms and hands...the blood would have spread out again."

"So we've two options to look at?"

"Well, because I suspected a hanging I did a tox screen because this guy's in shape Joe. To put a noose around his neck I think the perpetrator would have had to subdue him first. Force him to swallow something...get him docile and compliant."

"You find anything?" Johnson asked.

"Flunitrazepam," said Firth.

"Which is what in layman's terms?"

"Rohynol...Roofies."

"The date rape drug?" Abramo asked.

"Yes," said Firth. "It's a pre-operation anesthetic or strong sleeping pill but stronger doses can bring on amnesia. And because it's an odorless and tasteless pill it can be ground down easily and dropped into somebody's drink. But even more disturbing is that it disappears completely from the system within twenty four hours which as you both know makes prosecution very difficult."

"How long would it take before it kicks in?" Johnson asked.

"It could be as quick as ten minutes but it reaches its peak after eight hours at which point it can render a person totally unconscious."

"Just say we were comparing it to Valium, how much stronger would it be?"

"About ten times stronger," said Firth.

"So somebody drugs him, hangs him and then shoots him for good measure, is that what you're saying?" Abramo asked.

"No, I'm saying that there was Rohypnol in his system when he was either strangled or hung and then afterwards shot. How the Rohypnol got into his system I do not know because Rohypnol is also used in combination with other drugs."

"Such as?" Abramo asked.

"It enhances the effect of low grade heroin, mellows the buzz of crack and is often used to soften comedowns...especially from coke. But it's also got a reputation as a 'love drug' because it's an aphrodisiac that gives you a drunk feeling for a long period of time."

"We found cocaine in the victim's pants pocket," said Johnson.

"So you've two options. Did he use Rohypnol the next day after taking cocaine or was he drugged."

"What about the circular indents on the face?" Johnson asked. "Were you able to identify what caused them?"

"As of yet...no. All I can say is that it was something hard with a circle at the top."

"Caliber of the bullet? Type of gun?"

"No, sorry. Without the bullet there's no way of knowing which gun."

"Did the wife come down and identify him?"

"Yes, first thing this morning at nine o' clock."

"What you think of her?" Abramo asked.

"She seemed sincere, very upset."

"Not acting?"

"I don't know. That's your job Detective but from what I saw I thought she showed genuine signs of grief."

Chapter 9

Once they were back in the car and stuck in traffic again Johnson filled Abramo in on what he wanted to do next.

"I think we should talk to one of the Narcotics boys, see who sells Rohypnol at Vanity."

"Why?"

"We need to know if Richard was drugged by his killer or if he took the Rohypnol himself."

"So, what? We go up to the dealer and ask him who he's selling to?"

"You're Italian, aren't you?"

"Yeah."

"Then we'll make him an offer he can't refuse."

Abramo laughed at this.

"I like your style Joe, you can be an honorary Italian for the day."

As Johnson drove along one handed he opened the contacts in his phone then rang Eric Anderson, an old friend that worked on the floor below him in the Narcotics Division. Eric answered on the second ring.

"Yes Joe, what's up?" he asked.

"I need a bit of help Eric. You mind if me and my partner call round and see you?"

"When?"

"Now."

"Okay, no problem. I'm at the Precinct Joe."

"Right, we're on our way."

It took nearly thirty five minutes to get back to Midtown North. By the time Johnson pulled into one of the parking spaces out front his knee was aching and Abramo was ready to shoot every yellow taxi driver in New York.

"Those bloody yellow cabs think they own the road," he complained.

"They're an icon," Johnson said.

"Icon? No way Joe. They're a pestilence...like cockroaches infesting the city. I mean, do you know how many of them there are?"

"No idea."

"Thirteen thousand. I mean, is that overkill or what? And that's without counting the other taxis. Altogether, there's about forty thousand of them Joe. Forty thousand! I mean, come on. No one can justify that amount of taxis."

"It's only people out making a living Sal."

"Out clogging the streets you mean."

"Do you not realize thousands of cops moonlight as taxi drivers? My Dad did."

"Oh so that's why you like them. Good old Rocky was a taxi driver."

"Yes that is why. And he had a tough time of it too. Got robbed three times."

"Well, obviously I don't agree with that."

"Come on Sal, what's really eating you about the yellow cabs?"

Abramo rolled his eyes then sighed heavily.

"Am I really that easy to read?"

"Yes. Now spill."

"You know my sister Bonfilia?"

"Yes, the one that's in a wheelchair."

"Nissan got the new contract to build the new yellow taxis but guess what? None of them have wheelchair access. And if they don't have wheelchair access how are the disabled supposed to get about?"

"But sure the next four thousand taxi medallions are going to taxis that do have wheelchair access."

"Really? I didn't hear that."

"The Mayor announced it a few months back."

"Well, good. As long as my sister's able to get about then I'm happy...means I don't have to drive her everywhere."

After they walked into the station they took the stairs to the second floor. When they entered, the smell of coffee immediately hit them up the face. Abramo wrinkled his nose.

"Smell that Joe?" he said. 'Reckon we could get a cup?"

"Behave you."

Six Detectives were in the room, five of them huddled in a circle discussing something. The sixth one, Eric, was at his desk reading a letter.

"Looks like something's up," said Abramo.

Johnson strode across the room. Sensing someone approaching Eric looked up then smiled automatically when he seen it was Johnson.

"Long time no see," he said then he stood up with the letter in his hand.

Six foot tall and extremely broad he had tight knit curly black hair and a lantern jaw. As always he sported his trademark dark stubble because he loathed shaving. Around his neck was a gold chain that disappeared beneath his shirt. Johnson knew what dangled from the necklace. Two small boxing gloves. Gold boxing gloves. Toughness and streetwise New York oozed from every pore of Eric's skin.

"Come on, don't be holding back," said Eric.

"Never," said Johnson then at the same time they started jabbing and throwing pretend punches at each other. It was their own personal greeting and had been since their days at Arnold's Boxing Gym in Hell's Kitchen where they'd first met as scrawny ten year olds. After a couple of seconds they stopped, burst out laughing and embraced each other. When they separated Johnson pointed at the impromptu meeting in the corner.

"What's going on?" he asked.

Eric waved the letter in his hand.

"We've all to do SNEU training," he said.

"Which stands for what?

"Street Level Narcotics Enforcement Unit Training. Brought out three years ago...so even if you've been doing undercover for ten years like myself ...you've still to go back and do it."

"Why?"

"That guy that got shot three weeks ago with the sweets in his hand instead of a gun. The cop that pulled the trigger...Barry Holland...ends up he wasn't trained properly...which means the Department's up shit creek without a paddle and are about to get their asses sued. So from now on...according to this letter...anyone without SNEU training can't work the street."

"Bolting the stable door after the horse has escaped," said Johnson.

"Exactly but that's enough of our woes," said Eric. "How's you?"

"Can't complain...sure nobody would listen."

Eric laughed then swung one of his meaty arms around Johnson's shoulders.

"You remember the last time we had a drink together Joe?"

"Remember it? I wake up in a cold sweat thinking about it."

Eric looked across at Abramo.

"It was Joe's fortieth birthday so I arrive round to his house with a big forty ounce bottle of whisky...one ounce for every year. Huge this thing was. Now usually it'd take ten men to drink this monstrosity but because me and Joe are practically superhuman we finish that baby in one night with two whisky glasses and a smile."

"Tyrone crystal whisky glasses," said Johnson.

"Yeah, your fathers, Rocky's," said Eric blessing himself. "May he rest in peace."

"Amen to that."

Eric tilted his head back and spoke to the heavens.

"Gone but not forgotten Rocky," he said jabbing his finger up into the air.

"The whisky glasses were a wedding present from my Uncle Kevin," Johnson explained to Abramo.

"Beautiful they were. Really set the tone," said Eric. "Created an ambience."

Johnson shook his head.

"Not the next day they didn't," he said.

"Next day?!" said Eric. "Try the next week. I felt like someone had plucked my eyeballs out and dropped them in vinegar."

Johnson gave an empathetic nod.

"That was a man's night of drinking," he said.

"Bushmill's whisky mixed with ginger ale."

"Which ran out."

"So we switched to Diet Coke. Eight at night until ten the next morning."

"Then Jane came down."

"Like a fire breathing dragon," said Eric. "Shouted at you because you'd smoked in the kitchen and the smell was all over the house."

"I didn't know you smoked Joe," said Abramo.

"I don't usually but on that night I did."

"You see, I smoke," said Eric. "And because I looked so happy and content with a cigarette in my mouth...Joe here...who can't see green cheese...decides to join me. But you see, I was going out the back to smoke...but see when Joe lights up...he sits right where he is in the kitchen. Which in hindsight was not a good idea."

"Well, in my defense I did have near a liter of whisky down my neck at that point. I couldn't stand never mind walk."

"Poor Jane, remember her face...you were a rebel that night Joe."

"Yeah, a rebel without a clue, she still brings it up. Says I disrespected her."

"Too right you did...especially when you sparked up another Marlboro with her there."

"Really Joe?" said Abramo. "You lit up in front of her after she'd shouted at you?"

"I was as pissed as a fart...my brain may as well have been in a jar Sal because it certainly wasn't in my head."

Eric clutched Johnson tighter, a massive smile on his face.

"Jesus," he said. "I thought Jane was gonna kill you there and then."

"This is my house as well," you said. "I'll smoke in my own kitchen if I want and you'll not stop me!" Priceless, all I could do was laugh."

"Jane still hasn't forgiven me."

"And rightly so Joe. You were a bad' un that night."

"I haven't touched whisky since. Jane says I'm not allowed to drink it anymore."

"Me neither but it's because I'm too afraid of the after effects," said Eric laughing. "Anyway come on, introduce me to your friend."

"This is my partner Salvatore Abramo. Sal, this is my childhood friend and the man that continually leads me astray, Eric Anderson."

Abramo stuck out his hand.

"I've seen you around the station," he said as they shook hands. "It's good to put a name to the face."

"Likewise. I've heard a lot about you," said Eric attempting to crush Abramo's hand.

Abramo squeezed back forcing Eric to relinquish his grip. He wrung his hand with a rueful smile on his face.

"Joe wasn't lying, you're a strong big brute," he said.

"Only when I need to be," said Abramo.

"Well, don't worry, I'll not be trying that again."

"Good."

The three of them sat down around Eric's desk.

"So what can I do for you Joe?" Eric asked, his big friendly face eager to help.

"Who sells Rohypnol in our Precinct?"

"The forget me pill. Tons of people Joe. You'll have to narrow it down."

"Vanity Hotel."

"Germaine Grant's the man you're after. That's his patch."

"What's he like?"

"Black dude...flashy dresser...cross eyes."

"You know where we can find this upstanding member of the community?"

"He lives in an apartment on 10th Avenue, top floor."

"Do you think he'll speak to us?"

"Not a chance of it. If he knows you're a cop he'll spit in your eye then cut your throat...likes to use a knife."

"Then what do we do?"

Eric thought about this for a few seconds.

"I've a snitch," he finally said. "A loudmouth that I don't like...but I know he's in tight with Grant. We could get him to set up a buy with you then we could arrest Grant, threaten him with jail and get him to spill."

"Much will I need?"

"Two hundred dollars should be enough, he'll definitely come running for that."

"Okay, grand, I think I can manage that."

"This is going to burn my snitch but you're lucky. He wants to return to Argentina to see his mother...she's dying from cancer...has only a few months left to live. If I tell him all he has to do to get his plane fare is to set up a meet then I think he'll do it."

"Thanks Eric, you're a star."

"You owe me Joe because this snitch is a complete asshole. Riles me every time I see him."

Chapter 10

Five minutes later they were in Johnson's car and headed to see Eric's snitch. As the "Ninth Avenue International Food Festival" was on they had to park then go on foot to meet him as Ninth Avenue was closed to vehicles for the duration of the festival. As they walked along they were surrounded by an assortment of ethnic food shops and fine restaurants all offering a mixture of national and regional foods. Street vendors also lined the streets doling out alligator burgers, Kangaroo hotdogs and various other exotic meats. Thousands thronged the streets amidst the loud noise, bright colors and various smells sampling the wares of the traders.

"You ever go in there Joe?" Eric asked as they passed the Esposito Pork Shop at 38th.

"Not in a while."

"Then make sure to go. They do the best sausage and pepper hero ever...melts in the mouth."

"I'll take you next week as a thank you for doing this."

"Me as well," said Abramo. "You know I like my grub Joe."

"Okay, you as well Sal."

"Or that place there, Chantale's Cajun Kitchen...spicy gumbos, crab cakes, chicken curry...to die for Joe."

"I believe you but you're only getting the one meal out of me as a thank you."

Eric laughed out loud at this.

"Worth a try," he said.

All around them street fair vendors were busy selling a concoction of items; clothes, sunglasses, jewelry. Even socks.

"Last time I was here was two years ago with the kids," said Johnson.

"Did they like it?" Abramo asked.

"Absolutely loved it. They always put a big pavilion up on 53rd and 54th for children. All sorts of games and activities."

"How long's it on for?" Abramo asked, the expression on his face revealing he liked what he was hearing.

"I think tomorrow's the last day," said Johnson.

"In that case I'll get Gabriella to bring Angelo down during my lunch hour tomorrow. I'll meet them here."

Ten minutes later they stopped outside the Siam Grill near 42nd. Eric took out his phone and called his snitch. After a brief conversation he hung up.

"He's on his way."

"How long's he gonna be?" asked Abramo. "All this talking about food is making my stomach rumble."

"When he gets here we'll have lunch," said Johnson. "I'll buy."

Twenty minutes later the snitch arrived. He was a tall, lanky Latino with sunken eyes, greasy hair and a cruel mouth. In his right hand was a large slab of cornbread filled with Texas Chilli. Dressed in a bright yellow shirt that hung on him like an ill-fitted sheet he sauntered up to them like he was out for a stroll.

"What kept you?" Eric asked, unable to disguise the anger in his voice.

"If you must know I was watching an Egyptian belly dancer up on 55th...fancied me too."

"You told me you'd only be five minutes."

"Five minutes...twenty minutes....does it really make a difference?! I'm here now aren't I."

"Better late than never," said Johnson in an effort to diffuse the situation.

"Exactly," said the tall Latino firing Eric a dirty look.

When Eric went to say something back Johnson quickly intervened.

"Can you introduce us Eric?"

Eric bit down on his retort.

"This charming young man is Alfonso Lopez," he said. "Alfonso, this is Detective Joseph Johnson and his partner Detective Salvatore Abramo. Both from homicide."

"Oh, the big boys, real Detectives."

"We need your help Alfonso," said Johnson.

"As long as Bad Breath over there does what he said he would do then I'll give you all the help you need."

"Don't be calling me that," said Eric.

"Sorry Detective Halitosis but it's true, your breath is like a sewer. Seriously gross. Why don't you buy some breath mints...deodorant too...you fuckin' reek man."

"You do realize I can rescind our agreement asshole."

"Just take it easy Eric," said Johnson.

"Yeah Eric, stop being such a sensitive whore," said Alfonso. "It's unbecoming."

Johnson swung back to the big Latino.

"You! Keep it shut and grow up," he said.

Alfonso grinned then raised his free hand slowly into a sarcastic salute.

"Yes Sir, three bags full Sir, I'll do anything you fuckin' want Sir."

As he finished his salute with a flick of his hand Abramo stepped up close and slapped him hard across the face. The big Latino reeled back.

"What the fuck?" he said clutching his cheek.

Abramo grabbed him by the shirt collar and raised his fist.

"Learn some manners," he said.

"What the fuck...that's assault."

"No, that's tickling. You'll know all about it when it's assault."

Alfonso tried to break free but it was pointless even trying. Abramo's grip was like a vice.

"Let fuckin' go of me," he said.

"You going to behave?" Abramo asked.

"No, I'm fuckin' not...now let go of me you fuckin' monkey."

Abramo grabbed the snitch's neck and gave it a hard squeeze.

"Manners cost nothing," he said.

Alfonso yelped with pain.

"Aaagh, let go, let go...that fuckin' hurts man."

Abramo eased the pressure but didn't fully relinquish his grip.

"You going to be good?" he asked.

"Yes," said Alfonso, his voice no more than a squeak.

"Good boy," said Abramo then he released him and stepped back although he stayed within striking distance.

"Okay, we'll start again," said Johnson. "Alfonso, we need your help."

Alfonso glanced nervously at Abramo. The big cop's face was inscrutable. Alfonso rubbed the back of his neck.

"Do I get the plane fare I need to get back to Argentina?"

Johnson nodded.

"Yes," he said.

"Okay, what is it you need?"

"I need to make a buy from your friend Germaine Grant."

"What? Are you fuckin' crazy man? If Germaine realizes you're a cop he'll cut your fuckin' throat...mine too."

"That's where you come in. You're gonna vouch for me, tell him I'm your friend then go to the meet with me to make the buy."

"No fuckin' way man," said Alfonso, his face twisting at the mere thought. "I like breathing way too much to do something stupid like that."

"Tough, you're doing it," said Johnson.

Alfonso shook his head emphatically.

"No I'm not," he said.

"You are," Johnson insisted, his voice brooking no dissent.

"Listen man," said Alfonso. "You don't understand. Germaine is a crazy motherfucker...likes killing people...does it for fun."

"Not this time, we're taking him down."

"No, fuck that man. I'll get the money to see my Madre another way."

After saying this Alfonso turned to walk away but Abramo raised his hand. It was enough to stop the tall Latino dead in his tracks.

"We're not finished with you yet," he said.

"This is illegal," said Alfonso. "I'm gonna sue your ass for assault."

Abramo seized his neck again and squeezed.

"Shut up and listen," he said.

"Okay, okay," said the big Latino, his face screwed up with pain.

Satisfied, Abramo released him then on cue Johnson took the lead.

"How'd you flip this guy?" he asked Eric.

"Caught him with half a kilo of coke so I gave him an option. Either work for me or do twenty years."

Johnson turned back to Alfonso.

"You hear that?"

"I've got ears haven't I."

"Yes but have you got a brain?"

"Yeah...as a matter of fact I do which is why I'm not fuckin' doing this. It's suicide."

"So you'd rather go to jail for twenty years?"

"You can't do that, I'm not your snitch."

"But you're mine," said Eric, "and I've had enough of that loud mouth of yours to last me a lifetime. Time for you to go to the slammer where your breath'll be bad from sucking things you don't like. Then again, maybe you will like sucking them."

"That was only a joke about your breath."

"Mine isn't."

Alfonso looked at the three Detectives, gauging how serious they were. Reading the truth in their unflinching stares he realized he was trapped.

"Okay, okay, I'll do it," he said, "but I want the money first, up front. Five hundred dollars."

"Already sorted," said Eric tapping his breast pocket.

"Good...show me it."

Eric took a bundle of notes out of his inside pocket. He fanned them in his hand showing them to Alfonso. Alfonso reached out to take the money. When he did Eric pushed him back and stuck the money away.

"After, not before Alfonso."

"Up front man, that's what was agreed."

"Do I look stupid?"

"Do I have to answer that?"

"No but you're not getting the money. Now are you doing it or not?"

"I don't really have a choice do I?"

"Everyone has choices. Yes or no?"

"Yes."

"In that case I'm buying," said Johnson. "Pick a restaurant Alfonso then we'll go have a chat, plan this thing out and get something to eat."

"But sure he's already eating," said Eric.

"This is just a snack man," said Alfonso stuffing the rest of the cornbread into his mouth.

When he swallowed it he opened his mouth as wide as he could.

"All gone...see," he said. "Plenty of room for more."

"Good," said Johnson. "Pick somewhere."

"Empanada Mama."

"Between 51st and 52nd?"

"Yeah, that's it man. Great food...but even better...big ass waitresses with even bigger tits."

"You're all class Alfonso," said Eric.

"Fuck you man."

"Right, lead the way," said Johnson.

"Yeah, I'm hungry," said Abramo.

"In that case. Follow me Officers," said Alfonso.

When they reached Empanada Mama and took their seats a Cuban waitress with long, lustrous hair and exceptionally white teeth approached their table. Alfonso nudged Abramo who was sitting next to him.

"Booty call," he said with a wink.

Abramo grabbed his knee underneath the table. When his hand tightened like a steel clamp Alfonso yelped with pain.

"Aaagggghhh man, let go...let go!" he squealed.

Abramo released his grip.

"Manners cost nothing," he said.

The waitress, who'd heard Alfonso yell, handed them their menus with a bemused look on her face. Across the top of the menus was written:

Big flavors in small packages!

After he recovered Alfonso perused the menu. He picked the Pastelon, a Caribbean style beef lasagna with fried sweet plantains. Abramo, who was like a kid in a sweet shop, couldn't decide so Johnson recommended the Pollo Guisado, a Latin style chicken stew that he'd also decided to get. Eric ordered a pan grilled sirloin steak.

"Am I allowed to have a beer?" Alfonso asked.

"Fill your boots," said Johnson.

After they got their drinks and were waiting on their food Johnson outlined their plan to Alfonso.

"What we need you to do is to phone Grant and tell him that you've met an old friend that's looking to score some Roofies."

"Roofies, they're fuckin' shit man...coke is the way to go...far better."

"No, Roofies, it's got to be Roofies."

"Seriously? Roofies? You guys are fuckin' amateurs."

"Listen, Roofies, Rohynol, that's what we're after. Nothing else."

"Okay, okay. Keep your hair on. Roofies....for the goofies."

After saying this Alfonso laughed out loud at his own joke.

"Roofies for the goofies...fuck am I funny or what?"

"Or what?" said Eric.

"You just don't have a sense of humor Detective."

"Can we stay on track please," said Johnson.

"Just making a joke."

"Well, don't."

"Okay, okay. No jokes...no fun. We'll do it the police way."

"Tell Grant you've a friend with two hundred bucks looking to score Rohypnol tablets."

"What if he asks me to go alone and get them? He's did that before."

"No," said Johnson. "You tell him your friend, which is me..."

"What name?"

"Rocky Magee."

"Nice name...tough...he'll like that."

"Tell him I'm an ex-boxer..."

"Where do I know you from?"

"You tell me?"

Alfonso thought about this for a second.

"The MCC," he finally said. "I was there in 2006...Germaine knows that."

The Metropolitan Correctional Centre was a Federal Bureau of Prisons remand center in downtown Manhattan. Located on Park Row behind the Thurgood Marshall United States Courthouse at Foley Square it housed seven hundred and fifty inmates at capacity, both male and female.

"Okay, the MCC," said Johnson. "But tell him I have to go personally because I don't trust you and think you'll split with my money."

"Yeah man, that's good. He'll believe that because that's exactly what I'd do."

"Perfect."

"But look man, I don't think you fully understand what you're getting yourself into. Germaine is a paranoid fuckin' lunatic...a total whack job...off his head. I mean, not only does he sell coke by the bucket load...but he also sniffs it up his nose like it's going out of fashion...line after line...hour after hour...night after night. He's fucked up man...away in the fuckin' head...totally crazy."

"Okay, okay...relax...I get the picture," said Johnson.

"No man, you don't. You're not listening. When I said Germaine kills people for fun I fuckin' meant it...I'm not joking...he's the scariest motherfucker on the planet."

"Okay, okay...I understand. He's a bad dude."

Alfonso waved a hand at Johnson in disgust.

"Fuck you man."

"What's wrong?"

Alfonso leant across the table.

"What's wrong? I'll tell you what's fuckin' wrong. You're not fuckin' listening, that's what's wrong. Now open your big stupid police ears and pay a-fuckin' attention."

"Will you take it easy."

"No man...I fuckin' won't take it easy... can't take it easy. Not until you take this serious."

"I am taking it serious."

"No you're not. I can tell by your eyes."

"Okay, I'm paying attention now and I'm taking you serious."

Alfonso studied Johnson's eyes. Johnson felt like his soul was being scanned. Alfonso nodded, happy now that he had Johnson's full and undivided attention. He started speaking rapidly.

"I've seen Germaine gut people man...real bad...like a fish flopping on the floor...and he doesn't care man. They're bleeding out in front of him and all he's worried about is snorting some more shit up his nose."

"You've seen him do this? Been a witness to a murder and you've never told me," said Eric.

"Yes, I fuckin' have Detective Halitosis...because if Germaine found out I was snitching on him he'd stick me too. It's called self-preservation."

Eric's bottom lip protruded in anger.

"Let's stay on track," Johnson said quickly.

"Exactly...because you have to know this," said Alfonso. "Germaine keeps a big fuck off Bowie knife down the inside of his boot. That's what he uses to stick people with. If you see him going for that...then it's goodnight Irene...body-bag time...trip to the morgue."

"Which boot?" Johnson asked. "Right or left?"

"I don't fuckin' know."

"Has he ever frisked you?"

"Of course he's fuckin' frisked me man, this isn't the movies. Germaine would search his own Mama...stick his hand right down her big old knickers and fiddle about."

"So a wire's out?"

Alfonso was horrified at this idea.

"A wire? Are you fuckin' crazy man?! You wear one of them...you may as well sign your own death warrant. And whatever you do, don't say anything about his wobbly eye."

"Wobbly eye?"

"He's cross eyed man, goes berserk if you even mention it."

Chapter 11

After they finished their lunch they walked back through the crowds to the car. Abramo got into the back with Alfonso whilst Johnson and Eric climbed into the front.

"Right, phone him," said Johnson. "And put it on loud speaker so we can all hear."

"Now?"

"Yes now."

Alfonso took out his cell phone and rang Grant. As ordered he kept the loud speaker on. Grant answered after three rings.

"Alfonso, my old buddy, how's life as a giraffe?"

"Ha ha very funny Germaine."

"I know, I should do stand up shouldn't I."

"No, you shouldn't."

"Well, we'll agree to differ. What is it you want?"

"I've an old friend of mine looking to buy two hundred bucks worth of whisky," said Alfonso, using Grant's code word for Rohypnol.

"Okay, get you the money from him then ring me and we'll meet."

"No man, he says he has to go himself...reckons I'll stitch him up and do a runner with his money."

Grant laughed at this.

"Which you would Giraffe, isn't that right?"

"No, not me man. Sure you know how honest I am Germaine."

"Yeah right and pigs can fly. How well do you know him?"

"Met him in the MCC back in 2006. He's solid G, a gold brick."

"His name?

"Rocky Magee...he's an ex-boxer...was in for armed robbery."

"My old job. Okay, meet me in an hour at Birdland. You be with him."

The place Grant was referring to was a restaurant and bar on 44th Street between 8th and 9th. Named after the father of bebop, Charlie Parker, aka "Bird", it was a jazz mecca that had played host to scores of luminaries in the 50's and 60's. Now their photos as well as their spirits adorned the walls. Back in the day Bird had headlined the opening night. After that, other musical greats like John Coltrane, Miles Davis and Dizzy Gillespie had also topped the bill. Now it was a classy supper club where hot jazz was served daily alongside baby back ribs.

"Inside or outside?" Alfonso asked.

"Inside, at the bar."

"Sound man, see you then."

"And remember Giraffe...any funny business and that long neck of yours will be gettin' snapped in two."

"Don't worry man, this is cool...everything's above board."

"For your sake I hope so."

Grant disconnected. When Alfonso closed his own phone he was visibly shaking.

"He fuckin' knows," he said.

"He doesn't. Relax," said Eric.

"He does, I could hear it in his voice."

"All drug dealers are suspicious," said Johnson. "It's normal."

"What about if I just walk up with you, introduce you and then leave?"

"No, you have to stay with me," said Johnson, "otherwise he'll get suspicious."

"Fuck that man, you don't know this cat, he's got a sixth sense when it comes to 5's," said Alfonso using the nickname for the NYPD derived from the police follow up 'Form DD-5', a standard report filed by detectives during active cases.

"Look, I'm not gonna have a gun, a badge, nothing that will identify me as a police officer," said Johnson. "So just look at it as a normal buy. We walk up, go in, buy the Roofies and then leave. Simple. It's only afterwards we'll go back and arrest him."

"Okay," said Alfonso after a few seconds of deliberation. "But you motherfuckers better watch my back."

An hour later Johnson and Alfonso were parked around the corner from *Birdland* in the Detective's Fusion. Twenty minutes earlier Abramo and Eric had entered Birdland together and ordered drinks. They were the back up team and were both carrying their service weapons. Sal, a Sig P226. Eric, a 'Chief's Special', a snub-nosed Smith and Wesson Model 36 with a two inch barrel. Perfect for concealing easily underneath clothing Eric had 'grandfathered' the weapon when the transition to semi-automatic pistols had happened at the start of 1994.

To make himself look like someone that bought drugs Johnson had quickly driven home after dropping Abramo, Eric and Alfonso round the corner from Birdland. Jane, seeing him arrive home, had tried to talk to him but he'd waved her away and raced upstairs to the wardrobe in his bedroom. Now, he sat in the driver's seat of the Fusion wearing a pair of faded jeans and a blue t-shirt. Over this he'd pulled on an old brown leather jacket that was scuffed at the elbows. Alfonso was sitting beside him.

"Right, that's us, let's go," said Johnson.

Alfonso's eyes were huge and round, filled with fear.

"Are you sure you really need me man?"

"Yes, I am. Now get out."

"No, no, wait."

"What for?"

"Look, Eric doesn't like me."

"What's that got to do with anything?"

"Everything."

"What are you talking about?"

"Eric doesn't like me...thinks I'm a big mouth...which I'll admit I am... but either does your partner Sal."

"You're talking through your ass, Sal likes everybody."

"Then why'd he slap me?"

"Because you were giving me grief."

"Yeah but he also grabbed me by the back of the neck...not once but twice."

"Yeah, to stop you getting away."

"No, Sal doesn't like me...I know...I can feel these things...and either does Eric...which means if the shit hits the fan in this place I'm fucked."

"Sal and Eric are professional Police Officers, they'll come to your rescue...our rescue."

"But did you not see the look they both gave me before they left?"

"No I didn't. It's all in your head."

"It's not."

"It is, you're imagining things."

"I swear man," he said holding his right hand up to God. "I'm not. They both looked at me real funny....especially Sal...he had a big smirk on his face."

"Sal smirks like that all the time, that's just the way he is."

"Really?"

"Yes, really."

"There is something weird about him, isn't there."

"No, there's not, he's just naturally happy, that's why he smirks."

"Well, you have to admit he does look like a gorilla."

"Now look what happened when you said that last time. Don't be making the same mistake twice."

"He doesn't like being called that, does he?"

"Would you?"

"No, I suppose not."

"Right, come on, we're wasting time, let's go."

Alfonso opened the passenger door and got out. Johnson climbed out on the opposite side and locked the car. When Alfonso didn't budge Johnson walked round and grabbed him by the elbow.

"Start walking Alfonso."

The snitch dug his heels in and leaned back.

"Hold on, hold on," he said.

Johnson stopped trying to force him.

"What now?"

"Do I look scared?"

"No, you look fine."

"No seriously man, answer me truthfully because our lives could depend on this. Do I look scared?"

Johnson stood back and looked at him. Finally, he nodded slowly.

"Yes, you look scared, a bit pale."

"Fuck!" said Alfonso then immediately he raised his hands and started slapping himself on the cheeks.

"What are you doing?" Johnson asked.

"Getting the blood back into my face man. If I walk into Birdland looking like I've just shit myself Germaine will know something's wrong...pull that big fuckin' Bowie knife and do a Taliban on me."

"Taliban?"

"He'll cut my fuckin' head off man."

Oddly enough, this made sense to Johnson so he decided not to interfere. Instead, he folded his arms and watched Alfonso hit himself. After about ten slaps on each cheek the snitch's face was roaring red.

"How do I look now?" he asked.

"Like an Apache with sunburn."

"But do I still look frightened?"

"No, you actually look calm now...except you've got a big tomato for a head."

"Well, I'd rather have a big tomato for a head than be dead."

"That rhymes."

"Yeah I'm a poet and didn't know it."

"Right, let's go," said Johnson then side by side they walked round to Birdland with Alfonso adopting a streetwise strut and swagger that to Johnson looked exaggerated.

When they reached the entrance, a large poster on the front door advertised "David Ostwald's Louis Armstrong Centennial band" on Wednesdays and "The Birdland Big Band" on Fridays. Johnson pulled open the door and held it ajar so that Alfonso could enter first but he declined the offer.

"No man," he said. "You go."

Johnson nodded and stepped into the restaurant. Alfonso followed him in. Inside, Johnson looked around and was suitably impressed. The restaurant was wide and spacious with white clothed tables surrounding a stage that contained a black, grand piano sitting on a polished mahogany floor. The place oozed style and class. A black man in a tuxedo was playing Nat King Cole and Irving Mill's famous "Straighten up and fly right" on the piano. A miscellaneous mixture of heavenly smells filtered around the room making Johnson want to book a table and order a meal despite having just eaten in Empanada Mama. Around fifty people were seated at tables in the middle of meals with a further ten standing at the bar.

"Nice," Johnson said.

Alfonso's eyes darted around the room.

"Germaine loves this place," he said.

"Is he here yet?"

Alfonso shook his head.

"No but your friends are."

Johnson glanced across. Eric and Abramo were at the center of the bar nursing drinks seemingly in the middle of a deep conversation.

"Don't be looking at them," he said.

Alfonso fidgeted nervously and his shoulders twitched.

"Well they better be fuckin' looking at us man," he said.

"They are, they're just not making it obvious. Now stay cool."

"Cool? I'm the fuckin' King of cool. Arthur Fonzarelli cool."

Then, out of nowhere Alfonso burst into the Happy Days jingle.

"Sunday, Monday, Happy days, Tuesday - "

Johnson grabbed him by the arm.

"Will you relax, take it easy," he said.

Alfonso's words rushed out in an anxious stream.

"What, you never liked that show?" he said. "Fuckin' grade A comedy man. Henry Winkler as the Fonz...fuckin' great man...the coolest cat on the prowl. One click of his fingers...the broads came running?! Just like me man."

Alfonso clicked his fingers.

"One click and the bitches appear," he said, his face manic.

"You're rambling...stop it."

Now, Alfonso clutched Johnson's arm.

"Sorry man, but this is so fucked up. I know I'm going to die. I can feel it right here," he said jabbing his index finger into his stomach.

Johnson gently took a hold of the hand gripping his arm and pried it loose.

"Calm down, you're gonna screw this up."

"Sorry man...sorry...but I know this motherfucker, he's got a freaky antenna."

"Look at me Alfonso. Look at me."

Alfonso's eyes were all over the place. Johnson grabbed him by the elbows.

"Look at me!" he said.

Alfonso managed to focus on him. When Johnson looked into the snitch's eyes he realized Alfonso was close to bolting for the door. Johnson shook him.

"Listen to me," he said. "You've got to chill out. If you don't you're gonna fuck this up."

"I know...I know...I'm sorry."

"Breathe in through your nose and out your mouth."

Alfonso clamped his mouth shut and started to breathe through his nose but as he was halfway through his first breath he jolted upright as though stung by a cattle prod. His eyes bugged wide and he stepped out of Johnson's grasp.

"Too late man," he said. "Too late. He's fuckin' here."

Chapter 12

Johnson got his game face on and turned slowly. A tall black man wearing a crisp blue suit over a white shirt strutted into the bar. Unlike Alfonso's artificial attempt earlier this man's walk had a cocksure feel to it that exuded both confidence and danger. His face was hard and mean with callous eyes that in one sweep absorbed every detail of the restaurant. Johnson glanced down quickly to see if he was wearing boots. He was but his pants were pulled down over the top of them. A small noticeable bulge alerted Johnson that the Bowie knife was down the inside of Grant's right boot. When Grant swaggered up to them he gripped Alfonso by the shoulder.

"Giraffe, how's it hangin' skinny man?"

"Long, loose and full of juice Germaine."

Grant pretended to hug Alfonso but as he did so he swept his hands over the snitch's back and ass then down his legs. Next, he moved his hands round to the front and repeated the process. He finished by groping Alfonso's crotch. Afterwards, he stepped back.

"That's a mean piece of weaponry you're packing there Alfonso," he said.

"The bitches like it," said Alfonso.

"I'm sure they do."

Grant turned his gaze on Johnson, his eyes hard.

"Is this your friend?" he asked Alfonso over his shoulder.

"Yes, this is Rocky Magee. He's a good man Germaine...a cool cat."

"I'm sure he is."

Grant stuck out his hand. Johnson took it. As they shook Grant stared straight into Johnson's eyes.

"You a cop?" he asked.

"Hell, no man," said Johnson. "Of course not."

"In that case, I'll show you some love," said Grant then he stepped in close and frisked Johnson quickly and thoroughly just like he'd done with Alfonso. When he'd finished he took a step backwards.

"You obviously work out," he said. "Those are some nice buns you've got."

Johnson tried to give him what he hoped was a pleasant, care-free smile.

"Thanks," he said displaying his teeth.

"So what do you do Rocky?" Grant asked, staring into his eyes.

Johnson shrugged.

"I do a lot of things," he said.

"Work ways I mean."

"I'm a bouncer in a local night club."

"Which club?"

"Babalu."

"West 44th Street between 8th and 9th?"

"Yeah, you been?"

"Saw a show there about a Cuban singer…Celia Cruz I think her name was."

"Yeah, it was on a few months back."

"Big Rodrigo still doing the door there?"

Because Johnson's older brother Paul did the door in Babalu Johnson knew the staff that worked there. He realized immediately Grant's question was a trick one.

"There's no Rodrigo works in Babalu."

"No?"

"No."

"Who does work with you then?"

"E.T, you know him? Real name Elliot Teague?"

"Big guy, red hair?"

"No, stocky, blonde hair, used to be a wrestler."

"Anyone else?"

"Armando Dominguez, you know him?"

"Yeah, tall, black hair…one of them MMA fighter's?"

"No, he used to be a Marine and he's brown hair."

"Name me some bar staff," Grant ordered, anger and impatience apparent in his voice.

Johnson answered, trying to sound breezy, relaxed.

"Joanna Delaney, Margaret Towl, Marcus…"

Abruptly, Grant raised his hand.

"Okay, stop, stop, I've heard enough," he said.

Grant turned to Alfonso.

"Giraffe, come into the toilets with me," he said.

Alfonso's face drained of color.

"What?" he asked, his voice high pitched and squeaky.

"You fuckin' heard me," said Grant. "Come into the toilets with me."

"What for?" Alfonso asked, his head swiveling between Grant and Johnson. "He's the one buying."

"Because first I don't know him, second I don't like him and third I'm gettin' a bad fuckin' vibe of this motherfucker. Now get your fuckin' ass into the toilets before I break your skinny, dying lookin' neck."

"I'll go in with you," said Johnson.

"No you fuckin' won't," stormed Grant. "You'll stay right where you are Rocky Magee."

"Look, I asked him to set up this meet as a favor."

"And what? He can't go into the toilet with an old friend?"

"No, that's not what I'm saying."

"Then what the fuck are you saying?"

"That I'm the one buying the Roofies. I should be the one going into the toilet."

"For what? You lookin' your dick sucked? I'm not a fag man."

"Listen, I'm the one came to make the buy so let me do it."

"Know what...you don't smell right to me...you've cop written all over that stupid fuckin' face...but know this Mr. Policeman...I didn't bring any drugs with me in case this was a set up so go ahead and arrest me...because you'll find fuck all on me."

Johnson knew then he was blown and that they'd lost their chance but he tried one last time anyway.

"Look, I'm not a cop...I'm a bouncer."

Grant pointed at the entrance.

"In that case bounce along white boy...bounce right the fuck away from me out that fuckin' door!"

Desperate to salvage the operation, Johnson remembered what Alfonso had said about Grant's cross eyes and how it set him off. He knew it was a risky strategy but he'd ran out of options.

"Know what?!" he said. "You've sniffed so much of your own product up your big fuckin' nose it's turned you cross eyed...you can't even see straight anymore."

Grant snarled then lightning quick he flashed his hand down to his boot and pulled up the leg of his pants. Grabbing the hilt of the Bowie knife he whipped it out in one fluid movement. It looked massive as it swayed around in front of Johnson's eyes. Like a cobra seeking an opportunity to strike. As it moved back and forth the blade twinkled beneath the overhead lights. Grant gave Johnson a ferocious grin.

"I don't give a fuck if you're a cop," he said. "I'm gonna cut your tongue out then wrap it round your fuckin' head white boy."

"Stop! Police!" shouted Eric, his gun pointed at Grant's chest but again Grant moved unbelievably fast. Stepping sidewards he wrapped his arm around Alfonso's neck and held the knife to his throat.

"Stay the fuck back man or I'll slit this motherfucker from ear to ear," he yelled.

Johnson glanced at the bar. Abramo and Eric both had their arms extended holding their guns double fisted. The rest of the people at the bar ran towards the exit, loud screams intermingling with running feet. On stage the pianist stopped playing and suddenly everyone in the room was watching the drama unfold. Women screamed and a few ran into the toilets but most people stayed seated, too terrified to move.

"Put the knife down Germaine," Eric shouted. "There's no way out of here."

"Fuck you cop!"

Johnson held his hands up open palmed to show he intended no harm, an ancient sign of peace dating back to the Middle Ages when people carried swords and knives.

"Germaine, listen, there's no need for this," he said.

Grant ignored him and instead snarled into Alfonso's ear.

"You set me up motherfucker. I'm gonna gut you like a fish you skinny fuck."

"Please Germaine, they forced me to do it, I had no choice."

"Shut the fuck up or I'll end you now."

"Just take it easy Germaine. There's no need for anyone to get hurt," said Johnson.

Grant shook his head.

"I'm leaving with this bitch and if any of you so much as take a step towards me I'll send this motherfucker to hell," he shouted then he lifted his leg to take his first step towards the exit.

When he did Eric shot him in the leg, the sound of the gunshot deafening in the confines of the restaurant. Squealing with pain, Grant did a half pirouette then landed heavily on his ass, the knife still in his hand. Seizing his opportunity, Alfonso scuttled to safety behind Eric whilst on the dark mahogany floor Grant screamed in agony.

"My leg!" he cried.

"Drop the knife," Eric roared. "I will not ask you again."

Grant opened his arms wide.

"Fuck you cop! You gonna shoot me like Darrius? Come on!" he said. "Do it man, do it!! Think I give a fuck!!"

Grant was referring to Darrius Kennedy, a 51 year old black man that had been shot dead by police after wielding a knife in Times Square.

"Nobody wants you dead Germaine so be smart and throw the knife away," said Johnson.

"How many times did you motherfuckers shoot Darrius? Ten? Twelve? Fifteen? And for what? Smoking weed? Overkill man. Over fuckin' kill!!"

"Last chance Germaine. Drop the knife!" Abramo shouted.

Grant pointed his knife at Abramo.

"Oh yeah man, I see you want to kill me but do you know what? I'm too smart a cat to get fucked by a kitten. Here!" he yelled then he flung the knife away from him. It clattered against the wall behind Johnson, bounced off then landed at Johnson's feet. Johnson bent down and picked it up. After examining it he wondered where to put it. Not having a pocket big enough, he pulled up his trouser leg and stuck the knife down the inside of his boot. It fitted perfectly.

"Hands behind your back Germaine," Eric shouted.

When Grant complied Eric holstered his weapon then walked behind the drug dealer and cuffed him. He hauled Grant to his feet.

"Aggghhhh! What are you doing?" Grant screamed. "Can't you see I'm in fuckin' pain?"

"Hop over to that bar stool so I can get a look at it," said Eric.

As he did Johnson took out his cell. When the Dispatch Operator answered he asked for back up and an ambulance.

"Paramedics and back up are on the way," he said after he hung up.

Eric, who was busy examining Grant's wound, glanced back over his shoulder.

"It's a flesh wound Joe, nothing serious."

"Nothing serious?!" shouted Grant. "My blood's spilling out everywhere!"

Johnson walked across to him as Eric tied a dish towel from behind the bar around his leg.

"Are you a man or a mouse Germaine?"

"Squeak fuckin' squeak cop," said Grant through gritted teeth, in obvious pain.

"They just don't make them like they used to, eh Sal?"

Abramo, who'd re-holstered his gun stood beside Johnson with his arms folded.

"A pretend hard man," he said. "Dime a dozen all over the city."

"Anyone ever tell you, you look like a fuckin' ape," Grant said. "I'm sure there's a couple of bananas out back. Why don't you go get them!!"

Before Johnson could stop him Abramo shot out his arm and grabbed Grant by the throat. Slowly he tightened his grip until Grant started to splutter and his face turned purple. Johnson grabbed his partner's arm.

"Sal, let him go," he shouted but Abramo refused to listen and instead increased the pressure. Ever so slowly Grant's eyes began to close then they rolled back in his head and his tongue protruded from his mouth.

"Sal! Let him go!" Johnson shouted.

Abramo released the drug dealer and stepped back. When he did Grant's head wobbled like a rosebud on a broken stalk then he slumped forward and started to slip from the stool. Johnson caught him and pushed him back. As Grant was semi-conscious Johnson smacked him hard across the cheek to revive him. After the third slap Grant's eyes shot open. His breathing was rapid and scared.

"What happened?" he asked.

"You had a panic attack," Johnson lied.

Grant's eyes swept the room as he gulped air into his lungs.

"Fuck, fuck," he gasped.

And then the pain came back to his calf.

"Aaaaghh," he yelled looking down.

"You'll be alright. The ambulance is on its way," Johnson said.

"Fuckin' cops."

Johnson grabbed him by the shoulder.

"Listen Germaine, if you don't want to go down for attempted murder then I suggest you open your ears."

Grant's face contorted with hate.

"Fuck you pig," he said.

"You're not playing the game Germaine. Use your head."

Grant sniffed a large glob of phlegm to the back of his throat. As he prepared to launch it into Johnson's face Johnson grabbed him by the chin and shoved his head back. At the same time he used his other hand to pinch the drug dealer's nose closed forcing him to swallow his own mucus. After a few seconds he relinquished his grip.

"Nice?" he asked.

Grant's face was contorted with hate and rage.

"Fuck you pig!" he yelled.

"You do realize you just pulled a knife on me Germaine?" said Johnson. "That's attempted murder, possible life sentence."

"You insulted me. Nobody insults Germaine Grant."

"Get real Germaine. This isn't some tower block where you rule the roost. This is my world you're in now...where I make the rules...where you dance to my tune."

Behind Johnson the sound of the ambulance's siren could be heard getting closer. Germaine's face twisted with pain.

"That's my ride," he said.

Johnson glanced over his shoulder at Abramo.

"Sal, go outside and tell the ambulance we don't need it now. Tough guy here's going back to the Precinct with us."

Abramo made to exit the restaurant.

"You can't do that cop. I need medical attention," Grant shouted.

"My world Germaine...my rules," said Johnson.

"I'm hurting man...tell him to come back."

"And you'll talk?"

"Yes."

"Sal, it's okay. He's going to the hospital."

Abramo turned back. Johnson got straight to it.

"You sell drugs in Vanity Hotel, correct?" he asked.

"First," said Grant, "I want some assurances."

"About what?"

"No jail time."

"You pulled a knife, a gun was discharged plus you're wounded. We can't make that go away. There's a restaurant full of witnesses."

"Then I'll plead to common assault...nothing else."

Johnson pretended to deliberate. After a few seconds he gave a begrudging nod as if it pained him to accept the deal.

"That's a big ask Germaine...but okay, agreed."

"Call the bar man over. I want a witness."

Johnson did as he was asked.

"Happy now?" he asked after the barman had witnessed their agreement.

"You renege, he'll back me up."

"Don't worry, I won't renege."

"What do you want to know?"

"You sell drugs in Vanity Hotel. Correct?"

"Yes."

"Do you work alone or do you work for somebody else?"

Grant hesitated.

"It's okay," said Johnson. "We already know. We're just looking confirmation."

"I work for somebody else but I don't want to say his name."

"Then let me say it for you. Vitaly Yerzov. Am I correct?"

Grant glanced around to make sure nobody was watching then ever so slightly he inclined his head in a barely perceptible nod.

"Who do you sell to?" Johnson asked.

"Tons of people, it's a big hotel."

"Owned by who?"

"Richard and George. Sure everyone knows that."

"Did Richard ever buy anything from you?" Johnson asked.

"Yeah man, all the time. Coke...Weed...Ecstasy...Roofies now and again."

"What did he want the Roofies for?"

"Richard sniffs a lot of coke...the Roofies were to ease the next day jitters."

"Okay, thank you Germaine."

"What? That's it?"

"Yes."

Grant was incredulous.

"That's all you wanted to know?"

"Yes."

"Fuck me man. I got shot for that?"

"You did pull a knife."

"Fuck you pig."

Johnson turned and walked over to Eric. As they stood in conversation, two paramedics, a male and a female, entered. Johnson pointed across at Grant perched on the stool.

"He's over there," he said.

The female paramedic nodded her thanks then she and her partner crossed to Grant. Johnson shook Eric's hand.

"As always Eric, a pleasure," he said.

Eric gave him a big grin.

"It's never dull Joe."

"Three weeks until your birthday. Will I call round with some whisky Eric? Return the compliment?"

"If you do I'm not answering the door."

They both laughed.

"Let me know if you find out who killed Wright," Eric said.

"Don't worry, I will."

After saying their goodbyes Johnson and Abramo exited *Birdland* and returned to the Fusion with Johnson getting behind the wheel.

"I was hoping it'd go the other way," he said.

"What other way?" Abramo asked.

"That the killer was the one that had bought the Roofies, would have been easier to find him."

"So what's our next move?"

Johnson pulled on his seat belt.

"I'm gonna pay a visit to Yerzov's strip club," he said.

Abramo swung around in his seat to look at him.

"I hope you're taking me with you Joe," he said.

"Sorry Sal, you're a married man with a son and a pregnant wife. I couldn't subject you to the temptation."

"No way Joe, I want to go."

"Sorry buddy, I need you to go over to Forensics, talk to Donato, see what he's come up with."

"Why do I feel like I just got the shitty end of the stick?" said Abramo.

Johnson grinned.

"Because you just did," he said.

Chapter 13

'Flawless' strip club was on West 51st Street between 11th Avenue and West Street facing a construction site. When Johnson walked up to the entrance there were two bouncers at the front door. The one on the right hand side was by far the scarier of the two. Just below six foot he looked like he wrestled alligators for fun in his spare time. The smaller Bouncer on the left was a couple of inches shorter with a massive square head. When Johnson reached the door the larger one barred his path with a huge hand that resembled a catcher's mitt. Johnson recognized him from mug-shots. Dimitry Garin.

"Twenty dollar cover charge," said Garin.

Johnson glanced at him quickly and summed him up. Callous and cruel. Used to having his own way through brute force and ignorance. Johnson pulled out his wallet, extracted two tens then held them out like he did this every day of the week. For good measure he slapped a big smarmy grin onto his face.

"Cheap at twice the price," he said.

"You don't pay me," said Garin, folding his arms. "You pay the woman inside at the ticket desk."

"Then why'd you ask?"

"Because it's my job. You a problem with that?"

"No."

"Didn't think so."

Johnson walked in feeling small and crossed to the ticket booth. A beautiful brunette with movie star hair and chocolate colored eyes sat behind the counter filing her nails. She looked up at Johnson with a bored expression when he stopped in front of her.

"Twenty dollars please," she said, her voice a disinterested monotone.

Johnson smiled at her but she didn't smile back so he held out the two tens feeling like a jerk. She plucked them out of his hand, slipped them into a green cash box then once more gave him her dead-eyed stare.

"Straight up the corridor then go through the doors on the right," she said.

Because of her disinterested manner Johnson didn't bother to respond. Instead, he turned and walked along the threadbare carpet to the doors she'd just pointed at. When he pushed through them his attention, like every other man's in the room, was immediately drawn to a stripper coiled around a pole on the stage up at the front. Dressed in a silver bra and thong she was hanging upside down, her long blonde hair falling down from her face. Even upside down Johnson could tell that she was stunning looking. She slid down the pole effortlessly, one leg clamped round the pole acting as a brake, the other straight out at a ninety degree angle. Johnson sat down unable to take his eyes of her. Within seconds, a waitress materialized out of thin air with her smile cocked and ready.

"What type of drink would you like Sir?" she asked, her manner polite and courteous like an ordinary waitress.

The difference however was that she was only dressed in black stockings, stilettos and a tiny matching thong. Up top her breasts were bare, her nipples jutting out proudly.

"How much is a pint of Guinness?" Johnson asked, doing his best to maintain eye contact.

"I'm sorry Sir, we don't serve that."

"What about Bushmill's?"

"I've never heard of that Sir."

"It's a whisky."

"Sorry...no...but we do have Jack Daniels."

"That'll do rightly. Bring me a double."

"What Mixer would you like?"

"None...on the rocks."

"Is that all Sir?"

"Yes, thank you."

The waitress turned and walked back to the bar, her butt cheeks munching vigorously like a teenager chewing gum. When she returned a minute later she set the drink on the table in front of Johnson.

"That'll be fifty dollars please," she said.

Johnson glanced at her to see if she was joking. She wasn't.

"Tell me you're not serious," he said.

"It's a double," she said.

"I know it's a double. Do I get a car with it?"

"Sorry?"

Johnson shook his head in disgust.

"Never mind."

Sickened, he checked through his wallet worried he hadn't enough. Thankfully he had. Just about. He extracted two twenties and a ten then at the last second thought what the hell and swapped the ten for his third and last twenty. He handed the money to the waitress. When she made a show of getting him his change Johnson waved her away.

"That's okay," he said. "Keep it."

"Why thank you Sir," she said then as a reward for his generosity she bent forward, brushed his shoulder with one of her breasts and kissed him on the cheek.

"If you need anything else then please let me know," she said into his ear.

"I think I'll be okay," said Johnson.

The waitress straightened up, gave him a disparaging look then turned and sashayed back to the bar. Determined to relax, Johnson leaned back in his chair, picked up his glass of Jack and watched the stripper on stage perform her routine. She was young, maybe nineteen, but the contortions she was getting her body into convinced him that at one time she had to have been a gymnast. No way could an ordinary woman do what she was doing. As he lifted his glass for another sip a leggy brunette wearing a blue thong and a red bra strode up to his table in red high heels. She stared down at him with her hands on her hips and her legs spread reminding Johnson of Wonder woman only without the costume.

"Hi there Sexy," she said. "Would you like a lap dance?"

Johnson was curious.

"How much?" he asked.

"Twenty dollars for one song but if you want a private dance upstairs it's five hundred dollars for half an hour."

"Five hundred dollars? Are you telling me people actually pay that?"

"All the time Sir."

"Well, not this time."

"What about an ordinary lap dance then? Twenty dollars."

"Sorry...I don't even have twenty dollars but I've ten if you fancy doing half a song?"

"That's not allowed."

"Sorry. This drink and the door charge have wiped me out."

"I'm sorry to hear that. You're very handsome," she said then she turned and walked away.

Johnson watched her go, her accolade ringing in his ears. Even though he knew it was a line she fed every punter he'd still gotten an ego boost from the compliment. He looked back at the stage. Ahead of him, sitting two tables down, was a man with broad shoulders and shoulder length hair. For some reason he turned suddenly and looked directly at Johnson through dark shades. Johnson stared back but the man spun away. Up on the stage the stripper unclipped her bra with one hand then chucked it at an old bald guy sitting at the front table. It wrapped around his head but the huge grin on the old man's face revealed he didn't mind. He grabbed the bra with both hands. After a furtive glance around the room he sniffed it then put it into his jacket pocket. On stage the stripper began to do the splits.

In front of Johnson, the broad man with the sunglasses got up and made his way towards the exit. Johnson watched him wondering why he was acting so strangely. When the man got to the glass paneled door he stretched out his hand to open it only for it to be pushed open from the opposite side by Garin. The bouncer filled the doorway blocking the man's path. Angry words were exchanged but because of the staccato thump, thump, thump of the dance music Johnson couldn't hear what was being said. Then, suddenly, Garin reached down and grabbed the man by the shoulders. But immediately he retracted his hands like he'd just burnt his fingertips on a stove. With his face drained of color he stepped aside allowing the man to exit. Having seen enough Johnson decided it was time to introduce himself properly. Getting up he walked over to Garin and took out his shield.

"What happened there?" he asked.

Garin, whose face was still pale, shrugged his massive shoulders.

"Nothing," he said.

"Don't bullshit me Garin," said Johnson. "Who was that man?"

Garin shrugged.

"A customer."

"Why did you try and stop him leaving?"

"I didn't. We simply bumped into each other."

"You think I'm stupid Garin?"

"You want me to answer that truthfully or is that a rhetorical question?"

"Where's Yerzov? I want to talk to him."

"He's not here."

"Where's his office."

"I don't know."

"What do you mean you don't know? Don't you work here?"

"I only stand at the front door letting the perverts in."

"Okay then I'll find him myself."

Johnson went to turn away but Garin grabbed him back by the shoulder.

"Look, okay, I'll take you to him but I have to speak to him first, let him know you're here."

"Fair enough, lead the way."

Garin walked ahead of Johnson up to a side door at the back of the hall. When he opened it and stepped through Johnson followed after him emerging into a narrow hallway. Garin strode to the bottom and stopped outside a heavy, oak paneled door.

"Just give me a minute," he said, "So I can let him know you're here."

"Make it quick."

Garin rapped the door and a voice answered from inside.

"Who is it?"

"It's me...Garin."

Johnson heard footsteps then a bolt was drawn across. The door opened an inch. Behind it, a vicious looking man with a bald head peered out. Yerzov. He looked Johnson up and down then glanced up at Garin.

"Who the fuck is he?" he asked. "I don't know him."

"Look I'm sorry Boss, if you just let me in I'll explain," said Garin.

But before he could move Johnson grabbed the huge bouncer by the shoulder and pulled him back.

"Out of the way big man," he said.

Caught unawares Garin was thrown backwards.

"Hey, you said you'd let me talk to him first," he shouted.

"I changed my mind," said Johnson, already pushing the door open and stepping into the room. There was no one else inside. Garin stormed in after him, his face red with rage.

"You fuckin' lied cop."

Johnson turned and stared at him.

"Don't curse at me Garin or I'll run you in," he said.

Garin bent forward, his face now only inches from Johnson's own.

"Fuck you!" he said deliberately and slowly.

Johnson smiled at the big, savage face.

"I think you need to go to some anger management therapy. That attitude of yours is atrocious."

"What's this about?" Yerzov asked, his face mean and hard.

"I'll get to that soon enough but only when we're alone," Johnson replied.

Yerzov nodded at Garin.

"Go back round to the entrance," he said. "Annabelle's probably having a heart attack at being left round there on her own with Jones."

Garin nodded then stepped over to the door and opened it with one of his shovel hands. Before he departed he looked back at Johnson.

"Thought you smelt fuckin' funny on the way in," he said.

Johnson, knowing it would annoy him, didn't even bother to turn around.

"Close the door on your way out," he said, purposely being dismissive.

"Fuck you cop!" said Garin, all the pent up anger and rage shooting out in his words.

Knowing he was on the point of losing it Johnson stayed silent, but every fiber in his body was tuned and ready lest Garin suddenly attacked. But he didn't. Instead he opened the door with an infuriated snarl then slammed the door shut, almost taking it off its hinges.

Back in the room Yerzov shook his head.

"I think you've made an enemy," he said.

Johnson shrugged.

"Occupational hazard."

"Stupid though," said Yerzov. "You'd have been safer poking a tiger in the eye with a stick."

"No, not me, I like tigers."

"You're a cool bastard, aren't you."

"Like ice."

"So, tell me, what do you want?"

Johnson pointed at the brown chair behind the desk.

"First of all I'd like you to take a seat."

Yerzov shook his head.

"No, I prefer to stand."

Now Johnson knew why people were afraid of Yerzov. Up until this moment he'd only ever been a name to Johnson, a notorious bad guy to talk about during a shift. But up close and personal was a different matter. Now, the animal savagery that was part and parcel of Yerzov's being emanated off him like heat from a fire. Johnson was instantly wary. Yerzov wasn't a man to be trifled with.

"You always this welcoming?" he asked.

"Fuck the small talk cop. Get to the point."

Johnson stepped over to the desk and lifted up a bottle of Jack Daniels. Yerzov grabbed it out of his hand then walked around and sat down. Surprisingly, rather than put it away he unscrewed the lid.

"You want one?" he asked.

Johnson nodded.

"Double, on the rocks," he said.

As Yerzov poured the drinks Johnson took a seat and scanned the room. The walls were a drab grey with peeling paint. On the floor a heap of porn DVDs were piled in one corner beside a plastic bag. Yerzov added ice to the drinks then handed one across to Johnson.

"So, what can I do for you Officer...?"

"Detective Johnson."

"Anything to Rocky Johnson?"

Although he tried to hide it Johnson visibly stiffened at the mention of his father's nick name. Yerzov read the tell and smiled. Johnson changed his mind about drinking the whisky. Instead, he sat forward and placed the glass on the desk.

"How do you know my father?" he asked.

"He arrested me years ago. A tough man."

Johnson scrutinized Yerzov's eyes searching for a clue, some hint of something more sinister behind the gangster's remark. He couldn't tell but he decided to bite the bullet anyway.

"You have anything to do with his murder?"

"Me? Of course not. I liked the man...respected him. Everyone did."

Johnson decided to drop it. Yerzov wouldn't admit anything anyway. He picked up the glass of Jack, sat back and took a sip.

"You're a loan shark, isn't that right?" he asked.

Yerzov frowned.

"Loan sharking is illegal," he said. "To admit I participated in that would constitute serious stupidity on my part."

"So you're gonna play the smart guy?"

"Smart guys stay out of jail."

"Okay, I'll re-phrase my question," said Johnson. "Have you ever lent money to particular friends?"

"That's my own personal business."

"Still the smart guy?"

Yerzov raised his glass.

"Didn't you hear me the first time cop?" he said. "Smart guys stay out jail."

"You ever lend money to Richard Wright?"

Yerzov's eyes flickered but he recovered quickly.

"Never heard of him," he said.

"No?"

"No."

"That's not what your face said."

Yerzov smiled.

"What's my face saying now?" he asked.

"That you're a lying son of a bitch."

"Sticks and stones Detective."

"How much is Richard into you for?" asked Johnson, purposely keeping his question in the present tense lest he tip Yerzov that Richard was dead.

"I'm sorry Detective but I've never heard of the man."

"Is he making his payments?"

"Listen Detective Johnson, son of Rocky...you're asking the wrong person. I'm a legitimate businessman."

"Don't be bringing my father into this."

"Touchy subject?"

"Is Richard making his payments? Answer the question."

Yerzov took a swig of his whisky.

"This is starting to bore me Detective. You're starting to bore me."

"Richard's wife told me you sent Garin round three weeks ago."

"Whatever Garin does in his own time is his own business Detective. Nothing to do with me."

"Where were you last night between the hours of 1am and 3.30am?"

Now, the penny dropped with Yerzov.

"Richard's dead, isn't he?" he asked.

"Thought you didn't know him?"

"I don't but if you're asking where I was it means he's dead. Am I right?"

"I can neither confirm or deny. It's a police matter."

Yerzov got up, his face red with anger.

"Bastard," he said. "I knew I shouldn't have lent that fuckin' hornball money."

"Who? Richard?" Johnson asked.

"Yes, fuckin' Richard."

"So you did know him?"

"Yes, I did. You happy now?"

"Ecstatic. Over the moon...but you still haven't answered my question. Where were you last night between 1am and 3.30am?"

"I was here drinking whisky with Dimitry."

"Ask my brother am I a liar."

"Well, it's the truth. Ask Laura, she was here too."

"Who's she?"

"The double-jointed stripper with the blonde hair."

Johnson imagined the three of them in this room drinking whisky, snorting coke and most likely having sex.

"Richard is dead and seeing as how he owed you money and wasn't paying it back that gives you a motive for killing him."

"Now that's a stupid assumption Detective. With Richard dead I don't get my money."

Mentally, Johnson conceded this point but he didn't admit it to Yerzov.

"Why'd you call Richard a hornball?" he asked.

"Turn of phrase," said Yerzov but Johnson could see the question had made him uncomfortable.

"Yeah, a turn of phrase for someone that really likes sex. Did Richard?"

Yerzov returned to his seat and sat down.

"All men like sex Detective. Sure aren't we known for thinking with our dicks!"

"What did Richard do that made him a hornball?"

"Look, it was a throwaway remark. Nothing was meant by it."

"What was he into? Bondage? S&M? Orgies? What?"

"How would I know?"

"You're the one called him a hornball. You obviously know something about his sex life."

"I'm sorry Detective. I don't know anything about Richard's sex life."

"So why'd you call him a hornball?"

"I call everyone a hornball. You're a hornball, I'm a hornball, big Dimitry's a fuckin' hornball. We're all horn balls Detective. Even the Presidents of this great country are horn balls. JFK...fucking Marilyn...hornball. Clinton getting his cock sucked in the Whitehouse...hornball."

Johnson let it drop but he wasn't fooled for a second. Yerzov was hiding something.

"When was the last time you seen Richard?"

"Last Tuesday."

"Where?"

"At his hotel."

"Richard ever come here?"

"No."

"Do you know anyone that might want to hurt Richard?"

"No."

"No?"

"Fuckin' no."

"Am I sensing hostility Yerzov?"

"Fuck yeah...but not at you Detective...at the bastard that killed my golden goose...whoever that may be."

"Golden goose?"

"Turn of phrase."

"So Richard repeatedly borrowed money from you?"

"Yes."

"And you've no idea who would want to kill him?"

"None...but I will find out...you mark my words Rocky Junior...someone's going to pay me."

"Don't call me that."

"Sorry, keep forgetting you're sensitive. I'll try and be more gentle with you."

"Just don't mention my father's name again."

Yerzov mimed pulling a zip across his mouth.

"My lips are sealed," he said.

"And don't be leaving the city. I might want to speak to you again."

Yerzov held up his tumbler.

"I'll be right here Detective...waiting with the whisky."

Chapter 14

Johnson walked back round to the entrance passing Annabelle who still sat with the bored expression in the cubicle. When he exited Garin looked at him like he was a piece of shit on the bottom of his shoe. Johnson stopped and stared at him.

"Where were you last night between the hours of 1.00am and 3.30am?" he asked.

Garin raised his middle finger.

"See this cop," he said. "Fuckin' spin on it."

Moving quickly Johnson grabbed Garin's outstretched hand then stepped behind him forcing Garin's arm up behind his back. Garin squealed. In turn, the other doorman with the square head advanced towards Johnson but Johnson was alert to the danger. Pulling his Glock he pointed it at the second doorman's face.

"Back up Fred Flintstone," he said.

When the bouncer stopped dead in his tracks, Johnson re-holstered his gun then spoke to Garin.

"Put your other hand behind your back or I'll snap this one in two."

Garin quickly obliged so Johnson freed his cuffs and quickly snapped them on. After he closed them tight he kicked Garin in the back of the legs and forced him to drop to his knees. Still wary, he stepped round in front of Garin with one eye on the second bouncer.

"Any more tough guy nonsense and I'll run you in for obstructing a police investigation," he said. "Understand?"

Garin glared up at him but didn't say anything so Johnson took out his Nokia and began to dial.

"Your choice," he said.

"Okay, okay," said Garin. "Put the phone away."

Johnson ended the call but kept the cell in his hand.

"Where were you last night between the hours of 1.00am and 3.30am?" he said.

"Here," said Garin.

"With who?"

"Yerzov."

"Doing what?"

"Drinking...fuckin'."

"With who?"

"Laura..."

"Hands in the air!" a female voice suddenly shouted.

Johnson raised his hands and slowly turned. Annabelle, the girl that collected the money, was pointing a small derringer at his face.

"I'm a cop," Johnson said.

"Show me I.D."

Johnson pulled out his wallet then flipped it open to display his gold shield. Annabelle lowered her gun but didn't put it away. Johnson stepped over and took it out of her hand.

"You have a permit for this?" he asked.

"Of course, I'm not stupid."

Johnson handed her the gun back.

"How do I find Laura?" he asked.

"Fuck you cop," Garin shouted across. "Find her yourself. Sure aren't you a Detective."

Johnson turned around.

"All muscle and no brain Garin. This is a murder investigation and if I have to I'll have ten squad cars down here filled with angry cops itching to rip this place apart."

"That's your prerogative pig. I'm just an employee so I don't really give a fuck."

"Stupid move."

"Look Detective, take your twenty dollars back," said Annabelle walking back to the counter.

Reaching behind it, she lifted the lid of the cash box and extracted two tens. When she turned around she walked back to Johnson and handed him the money. Johnson, never one to look a gift horse in the mouth, accepted the money and stuck it in his pocket.

"Thanks," he said.

Annabelle inclined her head sideways motioning for him to follow her.

"I'll walk you round to Laura," she said.

"You're way too smart for this racket," Johnson said.

"Don't I know it," said Annabelle.

"Hey, what about me?" Garin shouted.

Johnson stopped and looked back. After a momentary pause he crossed over and stared down into the big man's face.

"You gonna be a good boy?"

"Take the cuffs off cop."

"Answer the question."

Garin shook his head in frustration.

"Yes, I'll be good," he said.

Johnson walked behind him and unlocked the cuffs. When Garin stood up he rubbed his wrists and fired Johnson dirty looks but he didn't say anything.

"This way," said Annabelle.

Johnson let her take the lead then trailed behind her. Back in the main hall she led him over to a white door. A sign on it read: STAFF ONLY.

"She's in there somewhere," said Annabelle.

"Thanks," Johnson said.

"Just trying to keep the place running," said Annabelle then she walked away.

Johnson watched her leave, noting the fluid movement of her body beneath the red silk. When she disappeared from view he turned and opened the door. It was like entering a horny teenage boy's dream. Scantily clad women in high heels stood around semi-naked in deep conversation. Ahead of him a redhead with a snake coiled around her shoulders spotted him first.

"Can't you read?" she shouted. "Staff only."

Johnson took out his shield.

"Police," he said holding it up.

"5-O!" the redhead yelled.

Johnson stopped when he reached her. The snake around the woman's shoulders lifted its head and peered at him.

"I'm looking for Laura," said Johnson.

"Sure isn't everyone," replied the redhead.

"What's your name?" Johnson asked.

"What would you like it to be sweetheart?"

"Your real one."

"Monica."

"Where's Laura Monica?"

The redhead flicked her head towards a fire exit.

"She's outside having a smoke."

"Appreciate it," said Johnson stepping round her.

"You're not bad looking for a cop," the stripper shouted after him. "If you ever fancy a threesome with me and the snake then let me know, he's got a wicked tongue and so have I."

"I'll keep that in mind," said Johnson without looking back.

When he reached the exit door he pushed the horizontal bar and stepped outside. Laura, wrapped up snugly in a fluffy green bathrobe, was standing with another stripper, both of them puffing away happily on a cigarette. The second stripper, petite with black, bobbed hair and green eyes glared at Johnson when he stepped through the door.

"Hey!" she shouted, her free hand raised. "Staff only."

Johnson glanced at her hand. It was more like a claw than a hand with exceptionally long fingernails curled into talons. Johnson flashed his shield.

"Take a walk," he told her. "Laura, you stay."

In a small act of defiance the tiny stripper took a final draw of her cigarette. Just before she exhaled she stepped up close to Johnson then blew the smoke in his face. Afterwards, a look of utter disdain on her face, she dropped the butt at her feet. As she ground it out with the heel of her stiletto she clutched Johnson's face in both her hands digging her fingernails into his cheeks.

"If he touches you Laura just shout," she said. "I'll scratch his eyes out."

Johnson removed her hands.

"She'll be fine," he said.

"Yeah right. I've heard that before."

Her little show over, she pushed past him and vanished into the strip club. When Johnson turned back to Laura she was looking at him with worried eyes.

"What I do?" she asked.

Johnson noticed white powder underneath her left nostril. Cocaine. He glanced at the small gold clutch in her hand.

"Nothing," he said. "I just want to ask you about last night."

"What about last night?"

"Where were you between the hours of 1.00am and 3.30am?"

"I was here with Dimitry and Yerzov."

"Doing what exactly?"

"Drinking."

With Yerzov's alibi confirmed for a third time Johnson decided to change direction.

"Do you know a man named Richard Wright?" he asked.

"No," said Laura but her eyes glanced sidewards. A lie.

"Okay, we'll try that again," said Johnson. "But this time I want you to think about the consequences of lying."

"I don't understand."

"Your nose...underneath it...there's white powder which I'm guessing is cocaine."

"What?" she said dipping her hand into her handbag.

When it re-emerged she was holding a small compact mirror. She opened it then held it up in front of her face.

"That's just talcum powder," she said. "I was powdering my nose earlier."

After saying this she licked the tip of her index finger then used it to wipe away the incriminating evidence.

"There, all gone," she said after she'd checked herself in the mirror.

"Too late," Johnson said. "I already seen it."

"But sure it was only talcum powder."

"You think I came up the Hudson in a bubble?" Johnson asked.

"It was talcum powder," said Laura, her voice rising by an octave. "I'm not lying."

"So if I search that little handbag you have in your hand I'll not find anything?"

Panicked, Laura stuck her purse underneath her arm.

"This is my personal property," she said.

Johnson shot out his hand and snatched the purse from her grasp. When she tried to grab it back from him he turned around and flicked open the catch. Inside was a lipstick, hankies and a packet of cigarettes. He stuck his hand in and rifled around then as he was about to give up he noticed a red zip that matched the interior color of the bag. He opened it. Inside was a small translucent bag containing white powder. Johnson lifted it out and held it up. Cocaine.

"Now what have we here?" he said.

"I don't know. That's not mine," said Laura.

"What? It just happened to magically appear in your bag?"

"Anyone could have put it there."

"Cut the crap Laura. It's yours. So unless you want me to run you in and charge you with drug possession then I suggest you start answering my questions."

She thought about this for a second, her mind doing somersaults. Looking for a way out. A plausible lie about how the cocaine got into her bag. Johnson took out his handcuffs. Added incentive for her to come clean.

"Clock's ticking Laura."

Her brain continued going through the variations. A street girl weighing up her options. Johnson opened the handcuffs.

"Last chance," he said.

She glanced at him then at the handcuffs then back up to his face.

"Okay," she said. "What do you want to know?"

"Do you know Richard Wright?"

"Yes," she said. "Every girl working here does."

"Why's that?"

She hesitated.

"Answer the question Laura. Why's that?"

"Because we all work in his hotel."

"Doing what exactly?"

"This and that."

"Specifics Laura."

She sighed out loud. Looked to the side then back again. Resigned to the fact that she had to tell the truth.

"We're Escorts," she said.

"Hookers?"

"That's not a nice term."

"Then I'll use a nicer one. Call girls?"

"Yes."

"So was Richard in here often?"

"He used to come in regular with George before we started working in the hotel."

"Which was when?"

"Three months ago. From the big opening night."

"But he hasn't been back since?"

"No but Andrei's always here."

"Andrei?"

"Yerzov's cousin. Andrei Kosomo."

"And he fits in how?"

"He's the Manager at the hotel."

"At Richard's hotel? Vanity?"

"Yes."

"But he also comes over here?"

"He used to work here. Bar Manager. But then he got the job at Vanity. Now he does the rota for which girls work in the hotel. Comes over every Saturday night...puts it up on the wall in the dressing room."

"Does he bring anything with him when he arrives?"

"I don't know."

"Think Laura...and remember if I think you're lying then I'm running you in."

Her shoulders slumped in defeat.

"He always has a bag with him."

"What type of bag?"

"A shopping bag...one of them plastic ones...like you'd get out of "Save A Lot"."

"Do you know what's in the bag?"

"No, I've no idea."

"What's he do with it?"

"He brings it round to Yerzov."

Adrenalin shot through Johnson's body. A plastic shopping bag had been sitting on Yerzov's floor.

"Okay Laura, thank you for your co-operation," Johnson said knowing he had to hurry.

Turning quickly he pulled open the fire door and rushed inside. His blood was up and he could feel the rush, the adrenalin shooting through his veins. Striding through the pack of strippers, he marched back into the club then round to Yerzov's office. Not bothering to knock he barged in. Yerzov was on the other side of the door with his coat was on and the plastic bag in his hand. It was obvious he was about to leave.

"Going somewhere?" Johnson asked.

Yerzov spun and gawped at him like a kid caught shoplifting.

"I've a dentist's appointment, rotten molar," he said.

Johnson shook his head.

"Now why do I not believe you?" he said.

"I don't know. Maybe it's your suspicious nature Detective."

"What's in the bag?"

Yerzov's face drained of color.

"Old porn DVDs," he said.

"Then I'm sure you won't mind if I take a look."

"Do you have a search warrant?"

"Sure why would I need a search warrant. Did you not say they're only old porn DVDs?"

"Doesn't matter what they are. Unless you have a search warrant, you can't look in this bag."

Johnson made to grab the bag but Yerzov clamped it to his chest like a quarterback protecting the ball.

"Must be something important," said Johnson. "You're acting highly suspicious."

"I know my rights Detective. Fourth Amendment, remember. This bag is my property and unless you have a search warrant you can't look inside it."

"But you're forgetting something Yerzov. Exigent circumstances. That's evidence in your hand and I'm of the opinion that you're trying to destroy it so I'm allowed to take it of you."

"I'm not trying to destroy it."

"Your word against mine in a court of law. I think a Judge would believe me before you. Now hand over the bag."

Yerzov ducked his head and charged, his right hand held out in front of him like a linebacker trying to break a tackle. Johnson slapped his hand aside and stuck out his foot. Yerzov grunted and fell forward, his head hitting of the ground as he failed to break his fall. He rolled over with the bag still in his hands and blood dripping from a gash in his forehead.

"Give it up Yerzov."

"Fuck you," the gangster replied.

After saying this he pushed himself up onto his knees then used the desk as leverage to clamber to his feet. He eyed Johnson warily who was blocking the doorway and therefore his escape. Then, his shoulders slumped and he held out the bag.

"Here," he said. "You win."

Johnson stepped forward to grab the bag. As he did so Yerzov swung the whisky bottle from behind his back and smashed it over Johnson's head. A searing white flash blazed across Johnson's vision and he slumped sidewards, momentarily dazed. Seizing the opportunity Yerzov danced around him then pulled open the door and sprinted down the corridor. Behind him, left in the office, Johnson shook his head and cursed under his breath. Straightening up he gulped air into his lungs then turned and grabbed the door handle but as his fingers touched the brass a searing white flash blazed across his vision. Instinctively, he gritted his teeth and rode the storm. After a couple of seconds it started to subside so he continued what he'd been doing and yanked open the door. Still groggy, he stumbled out then weaved across the ground as he began to give chase.

"Yerzov!" he yelled but the Russian gangster was well ahead and already pulling open the door to the main corridor.

Hearing Johnson's shout he glanced back, his face a hate filled mask of rage.

"Fuck you cop!"

Galvanized, Johnson quickened his pace and lurched after him, his head still spinning. In the corridor he blinked rapidly to recover his vision but all he could see were flickering lights. Yellow and white they flashed off and on, emitting streaks of jagged pain behind Johnson's eyeballs. Fighting back with every ounce of will and determination he had, he screwed his eyes shut and clenched his fists. It worked and momentarily he gained a respite from the agony.

Now able to see he ran down the corridor then turned right and burst out the exit. Out of his peripheral vision he picked up Garin and the other Bouncer at either side of the doorway but ahead was Yerzov, the main prize, desperately trying to get away. Johnson reached him in two strides, seized him by the shoulder and spun him around.

"Not so fast," he said.

Yerzov, full of venom, snarled like an angry dog then swung his leg with as much force as he could muster and kicked Johnson on the shin.

Johnson stumbled back, streaks of fire racing up his leg. Simultaneously, a small grunt of pain escaped from his lips. But he recovered quickly.

"That's assault on a police officer," he told the Russian mob boss.

"Fuck you cop," was Yerzov's reply, the word's spat out with unleashed vitriol.

Stepping forward, Johnson grabbed Yerzov by the face, put his right leg behind the gangster's and pushed. Yerzov tumbled back and hit the ground hard. The bag, still clutched in his hands, landed on his chest. Johnson pulled out his Glock and pointed it down at him.

"No more games," he said, his chest heaving with exertion.

In response, Yerzov grinned then freed a hand and waved.

"Night night," he said.

Alerted, Johnson started to spin around but it was too late. Something hard hit him on the back of the head and he pitched forward, his face nose-diving into the pavement. But he didn't feel a thing. For on impact he was already unconscious by the time he hit the ground.

When Johnson woke up two minutes later, a grinning Garin was staring down at him. At the same time, Annabelle was washing his face gently with a face cloth. Johnson tried to get up but instantly he felt woozy and fell back again.

"Take it easy," said Annabelle.

Johnson's eyes started to re-focus and he looked at Annabelle. Up close she was even more beautiful than he remembered.

"Florence Nightingale," he said.

"Just lie still," she said. "Get your bearings."

Johnson took her advice and looked up at the New York sky. It was a pale blue flecked with white. Slowly, his strength started to come back and color returned to his face. As he gathered his wits he tried to piece together what had happened. Eventually, after three minutes lying prone he took a deep breath and sat up.

"You think you can stand?" Annabelle asked.

Johnson nodded.

"Only one way to find out," he said.

Using Annabelle's shoulder as a crutch Johnson stumbled to his feet. After holding onto her for a minute he told her to let him go.

"You sure?" she asked.

"Yeah," he said. "Just be ready to catch me."

"Don't worry, I will."

"Okay, on the count of three," said Johnson. "One...two...three."

At the same time that she stepped away from him Johnson took his arm from around her shoulders. After a slight wobble he steadied himself then smiled as his legs held and he remained upright.

"Well done," said Annabelle.

Johnson nodded, still a little wary and feeling nauseous. Beads of sweat formed on his forehead but he gritted his teeth and fought past it. Eventually, his vision solidified and full strength returned to his legs.

Garin walked up to him with a barely suppressed smile on his face.

"Here's your gun Detective," he said, holding out Johnson's Glock.

Johnson took it, flicked the catch and ejected the magazine. It was fully loaded. He inserted it again then stuck the gun back in its holster before staring at Garin for a full five seconds. Coming to a decision he turned to Annabelle.

"Did you see what happened?" he asked.

"No, Garin told me you tripped and fell, knocked yourself out."

Johnson glanced at the two CCTV cameras mounted above the club's entrance then took out his phone and called the station.

"Send over two squad cars to Flawless strip club in Hell's Kitchen," he said.

In the middle of speaking Garin started to edge backwards so Johnson pulled out his gun and walked up to him.

"Where do you think you're going?" he said sticking his gun against Garin's belly.

Garin stopped, a frustrated look on his face.

"I hate fuckin' cops," he said.

Johnson smiled up at him as he continued his phone conversation.

"I need help arresting someone," he said.

Chapter 15

Garin sat hunched over the table in Interview Room 3 of the Midtown North precinct. His hands were handcuffed behind his back but he wasn't unduly worried. The table, brown in color, was scarred and rutted with graffiti scrawled across it. Garin read the comments then laughed out loud at a wit's maxim in black ink:

"Anything you say will be held against you...."Tits."

He repeated it out loud, over and over again in an attempt to memorize it. The four walls hemming him in were a mottled, blemished white. Like the table they too had been mutilated by years of graffiti. The door opened and Johnson came in pushing a TV on a trolley with a DVD player underneath it.

"Thought we'd watch a film together," he said then he plugged the TV and DVD into the wall. When he was finished he lifted the remote control and pressed play. On screen Yerzov burst out the door with the bag in his hands, shouted at Garin and then kept running. Seconds later Johnson emerged and pulled Yerzov back. Then came the kick on the shin resulting in Johnson throwing him to the ground and pulling his gun. Two seconds later Garin could be seen punching Johnson on the back of the head laying him out cold. Garin then picked up the fallen Glock and turned back towards the door, a huge self-satisfied grin on his face. Johnson paused the video on the smiling thug's face.

"What you think? Good film?" Johnson asked. "Personally I think you should get an Oscar."

"Don't know what you're on about," said Garin. "That's not me."

Johnson grinned when he heard this.

"What...it's your evil twin? Frankenstein's monster?"

"Don't know but it isn't me."

"Oh, I get it," said Johnson. "That's your defense. The guy in the film caught assaulting me...a police officer...isn't you even though he's identical to you. Even has the exact same scar above your right eye."

Garin glanced at the paused close-up of his face on the screen. After a couple of seconds his shoulders slumped and he physically wilted.

"Reality hitting home yet?" Johnson asked.

"It isn't me," said Garin but this time there was no conviction in his voice.

Johnson leant forward, placed both his hands on the table and stared at the big enforcer. Garin, unable to hold his gaze, dropped his eyes after a couple of seconds.

"Okay, we'll do it your way," Johnson said. "It's not you. It's just somebody that looks exactly like you with the exact same scar and clothes on that you just so happen to be wearing now. Just a coincidence, isn't it. The truth is...you've got an evil twin out there somewhere running around pretending to be you...getting you into trouble."

Garin didn't say anything. Johnson let the stupidity of Garin's cover story permeate through to his brain. After a couple of seconds Johnson straightened up and folded his arms.

"Are you seriously still gonna try and deny that that's you on that screen?" he said.

Garin shook his head as he spoke but still he was unable to meet Johnson's gaze.

"It's not me."

"Then more the fool you," said Johnson, "because when you're standin' in the dock denying that's it's you the jury'll be thinking they're at "Caroline's" in Times Square watching the latest standup comedy routine. Then...after they've found you guilty the Judge'll nail on a couple of extra years for wasting his and the court's time. But then hey...who am I? Maybe I'm wrong. Maybe you'll get twelve blind jurors along with a blind Judge and you'll walk."

Garin dropped his eyes and chewed his bottom lip, his face contorted with worry. Johnson sat down in front of him. It was time to throw out the bait.

"Listen Garin," he said, "right now you're looking at four years guaranteed...rubber stamped...a slam dunk...but...if you use your brain and co-operate with me today I promise you now you'll be walking out that door in less than an hour."

Garin's eyes brightened at the mention of him walking out. Johnson knew then he had him.

"I'm listening," said Garin.

Johnson leant across the table. Subconsciously, on the other side, Garin mimicked his movements. Johnson kept his voice low and conspiratorial.

"No one knows we took the CCTV tapes except you," he said. "Now, if I decide to let you go you can simply say we had no evidence on you because you hid the tapes after you knocked me out."

"What do you want me to do?"

"First of all I want you to answer a few questions then afterwards I want you to work for me. Become my eyes and ears in Yerzov's organization."

Garin sat back.

"No," he said. "You don't know what Yerzov's capable of. I do."

"You'd rather do four years for him? I'm impressed with your loyalty but I'll not argue with you."

Johnson stood up then unplugged the TV and DVD and pushed the trolley towards the door. When he rapped it Garin called him back.

"Wait," he shouted.

Johnson stopped, his hand in mid-knock then walked back around and sat down.

"Change your mind?" he asked. "Decide to use that thing inside your head called a brain?"

"Yes."

"Good."

"I walk away? No jail time?"

"None...but that's provided you answer truthfully. If I think for one second you're lying to me then the whole deal is off."

Garin leant back in his chair, deep in thought then sat forward again.

"Okay, I'll do it," he said.

Johnson nodded.

"Okay, first question," he said. "What was in the bag Yerzov was running away with?"

"I've no idea."

Johnson looked at him wondering if he was telling the truth. Most likely not. Garin had probably never told the truth in his life. But Johnson needed to know what was in that bag. He could feel it in his water that it was the key to unlocking who had killed Richard Wright. He decided to have another go at the big enforcer.

"If I find out you did know what was in that bag then our deal is off. Straight to jail, no questions asked."

"Look, I don't know what was in it...I swear."

"You better not. There'll be no second chances."

"I'm not lying."

"Then why do I think you are?"

"I'm not."

"Look, just answer the question. What was in the bag?"

"I don't know," said Garin. "Honest."

"Honest? Don't make me laugh. You couldn't spell the word," said Johnson then he stood up, grabbed the trolley and pushed it over to the door.

When he stopped to give it a rap Garin swivelled around on his seat.

"Our deal's still on, isn't it?" he asked.

"No," said Johnson. "You had your chance. And sure...from what I hear...you're so tough you could do four years standin' on your head."

"Look, come back," said Garin but the door had already opened so Johnson pushed the trolley through and kept walking.

Chapter 16

Back in the Bullpen Johnson decided to make himself a cup of coffee while he let Garin stew. Picking up the kettle he crossed to the sink and started to fill it with water when his phone buzzed in his pocket. Afraid it might ring off before he answered he turned off the tap and set the kettle down. He dipped his hand into his pocket and pulled out his cell. On the small, rectangular screen three letters were displayed: JKO. Shorthand for "The Jacqueline Kennedy Onassis High School", the school his daughter Rachel attended. Now why are they ringing me he wondered? Since Rachel had started four years ago he and Jane had only ever been contacted through letters about school plays, parents' meetings or holidays. As he hit the green answer button, a tiny knot of worry formed in his stomach.

"Hello?" he said.

"Is that Mr. Johnson?"

"Yes, who's this?"

"I'm your daughter Rachel's form teacher...Mrs. Collins?"

"Yes, Mrs. Collins I've met you a few times. What is it? Something wrong with Rachel?"

"Actually, it's quite a delicate matter. I'm wondering if you could come around to the school."

The small ball of apprehension in Johnson's belly began to grow.

"When? Now?"

"Yes, if that's possible."

"What's it about?" he asked, the fear now a wrecking ball.

Mrs. Collins paused for a second then answered.

"Rachel was caught in the school toilets at lunchtime today smoking marijuana."

Relief flooded through Johnson's system. Rachel smoking a bit of blow he could deal with. At least nothing serious had happened to her. Relaxed now, he suddenly found himself becoming defensive.

"Marijuana? You sure? Doesn't sound like my Rachel," he said.

"I'm positive Sir because I'm the one that caught her with the reefer in her hand."

"To be honest Mrs. Collins. I find that very hard to believe."

"I assure you Mr. Johnson...so do I...but it doesn't change the fact that Rachel...and another girl...Susan Maxwell...were locked in a cubicle together smoking an illegal substance."

"You're sure it was marijuana?"

"Mr. Johnson, I've worked in this school for fifteen years now. It's safe to say that I know marijuana when I see it...or smell it."

"That other girl must have owned it. My Rachel wouldn't know where to get her hands on marijuana."

"No, I'm sorry Sir. That's not the case. Rachel has already admitted that she's the one brought the marijuana into school."

This shocked Johnson. Didn't make sense. He glanced at his watch then came to a decision. Garin could wait. It wouldn't do him any harm to stew a bit longer.

"Okay, Mrs. Collins, I'm on my way," he said.

"Thank you Sir."

Located at 120 West 46th Street near Times Square the JKO was only fifteen minutes away from the Precinct. As Johnson drove along he thought about Rachel. As far as he was concerned she was a great kid. Diligent, hard working, kind and generous. When she'd secured a place at the JKO four years previous he'd been over the moon. Proud as punch. The school had an exceptional academic record and was notoriously hard to get into but Rachel, to her credit, had sailed through the interview. Now in 11th grade she was currently studying International Business Studies, Hospitality and Tourism.

When Johnson reached the school he parked outside then walked up the steps and through the front doors into the foyer. Inside he approached the receptionist sitting behind a glass window.

"Excuse me?" he said.

Taken unawares, the receptionist, a brunette with large eyes, jerked upright in her seat. At the same time she pushed a book she'd been reading underneath a report but not before Johnson had seen the cover: 'Ten Blind Disciples,' by Kieron McQueen. A literary phenomenon the book had reputedly sold more copies than Harry Potter.

"Yes, may I help you?" the receptionist asked.

Her voice was high pitched and defensive.

"Good book?" Johnson asked.

"Pardon?"

"The book. Ten Blind Disciples...any good? Everywhere I go people seem to be reading it."

The receptionist blushed.

"It's okay," she said, a little tentatively.

Johnson got the impression she was hiding what she really thought. He tried to encourage her.

"My wife just finished it last week," he said.

This did the trick. She instantly opened up.

"Lucky you! Have you tried anything from it yet?" she asked.

"Pardon?"

Johnson's reaction wasn't what she'd expected.

"Sorry," she said. "I thought your wife would have talked about the story with you? About the ten blind disciples?"

"No, she didn't."

In truth Johnson had asked Jane what all the fuss was about but her answer had been short and curt: "It's a love story".

"Then maybe you should read it yourself," said the receptionist.

"I think I will," said Johnson. "You've made me curious."

The receptionist gave him a meaningful look.

"The book is filled with curiosity," she said.

Johnson nodded slowly.

"I'll take your word for it."

Noticing his reticence the receptionist got uncomfortable and reverted back to type. Straightening her posture, she lifted her chin and adopted an affected, professional manner.

"How may I help you Sir?" she asked.

Her tone now was polite and courteous.

"My name's Mr. Johnson. I'm here to see Mrs. Collins."

"Yes, she's waiting for you in the Principal's office."

"Which is where?"

The receptionist pointed through the glass partition across the foyer.

"Over there...that red door," she said.

Johnson thanked her then walked over to the door she'd just indicated. He knocked politely. Mrs. Collins, wearing a plaid skirt and a green blouse, opened the door. Her face, as every other time he'd met her, was stern and unforgiving.

"Ah Mr. Johnson. Please...come in."

Johnson walked in. In front of him sitting before the Principal's desk was his daughter Rachel. Beside her was another teenage girl that Johnson took to be Susan Maxwell. Unlike his own daughter, who was trim and healthy looking, this girl had the sallow cheeks and sunken orbs of a habitual drug user. Her large, staring eyes followed Johnson when he entered. Rachel, on the other hand, cast a quick glance at him then dropped her head and studied her feet. Johnson crossed over to her and gently rested a hand on her shoulder.

"You okay?"

Rachel looked up at him, her eyes contrite.

"Daddy, I'm really sorry."

"It's okay love, don't be worrying."

Johnson gave her shoulder a reassuring squeeze then looked at the Principal behind the desk. Her name was Imelda Donaldson. A petite lady with an infectious smile she was still attractive despite being in her fifties. Her brown hair, an obvious dye job, was cut into an appealing bob giving her the appearance of an aging elf beauty. Her make-up, nails and lipstick were applied perfectly. She pointed at the empty chair beside Johnson's daughter.

"Please Detective, take a seat."

When Johnson sat down Mrs. Donaldson leant across the desk with her hand out. Held between her manicured index finger and thumb was a spliff. Mrs. Donaldson passed the joint to Johnson.

"This is what we found in the possession of Rachel and Susan," she said.

Johnson examined it. The memory of the first time he'd smoked a joint rose from the depths of his mind: His sixteenth birthday. 28th September 1986. Back of the local shops with Stevie Vincent. Both of them high as kites. Johnson hid a wry smile and tried to look serious as he studied the cause of all the fuss. He held the joint up to his nose and took a healthy sniff.

"Certainly smells like weed," he said.

"If it looks like a duck, quacks like a duck and walks like a duck Mr. Johnson then it's most likely a duck," said the Principal.

Johnson gave her a resigned nod. Satisfied that she'd proven her case the Principal steepled her fingers. An authoritive gesture.

"Rachel has admitted she is the one brought the marijuana into school," said the Principal, "but I'm afraid Mr. Johnson she's refusing to tell us exactly where she got this 'joint' from."

"I did tell you. I found it," said Rachel.

The Principal shook her head in annoyance.

"Rachel, please," she said. "Don't insult our intelligence. People just don't leave 'Spliffs' lying around."

When the Principal said 'Spliffs' Johnson heard the pride in her voice at being so street. Savvy. Up to date with the latest lingo. The Principal was well chuffed with herself.

"I'm not lying," said Rachel. "I did find it."

"Where Rachel?" Johnson asked.

"I don't want to say Daddy."

This threw Johnson. Rachel was usually honest and forthright.

"Rachel?" he tried again.

Rachel folded her arms and clamped her jaw shut. Surprised at her reaction Johnson prompted her again.

"Rachel?"

She swung her head round towards him.

"I'll tell you Daddy but I'm not telling them."

Johnson was confused by his daughter's obstinacy. He looked at the Principal.

"Is that okay?"

Rachel interrupted.

"You can't tell them Daddy. Otherwise I'm not telling you."

"Okay love, just relax."

"I am relaxed," she said.

"Is it okay if Rachel tells me?" Johnson asked the Principal. "But I keep it to myself."

The Principal looked at Mrs. Collins. After considering it for a second Mrs. Collins shrugged her shoulders. The Principal returned her gaze to Johnson.

"Yes, that's fine."

Johnson nodded at Rachel then got up from his seat.

"Let's go outside into the corridor," he said.

Rachel got up and followed him out.

Once they were in the corridor and the door was firmly shut Johnson took both his daughter's hands in his own.

"Okay, first and foremost, just remember that I love you and that everything's going to be okay."

Rachel's eyes filled with tears.

"I'm really sorry Daddy," she said.

Johnson released her hands and gave her a hug.

"There's no need for tears love."

She sobbed a little as Johnson held her. After ten seconds he stepped back.

"You okay?" he asked.

She nodded her head.

"Yes."

Johnson held her at arm's length then noticing a tear sliding down her cheek he wiped it away gently with his finger.

"You ready?" he asked.

Rachel gave him a weak smile.

"Yes," she said.

"Where did you get the joint from Rachel?" he asked.

"In the back of Mom's car Daddy, that's why I didn't want to say."

"Your mother's car? You're sure?"

"Yes! It was in the big pocket at the back of her seat."

Johnson held up his hand as he tried to wrap his mind around what he was hearing.

"Whoa, just wait Rachel. When was this?"

"This morning...when Mom was running me, Amy and Rebecca to school."

"Okay, start from the start love...from the moment you got into the car."

Rachel's words raced out in an anxious stream.

"I have a file that I stick down the back of Mom's seat every morning. It has my English work in it. When I pulled it out of the pocket this morning to go into school the joint was stuck to the bottom of it. My file must have pressed against it."

"Was there anything else in the pocket?"

"I don't know. I didn't check. I only noticed the joint when I got into class and sat down."

Johnson's mind went into overdrive, all sorts of questions running through his head. First and foremost and certainly the most pertinent was why his wife had marijuana stashed in her car. What the hell was going on? Johnson double-checked with his daughter.

"You're sure about this Rachel?"

"Yes Daddy, I'm not lying."

"Okay, we keep this between the two of us....don't say anything to anybody...especially not your Mom."

"Why not?"

"Because I said so."

"That's not a reason."

"I don't care. You say nothing, understood?"

"Okay, you don't have to get angry."

"I'm not getting angry."

"You are. I can tell by your eyes...they're like slits. That's the way they go when you're angry."

Johnson stepped back and closed his mouth. Sucking air up through his nose he released it gradually out his mouth.

"Take another breath," his daughter said.

Johnson nodded, smiled then did as he was told. Slowly, the stress and anger building up inside his body began to recede. But a foggy residual cloud of anxiety refused to evaporate from the front of his brain. Something was going on and he knew he wouldn't be able to settle until he'd found out what.

Johnson walked back into the office with Rachel. Again the Principal asked them to sit down. When they did she explained why she had no other option but to suspend Rachel and the other girl for three days. As this seemed a fair punishment Johnson didn't argue. Ten minutes later he dropped Rachel home then returned to the station.

Chapter 17

The first thing Johnson did when he got back up to the Bullpen was fill the kettle again. When it boiled he made an extra strong cup of coffee then sat at his desk deep in thought. Half way through the cup Abramo strolled in.

"How'd it go at Forensics?" Johnson asked.

Abramo took out a typed up report and proffered it across to him but he waved it away.

"No, I've no time," he said. "Give me a quick rundown."

"Forensics identified the red hook. It's from a basketball hoop, the piece that connects the net to the rim."

"Right, good. That narrows the focus."

"They were also able to identify the minivan from the tire treads. It's a Renault Master."

"Okay, now we're whistling Dixie. A white Renault Master minivan with a New York Knicks bumper sticker on the back."

"Donato also identified those foot prints that were in the mud. They're from a Nike trainer. Size nine. Donato reckons our perp's height is between five foot seven and five foot eleven."

"Be happier if we had an exact height."

"He's good but he's not that good."

"Anything else?"

"The blood on the road wasn't the victims. It's Group A, the victim's was Group B."

"That's the girl's blood then."

"Yeah, that's what I was thinking."

Johnson set his cup down and stood up.

"Right, time I got back into character," he said.

"Why, what are you doing?"

Johnson explained quickly what had happened at the strip club.

"You want me to come with you?" Abramo asked. "Good cop, bad cop routine?"

"No, if he sees you he'll clam up. Get his hard man persona on."

"In that case I'm gonna copy you and get myself a cup of coffee. After that I'll update my report for the murder file."

"You do that," said Johnson then he straightened his shoulders and walked back round to the interview room. When he entered he was purposely abrupt.

"On your feet Garin," he said.

The big man looked up at him but refused to budge.

"Look, I was telling you the truth about that bag," he said. "I don't know what was in it but I do know who brought it over."

"That's okay. So do I. Andrei Kosomo. Every Saturday. Regular as clockwork."

Garin's face dropped.

"Right, come on. On your feet."

"Look, what about if I try and find out what was in the bag for you?"

"How?"

"I'll ask Kosomo...or Yerzov...either of them will tell me."

"Okay, phone Yerzov now."

"He's hardly gonna talk over the phone. He's not that stupid."

"What about Kosomo?"

"Nobody talks over the phone nowadays Detective."

"Okay, fair enough. That's your first priority. Now tell me what Yerzov shouted at you when he ran out of the club and I was chasing him?"

"Stop that fuckin' cop!"

"So you were simply following orders?"

"Exactly."

"What about the guy leaving the strip club? What happened there?"

Garin hesitated.

"What happened?" Johnson asked again.

"He pulled a gun on me," he said.

"Why?"

"I recognized him."

"Who was he?"

"Danny Riley."

When he said this Johnson had to hide his surprise. Danny Riley had been his best friend when he'd been growing up in Hell's Kitchen. Inseparable as teenagers they'd even sported the same permed hair in imitation of Bon Jovi. Perms they'd both had shaved of when they'd joined the Marines at eighteen back in 1988. The last time Johnson had seen Danny had been at his cousin Jack's wedding in the Sacred Heart Church two years previous. Afterwards, at the reception in The Gem Hotel, they'd caught up on old times over pints of Guinness, cocktails and Danny's favorite drink: Cruzan's aged Rum. Coming from a tight knit community like Hell's Kitchen they'd both been aware of each other's history: Johnson a policeman, Danny a reputed hitman and gangster. On that night however it hadn't posed a problem as the only reason they were sitting together was to shoot the shit and wish Jack all the best with his new wife. At the end of the night they'd even swapped numbers and promised to stay in touch. They never had.

"Why'd he pull a gun on you?" Johnson asked.

"Must have been worried I wasn't gonna let him leave."

"And were you?"

"Probably not. I'm sure the Boss would have wanted to talk to him."

"Okay, I'm gonna release you after you sign a C.I. agreement."

"I don't even know what that is?"

"Confidential Informant."

"You mean a grass?"

"No. I mean someone that just walked away from four years in the can."

Fifteen minutes later Johnson cut Garin loose with strict instructions to contact him when he found out what was in the bag. As soon as Garin was out of the Precinct Johnson walked back up to the Bullpen. Abramo was at his desk typing on the computer. Johnson walked over and read what he was writing over his shoulder. It was a summary on the findings from Forensics and Abramo's conclusions on what to do next.

"I'm gonna head home for an hour Sal so if anyone's looking me tell them to ring my cell."

"Okay Joe, no problem."

Twenty minutes later Johnson was back in the house. His wife was upstairs having a shower so he got her car keys and went out to her BMW that was parked in the driveway. After he opened one of the back doors he got in and stuck his hand into the pocket behind the driver's seat. When he withdrew his hand he was holding an unopened condom and a tobacco pouch. Instantly, Johnson's heart sank. He opened the pouch and the reek of grass hit him up the face. Johnson dipped his hand in and pulled out a small see-through bag with a green marijuana leaf printed on the side. He stuck the grass back in the pouch then got out of the car and went back into the house. In the kitchen he made himself a cup of coffee then sat waiting at the table for his wife to come down. When she did and she walked into the kitchen she jumped because she hadn't realized he was there.

"What are you doing home?" she asked.

"I know," Johnson said.

Her face screwed up in confusion.

"Know what?"

"About your affair."

The color in his wife's face drained completely and for a couple of seconds she didn't speak. After a couple of seconds she let out a resigned sigh, pulled out a chair and sat down. Johnson, his heart breaking, stared across at her, his face impassive.

"Do you want to explain?" he asked.

"Look Joseph, I'm really sorry."

"So you're not denying it?"

"No, you're right, I have been having an affair," she said.

"With who?" Johnson asked.

She hesitated then after a couple of seconds she spoke.

"Does it matter?"

Johnson felt the knife twist a little deeper as she tried to protect the identity of her lover.

"Yes, it does," he said.

Considering whether to tell him or not she finally nodded her head.

"John Kelly," she said. "He's a Patrol cop."

"How long has it been going on for?"

"Just over a year."

Johnson sat there stunned as the full impact of her adultery hit him. He shook his head, his heart now a leaden rock inside his chest. For a moment he thought he wouldn't be able to breathe let alone stand but somehow he managed to get to his feet.

"Where are you going Joseph?" his wife asked.

"Back to work," he said, the words delivered by rote but inside it felt like his organs were slowly compressing, squeezing, shutting down.

Jane's face was a mask of worry.

"I'll finish with him," she said.

"I don't care what you do. Just don't be here when I get home tonight."

"You're kicking me out?"

"No, I'm asking you to leave."

"But this is my home."

"No, was your home. It's not now."

"Look Joseph, it was a mistake."

"What? For over a year you kept finding him on top of you by accident?!"

"It was just sex."

"That's why you wouldn't let me touch you, isn't it? Because of him."

"No, I just couldn't do it with him and you at the same time."

"Well, I hope it was worth it."

"I wanted to stop."

"But you never."

"Please Joseph, don't do anything rash. We can work through this."

Johnson ignored her and crossed to the kitchen door. After opening it he left the house and got back into his car. When he reached the Precinct Abramo was still typing on his computer.

"How long will you be?" Johnson asked him.

"Why? What's up?"

"I want you to come over to Vanity Hotel with me....talk to this guy Kosomo...Yerzov's cousin...then the partner George Taylor afterwards.

"Printing now Joe."

After the summary was printed Abramo placed it into the Murder File along with the Forensics Report. Next, he logged off from his computer and stood up.

"Okay, let's go," he said.

Chapter 18

Vanity Hotel was dead center of Hell's Kitchen on 10th Avenue in an area renowned for its single bars and pretty women. When Johnson and Abramo reached it they parked in a side street then got out and walked up to the hotel side by side. Above the wide doorway the name "VANITY" was lit up in neon letters that were three feet tall. The building was ultra hip and modern with the ground floor having glass walls that allowed the guests in the foyer to look out at those still attempting to get in. The glass on each side had different patterns: Swirls and circles on the front, fluttering angels and capering devils both left and right then gyrating figures at the back. The hotel had twenty floors with a large basement underneath that had been transformed into an ultra modern nightclub. It was nine at night and already a long queue had formed at the entrance to the nightclub section. The two Bouncers at the front door were identical twins. Both handsome, square jawed and tan they had the exact same steroid muscles bulging out from beneath expensive tuxedos. Eye candy for the female clientele Johnson reckoned. When the two Detectives approached one of the Bouncers stuck out his arm.

"Sorry Gentlemen but there's a queue," he said.

Johnson flashed his shield.

"Who's the manager tonight?" he asked.

"Mr. Kosomo."

"May we speak to him?"

"Give me a second."

The Doorman shot his arm forward then spoke into the microphone peeking out from underneath his sleeve.

"Andrei, are you there?"

After a couple of seconds the manager replied, his answer filtering through to the transparent ear piece wrapped around the Doorman's ear.

"The police are at the front door," said the Doorman.

Again the Manager spoke. The Bouncer nodded then turned to the policemen.

"I'm sorry Detectives but the manager wants to know what this is about?"

"Tell your manager we'll tell him that when we see him."

"Andrei, they said they'll tell you that when you come down."

The Bouncer nodded at the Manager's reply, pulled his sleeve down then motioned for them to follow him into the hotel. In the foyer the Doorman pointed at a couch.

"If you just wait over there he'll be down shortly."

"Thanks," Johnson said.

As the Doorman returned to his post the two Detectives walked over to the seat he'd indicated before he'd left. Above it was a large framed photograph of a man in a tuxedo with his arm around a nonplussed Brad Pitt. The two Detectives stared at it.

"Hotel to the stars," said Abramo.

Johnson nodded then the both of them turned and sat on the red cocktail sofa. Abramo bounced up and down like he was in a furniture store and considering buying it.

"This is comfortable," he said.

"Behave," said Johnson. "This isn't Kindergarten."

Abramo bent down and stared at a small imprint on one of the wooden legs. His eyebrows rose in surprise.

"This is a Taylor Llorente," he said.

"Which means what?"

"Which means it cost about ten grand."

"Probably a fake."

"No, it's not. Look at the stamp."

Johnson didn't bother to look. If people were stupid enough to pay ten thousand dollars for something to sit on then no wonder the world was in the middle of a recession. He folded his arms.

"Ten grand for a couch...now I've heard it all," he said.

"Gabriella would love this," said Abramo, obvious admiration in his voice. "She was a fashion major at college."

"Sure ask the manager when he gets down. See if he'll let you take it," said Johnson.

Abramo grinned at this.

"That's not a bad idea," he said.

Johnson studied the foyer around him. The carpet was a luxuriant purple and the walls were a velvet green. Various oil paintings of famous dead musicians hung on the walls: Elvis, Michael Jackson, Pavarotti, Kurt Cobain, Notorious B.I.G, Sid Vicious, 2Pac, Otis Redding, Janis Joplin, Jim Morrison, Jimi Hendrix, Marc Bolan, Keith Moon and John Lennon. Johnson got up for a better look. Up close, the paintings were even more impressive than from a distance. Being a painter himself Johnson could recognize talent when he saw it. Whoever had painted these was in a whole league of their own. Johnson searched for the signature of the artist. It was in the bottom right hand corner of each portrait: Cynthia Harris. Johnson nodded and made a mental note to google her work later when he got home.

Straightening up he decided to walk around the foyer until the Manager arrived but when there was still no sign of him after five minutes he decided to ask the Bouncers to radio through to him again. As he turned to inform Abramo of his intentions a man in a neatly fitted tuxedo emerged from the elevator and strode towards him. The man's head was up and he walked with a jaunty spring in his step. Clutched in his hand was a venetian mask.

"Are you the police?" he asked when he reached Johnson.

Johnson took out his wallet then flipped it open to display his shield.

"I'm Detective Johnson," he said, "and that man on the sofa is Detective Salvatore Abramo."

When he heard his name being mentioned Abramo finished his love affair with the couch and stood up then straightened his spine and walked over but the man wasn't impressed. After giving Abramo a cursory glance he turned back to Johnson.

"I'm Michael Connors," he said. "The Assistant Manager."

"You're not the man we're looking," said Johnson. "Where's the Manager? Andrei Kosomo?"

"He's just popped out on important business. He asked me to take his place."

"Where'd he go?" Johnson asked.

"Pardon?"

"Kosomo? Where'd he go?"

"I don't know. I assume to his car."

"Which is where?"

"The back car park."

"How do I get to it?"

Connors pointed at a brown door.

"Out that way," he said.

Johnson ran to the door and yanked it open. A set of concrete steps led to a lower level. Johnson sprinted down with Abramo right behind him. When they burst out through the bottom doors into the car park there was no one in sight. The Assistant Manager followed them down, a stricken look on his face.

"What's going on?" he asked.

"What's your Manager's home address?" Johnson asked.

"I...I don't know."

"What do you mean you don't know? You work with him."

"I only know him a few months."

Johnson studied the Assistant Manager. Up close he had piercing blue eyes, a hawk nose and a thin line for a mouth. He looked to be around forty. They walked back up into the foyer.

"Do you have a photograph of the elusive Mr. Kosomo?" Johnson asked.

"That's him there," said Connors.

Johnson turned. The Assistant Manager had pointed at the photograph of the man with his arm around Brad Pitt. Johnson took out his phone and snapped a quick picture.

"What's going on?" Connors asked.

Johnson turned back and decided to enlighten him.

"Mr. Connors, I'm sorry to inform you of this...but your boss...Richard Wright...was shot dead in the early hours of this morning."

Johnson watched Connor's eyes closely as he said this. They filled with surprise first and then shock. As far as Johnson could tell the reaction was genuine.

"Really?" said Connors. "That's so hard to believe. I mean...I was talking to him last night standing right here...in the exact spot where you are now."

"So you were working last night?"

"Yes."

"What time did Richard arrive here to the hotel last night?"

"About half eight I think."

"Is George Taylor, the other partner here?"

"Yes, he's upstairs. Probably in the office."

There was a note of contempt in the Assistant Manager's voice.

"You don't like him?"

"Who?"

"The other partner," said Johnson. "George Taylor."

"He's okay...I suppose."

"Look, we're not going to tell him. Why don't you like him?"

"He's a drunk."

Johnson decided to switch direction and go on a fishing expedition.

"What about Richard's girlfriend? Was she here with him last night?"

The Assistant Manager hesitated.

"It's okay, we know he's married. It won't get back to his wife."

"No, she wasn't with him."

Bingo. Bulls eye with his first dart. Johnson took out his notebook.

"What's the girlfriend's name?"

"Nancy."

"Nancy who?"

"Moore."

Johnson jotted down the name.

"Do you have an address for her?"

"No."

"How do you know her?"

"She's been in here with Richard a few times."

"Would anyone have a number for her?"

"No, don't think so."

"Do you know how I might be able to contact her?"

"No, sorry."

Johnson switched direction again.

"Did you like Richard?"

"As bosses go he was all right."

"Do you know if he had any enemies?"

Connor's face scrunched up. It was obvious he was wondering whether or not to tell Johnson something.

"Spit it out Connors...with-holding information is an offence."

After a brief pause followed by a deep breath Connors started talking.

"Four men forced their way into the hotel on Thursday night," he said.

"In what way forced?" Johnson asked.

"With guns. Our doormen refused them entry but they pulled out weapons. Threatened to shoot Richard and Robin."

"Who are they?"

"The twin doormen that do the front door."

"The big tan gentlemen with the beautiful muscles and the thick necks?"

"Yes, that's them."

"So what happened?"

"They stuck guns against Richard and Robin's stomachs then made them radio through for Richard. I came down with him...met them in the foyer."

"Then what happened?"

"They forced us onto our knees...stuck guns in our mouths. One of them even said I looked cute with a gun barrel in my mouth...made lewd suggestions...extremely vulgar."

"What did they want?"

"It was a business call they said."

"What type of business?"

"Drugs. They wanted to sell them in the hotel."

"What did Richard say?"

"No."

Johnson smelt a rat.

"Even with a gun in his mouth?"

"Richard is...sorry...was a respectable man."

"You do understand it's an offence to lie to the police?"

"I'm not lying Detective. Richard was against drugs."

"Then why did I find a bag of cocaine in his pants' pocket?"

"I've no idea. I didn't think Richard took drugs. Maybe the doormen confiscated the cocaine and gave it to Richard."

"Is that the usual policy?" Johnson asked.

"Yes, any drugs found on the premises are either given to me, Richard, George or Andrei. We then place them in the drawer in the office and call the police."

"What do you keep the drugs in?"

"We always use large, white envelopes."

"Do you write anything on these envelopes?"

"Yes, that's also procedure. We put a date on the label and the type of drugs we suspect have been confiscated. If they're in tablet form we count them then write on the envelope how many there are."

"The drugs we found on Richard weren't in an envelope. They were in a clear see through bag."

"Still doesn't mean they were his."

"You're very loyal."

"Richard was a friend."

"So what happened when Richard told these men he wasn't going to let them deal drugs in his club?"

"They left."

"Just like that?"

"No, they said they'd be back...that it wasn't over."

"Why am I finding this whole scenario you've just outlined extremely hard to believe?"

"I don't know Detective. I'm telling the truth."

"No you're not," said Johnson.

"I am."

"Then we'll agree to differ but know this Mr. Connors. Once I catch you out in a lie I'll be coming back for you with cuffs."

"I'm not lying."

"Did these men say who they were by any chance?"

"They didn't have to, I knew who they were."

"So enlighten us then. Who were they?"

"Irish gangsters."

"You're sure?"

"Positive."

"Would you recognize these men if you saw them again?" Johnson asked.

"Yes, definitely."

"Then I want you to come to the station tomorrow to look at mug shots."

"Which station?"

"Midtown North."

"What time?"

"2pm."

"Okay, I'll be there."

Johnson scanned the foyer.

"How do we get down to the office?" he asked.

"There's stairs over this way."

When they walked down the stairs the Halloween party was in full throttle. A vibrant mix of customers in various costumes gyrated on the dance floor whilst two Smurfs at the bar were arguing with two men dressed as Superman and Batman. The Bouncers were in the middle of the melee trying to sort it out.

"The Halloween Ball," said Connors.

Johnson looked around at the women. He'd no doubt prostitutes were intermingled amongst the crowd.

"This way," said Connors.

Johnson and Abramo followed Connors round to a long bar in the far corner. Perched on a stool was a rake thin man with lank hair and a ponytail that ran down his back. A venetian mask was shoved up onto his head like a hat. The four barmen also wore costumes. Superheroes: Batman, Robin, Iron Man and Spiderman. Connors tapped the man with the ponytail on the shoulder. He swung round, his eyes bleary and only half open.

"Do you know where George is Mitch?"

"I think he's in the office."

"Would you lift your mask please," Johnson asked a barman dressed as Batman.

"I'm not allowed."

Johnson looked at the Assistant Manager.

"It's okay," said Connors.

The barman lifted his mask. Underneath was a fresh faced young man with high cheekbones and cobalt, blue eyes.

"What's your name?" Johnson asked.

"John Mathews."

"Were you working last night?"

"Yes."

"Then stay around. I want to talk to you in about half an hour."

"Okay."

"Call your friends over."

Mathews spun and shouted to his co-workers.

"Micky, Dan, Jimmy, over here."

The other three barmen glanced round then walked over.

"Lift the masks gentlemen," Johnson said.

When they hesitated Connors waved his hand.

"Go ahead, it's okay."

Together, the three barmen raised their masks. They were all young, early twenties, and extremely handsome."

"Were the four of you working last night?" Johnson asked.

They nodded in unison.

"Okay, stay around. I want to question you later."

Johnson turned to Connors.

"Where's the office?"

Connors pointed at a brown door.

"That's it over there," he said.

"Then lead the way," said Johnson.

"Do you have a search warrant?"

"Of course, we always come prepared."

Abramo took the search warrant out of his pocket and handed it to Connors. After the Assistant Manager skimmed over it he passed it back.

"Seems to be in order," he said, a begrudging look on his face.

"I'm glad you think so," said Johnson.

Walking in front Connors led them over to the office door. Abramo gave it a hard rap.

"Who is it?" a voice shouted out.

"Police," said Abramo. "Open up."

Chapter 19

A few seconds later the key turned in the lock and the door opened. A man with grey hair, a pot belly and heavy bags under his eyes stood in the doorway. The unmistakable reek of alcohol mixed with tobacco smoke hung on him like a cloak.

"Yes?" he asked.

"George Taylor?" Abramo asked.

"Yes."

"Police."

Taylor stepped back and opened the door.

"Come in," he said, his face weary.

When Johnson walked in and looked around he couldn't help but admire the room. No expense had been spared with the furnishings. A huge antique mahogany desk sat at the head of the room with an expensive computer and printer on top. A letter opener in the shape of an ancient sword sat at the corner of the desk, its hilt facing upwards. From the ceiling hung an overhead projector aimed at an interactive whiteboard that was fixed neatly on the bottom wall. An opulent sofa with sumptuous, velvet cushions ran along one wall whilst the other had a large painting of a civil war battle running along the length of it. Below the painting was a long rectangular fish tank with a warning sign attached to the glass:

BEWARE: PIRANHA

Johnson's gaze travelled around the room. On the back wall was an oil painting of Richard Wright above a desk. Johnson turned towards the Assistant Manager.

"Mr. Connors, I need you to do me a favor," he said.

"What is it?" Connors asked.

"Do you keep a list of the employees that work here on any given night?"

"Yes, in the Duty Register."

"Which is where?"

"In my office."

"Okay, I want to see that after I've interviewed George."

"Certainly," Connors said stiffly.

Conversation over Johnson waited on Connors to leave but the Assistant Manager stayed where he was. Johnson thrust out his hand.

"We'll take it from here," he said.

Connors slowly accepted the handshake.

"I would like to stay," he said.

"Sorry but this is a murder investigation Mr. Connors. We don't need onlookers."

"I realize that but I don't think it's right leaving you in here alone with Mr. Taylor."

"I don't care what you think. Now please leave. You're hampering a murder investigation."

Connors seemed about to say something else but at the last second he stopped himself then turned and exited, a disgruntled look on his face.

"Right, take a seat," Johnson said to George.

George sat down on the leather swivel chair behind the desk.

"Tell me about Yerzov," Johnson said.

When he said this George seemed to shrink into the seat as though he hoped it would absorb him and make him disappear. At the same time his face drained of color and turned a sickly grey.

"I don't know anyone called Yerzov," he said.

Johnson turned and looked at Abramo.

"Why is it that every time we talk to people all they ever do is tell us lies? Are there no honest people left in the world anymore?"

Abramo shook his head.

"Very few I'm afraid."

"But do you know what Sal? Even though they lie to us we always find out the truth, don't we?"

"Always, every single time."

Johnson pulled a seat over to the desk and sat down.

"Okay George," he said. "We'll start again...but before we do...I'd just like to tell you that your partner...Richard Wright...was killed earlier today...strangled or hung...we're not sure yet...then afterwards...to make certain...his killer put a gun right against his head...just below the ear...and blew his brains out. Not very nice."

As Johnson had hoped this got Taylor's attention. His mouth dropped open and for a few seconds Johnson thought he was about to burst into tears. Instead, his mouth worked up and down like a ventriloquist's dummy with no sound coming out.

"Cat got your tongue George?" Johnson asked.

Finally, after a few seconds Taylor found his voice.

"Richard's dead?" he asked, his eyes wide with disbelief.

Johnson nodded.

"As the proverbial door nail. On a slab at this very minute with an ugly big "Y" sliced into his chest."

"Who? When?" Taylor asked.

"That's what we're trying to figure out but every time we ask someone a question all we get is bullshit and lies."

"Has his wife been told?"

"Yes, she was the first to hear."

"This'll devastate her. Richard was her world."

"Then help us find his killer."

"I don't know anything."

Johnson straightened up in his seat and sat forward.

"We're not saying you do. All we're asking is that you be honest with us and cut the bullshit."

Taylor tapped an anxious finger against his chin. Then, suddenly, as though he'd had an epiphany he yanked open the bottom drawer of the desk and pulled out a bottle of vodka. *Absolut Miami.* Unscrewing the lid he held the bottle up high like it was a trophy then dramatically turned it upside down so that the vodka cascaded down like a miniature waterfall. When his glass was full Taylor slammed the bottle down then picked up the vodka and drank it raw in one go. When he finished he thumped the glass down hard on the desk then quickly refilled it again. This time however he sat back, nursed the drink in his lap and looked at Johnson.

"Go ahead," he said. "Ask me anything. I'll not lie."

"Tell me about Yerzov."

"He's a Russian gangster...a real bad man."

"And you know him how?"

"I first met him about six months ago. Richard introduced me to him."

"Why?"

"Because Richard had signed over ten per cent of the hotel to him...made him a partner."

"Why?"

"Gambling. Richard's downfall from the day and hour I met him."

"What about you? You gamble?"

Taylor held up his glass.

"No, this is my only vice Detective," he said. "That and knowing Richard."

"How did you feel about a gangster getting part of your hotel?"

"At first I actually thought it was a good thing because this place was a shit hole...going under fast...sinking. Then Yerzov started pumping money in...renovations...extensions...crowds coming back...he was a savior...Christ Almighty come to earth with a big wallet."

"You said at first."

"Things were too good to be true...miracles don't really happen Detective."

"Why?"

"He turned this place into a den of iniquity, gambling, strippers, prostitutes, anything to make a buck. He didn't care as long the customers were spending money."

"Why so moral?"

"At the start I wasn't...I thought I could handle it...turn a blind eye...take the money...but after a while it started to get to me."

"Did it get to Richard?"

Taylor laughed out loud at this. A short bark filled with resentment.

"No, the opposite Detective. Richard loved it. Running with the big boys...the tough guys. Gambling, whores, this place was a paradise for Richard. Heaven on earth. He just had to snap his fingers and he could have a Jacuzzi filled with six naked women waiting to lick him from head to toe as he watched the football."

"You seem annoyed at him."

"Oh don't get me wrong Detective...I loved the guy. He was like a brother to me...but he had his faults...he was no saint. I mean...if you knew Richard you'd understand...all he ever did was think with his dick and gamble...that's what should be written on his headstone..."Degenerate sex addict that always backed the wrong team!"

"You sound angry?"

"No, not at all. He was my best friend and an asshole that turned everything he touched to shit...but I'm gonna miss him."

"Tell us about this fight you had with Richard on the 19th June?" Johnson asked.

"That was personal," said Taylor, his face darkening.

"In what way?"

"Richard did something...I found out...so I confronted him about it."

Chapter 20

Johnson heard the door open and turned around. A man wearing a full faced venetian mask and a tri-corn hat stepped into the room. In his right hand was a revolver. He swung the gun between the three of them.

"Nobody move," he said, his voice extremely deep, almost like he was trying to disguise it.

Johnson glanced quickly at Abramo. Already, his partner's body was tensed and ready to pounce.

"Take it easy Sal," he said.

Alerted, the intruder settled his gun on Abramo's face. Johnson recognized the weapon as a Smith and Wesson .38 Special.

"Come on ahead big balls," the man goaded. "Let's be having you."

Abramo dropped his chin onto his chest and seemed about to attack.

"No Sal," Johnson shouted.

"Let him go," said the intruder. "If he's stupid enough to charge a man with a loaded gun then he deserves to die."

Abramo lifted his head and rolled his thick neck. Simultaneously, his body relaxed. The man holding the gun looked disappointed.

"Balls drop off cop?"

Abramo's mouth hardened at the insult.

"You must think you're a tough guy, do you?" said the masked man. "Able to stop bullets...fart thunder...shite dynamite. Fuckin' Superman reincarnated, is that it?!"

Abramo stared at him, flagrant hatred visible in his gaze. The man's eyes hardened.

"Anyone ever tell you look like a fuckin' gorilla?" he said.

"Fuck you," Abramo replied.

Hearing this, the man tightened his grip on the gun then leant forward onto the balls of his feet to combat muzzle flip. Johnson, in no doubt that the man was about to shoot, yelled to stop him from pulling the trigger.

"We'll do whatever you want," he shouted.

The man didn't even bother to look at him. Instead, he kept his concentration tightly focused on Abramo.

"Does that go for you too big balls?" he asked.

Johnson swung round to his partner, imploring him with his eyes to agree. After a momentary pause Abramo spoke.

"Yes, it goes for me too," he said.

Almost immediately the man visibly relaxed and the tension in his arms dissipitated.

"Take out your gun and place it on the desk," he said. "And do it slowly."

Abramo did as he was told, withdrawing his Sig P226 and placing it on the desk. Satisfied, the man swung his gun to Johnson.

"Your turn."

Johnson too followed the man's instructions, putting his gun beside Abramo's.

"Now take out your cuffs and put them on King Kong here with his hands behind his back."

Johnson pulled his cuffs out of his pants' pocket and stepped behind Abramo. As he fitted the cuffs round his partner's thick wrists he scanned Abramo's fingers for the lock-pick ring. It was on the second finger of Sal's right hand.

"Don't do anything silly Sal," he whispered.

Abramo didn't reply but even from behind Johnson could feel the frustrated energy pulsing of his partner's body. The man waved the .38.

"Now take his cuffs out of his pocket and give them to the drunk. He'll put them on you."

"Hey, that's not nice," said George.

The man turned and aimed his gun at George's stomach.

"You're a fuckin' drunk...now shut the fuck up."

George raised his hands defensively.

"Okay, okay," he said. "I'm a drunk."

The man swung the revolver back to Johnson.

"Hurry up."

Johnson dug the cuffs out of Abramo's pocket, handed them to George then put his hands behind his back.

"Sorry," George said as he placed the cuffs around his wrists.

The man stepped behind them and checked the handcuffs were properly shut. They were.

"Right, cops, on your knees," he ordered.

When the two detectives knelt down the man lifted their guns then stepped over to the fish tank containing the piranha and dropped them in.

"Better safe than sorry," he said then he walked back to Johnson and made to grab his tie.

Instinctively Johnson pulled back. The man pressed the muzzle of his gun into Johnson's left eye socket.

"I'm taking your tie," he said. "You okay with that?"

This time Johnson allowed him. The man undid the knot with one hand, his gun now jammed into Johnson's throat. He pulled the tie and it slid loose.

"Right drunk, over here."

George walked over weaving a little with each step he took.

"Turn around and put your hands behind your back," the man said.

George complied. Needing both hands the man stuck his gun into the waistband of his pants. He practiced pulling it out three times. On each occasion he was extremely fast.

"Don't be getting any ideas guys," he said as he slid the gun back into place. "Either of you so much as blink and I'll shoot you dead...so don't be stupid...especially you monkey man...no fuckin' about...because if you do...it won't be a banana I'll be giving you...it'll be one in the fuckin' head."

Content that the detectives were both equally cowed by his "Billy the Kid" demonstration the man started to wrap the tie around George's wrists. As he was about to finish Abramo surged upright, swiped the letter opener of the desk and ran at him. Hearing the sudden rush of footsteps the man turned but he was too late. Abramo was already upon him. Swinging his fist he plunged the imitation dagger into the top of the man's right arm. The man squealed with pain and stumbled back, the knife protruding through the fabric of his costume. Snarling viciously, Abramo closed in and swung a powerful hook at the man's head but the man managed to step back and somehow avoided it. Now, instead of connecting with the man's temple the looping right skidded across the top of the tri-corn hat and knocked it off the man's head. Stumbling sidewards the man quickly straightened and tried to reach for his gun. But Abramo was on him again. Slapping the man's hand away he threw another bomb. But again the man's reflexes were exceptionally quick and he managed to sway away.

Behind the man Johnson scrambled to his feet. As the intruder had his back to him Johnson kicked him in the back of the knee. At the same time Abramo launched another hook. This time the punch connected and ploughed into the man's cheek and rotated his mask. Blinded for a second because the eye holes had moved the man shoved Abramo backwards then scrabbled at his mask. Recovering quickly Abramo charged back in but the momentary respite had been enough for the man. Now the gun was in his hand and his mask was righted. At point blank range he pulled the trigger. Hit in the shoulder Abramo stumbled back then lurched forward. Taking no chances the man pulled the trigger three more times, the last bullet piercing Abramo's heart before exiting out his back in an explosion of blood.

"No!" Johnson screamed but already he knew it was too late.

The man pivoted quickly and pointed his gun at Johnson's face.

"You wanna act the hero too?" he asked, his chest heaving with exertion.

Johnson gazed down at his partner on the floor. Abramo's eyes were open, vacantly staring at the painting of Richard Wright above the hotel owner's desk. The man pressed the gun in against Johnson's forehead.

"Dead or alive cop?" he asked.

Johnson glared at his friend's killer unable to say anything. Anger washed through him and for a second he considered swinging for the man's head himself. The man read the intention in Johnson's eyes and pressed the gun in hard.

"Clock's ticking cop. Make a fuckin' decision."

Again Johnson couldn't trust himself to speak. The killer's irritation grew.

"Dead or alive?" he said. "I won't ask again. Your choice."

When Johnson remained mute the man pulled the hammer back on the revolver with his thumb. Beneath the mask Johnson saw the man's eyes harden with resolve. Just before he pulled the trigger Johnson spoke to save his life.

"Alive," he said.

The man kept the gun where it was. Johnson knew he was considering killing him anyway but there was nothing he could do about it. He waited helplessly staring into the man's eyes trying to give the impression that he wasn't afraid. Eventually, after five interminable seconds the man removed the gun and gently eased the hammer forward.

"Wise decision," he said then he turned and walked over to George.

Untying his hands he turned and pointed at the letter opener protruding from the top of his arm.

"Pull it out," he said.

Petrified, George wrapped his fingers around the tiny hilt.

"You ready?" he asked.

The man gritted his teeth.

"Pull the fuckin' thing," he said.

George wrenched the blade out quickly. There was a sickening suction noise as it slid free.

"Give me it," the man said.

George handed him the bloodied letter opener. The man studied it then stuck it in his trouser's pocket.

"Don't want to be leaving DNA eh?" he said to Johnson.

"There's more than one way to skin a cat," Johnson said.

"True," the man agreed then he used the tail end of his black cloak to stem the blood leaking from his arm.

"Looks like I'm gonna need stitches," he said.

Next, he pulled the keys for the handcuffs out of his pocket and handed them to George.

"Open his cuffs," he said nodding at Johnson, "Then take him over to the radiator and handcuff him to it."

George, his face sheet white, walked across and undid Johnson's cuffs. Johnson stepped over to the radiator and sat down, his hands behind his back. George slid one end of the cuffs through the pipe of the radiator then locked them again. When George stood up and turned round the man was squatting down beside Abramo scrutinising the dead detective's face.

"People look so peaceful when they're dead, don't they?" he said.

Neither Johnson nor George replied. Angered by their silence the man stood up and pointed his gun at George.

"Take his cuffs off," he said waving his gun at Abramo, "Then go over to the other side of the radiator and sit down with your hands behind your back."

George did as he was told. After he was in position the man strode over and locked the cuffs behind him. When he straightened up he took a long, slender key out of his pocket and held it up.

"Richard begged for his life last night before I killed him...told me all his dirty secrets and where his money is. Thought I was going to let him live you see. Such a fool."

After saying this the man walked over to the wall and squatted down. At first Johnson was confused because there was nothing there besides a treble wall socket. Then the man inserted the key he held into one of the holes. When he turned it and there was an audible click Johnson realized the wall socket was a hidden safe. With the key still in the man pulled. An open topped tray slid out of the wall. The man lifted the tray across to Richard's desk then dipped his hand in and searched around. His body language told Johnson he hadn't found what he was looking for. Angry now, the man pulled everything out and threw it on the floor. Next, he upended the tray and shook it. Nothing. Furious, he flung the tray at the ground then stormed across to George.

"Where's the key?"

"What? I don't know what you're on about?"

"Don't play fuckin' stupid with me George!"

"I'm not."

Infuriated, the man turned and stormed across to the portrait of Richard Wright. Ripping it off the nail it was hanging on he hurled it at George but instead of hitting him it bounced off the wall. When the frame hit the ground it split apart with one side dangling loose. Now, behind where the portrait had been, was a safe with an iron door and two keyholes side by side. The man pointed at the keyholes as he spoke to George.

"Richard told me his key was in that box and that you have the other one. Do you have both keys George?"

"I don't know what you're talking about. I never even knew that safe was there."

"Don't blow smoke up my ass George. You're Richard's partner and best friend...know everything about him...so don't sit there and act like you're stupid. Where are the keys?"

"I swear, I don't know."

The man shook his head then walked over to George and withdrew his gun. He aimed it at George's kneecap.

"Your friend Richard told me last night that there's a million dollars in that safe and that his key was in the socket safe...but as you can see...it's not...which means Richard lied to me. Must have known I was going to kill him anyway. But I think you know George...don't you? Where are the keys?"

"Please, you've got to understand. Me and Richard weren't really that close."

The man swivelled and looked at Johnson.

"What about you cop? You know where the keys are?"

"Fuck you," said Johnson.

"Oh, get your balls back...well done Detective. I applaud your audacity and bravery. Outstanding."

"I will hunt you down for this."

"No...please...I surrender! Here, take my gun! I give up," said the man before bursting into sarcastic laughter behind the mask.

Johnson's face turned red, anger and shame vying with each other to burnish his skin.

"You ever been to Thailand cop?" the man asked.

Johnson refused to speak.

"Oh, I get it...you're not feeling talkative because I killed your friend! Okay, I understand...it's a sensitive issue...you bonded together chasing bad guys, ate doughnuts together, talked shit together...probably even felt each other's balls...fucked each other's wives...all that type of stuff...but I'm telling you now cop...if ever you get the chance...go to Thailand. Beaches? Unbelievable. Women? Even better... fuck capital of the world."

The man started thrusting his hips.

"Isra Anuwat in the Sapphire Lodge in Pattaya...fan-fuckin' tastic....make sure you go and see her...best tits in the world...but see her mouth? Even better. Could suck a lemon through a straw. So if you go, tell her I sent you....she'll probably give you discount...loves me you see...I'm her favorite. At least, that's what she tells me...but you know how it is with sluts...all the fuckin' same...tell you what you want to hear as long as you're paying them."

Johnson stared at him, every ounce of hatred in his body directed towards his friend's killer. The man smiled behind his mask then turned and aimed his gun at George's knee.

Chapter 21

"Right George, back to you," he said.

"Look, there's no need to hurt me," said George.

"I'll be the judge of that."

"I'll tell you anything you want."

"Good because if you don't I'm gonna blow a hole in your kneecap."

"W...w...what? You can't be serious," said George.

"I'm deadly serious."

"B...b...but why? I'll tell you anything you want to know about Richard."

"All I want to know about Richard is where his key is...and yours."

"I don't know...I don't have a key...Richard lied to you."

The man tutted loudly.

"That's not good George...not good at all."

"Please, I'm not lying."

"You do realize I have to make sure you're telling me the truth?"

"I am telling you the truth."

"But I don't know that."

"Look, I wouldn't lie to you."

The man tucked the gun into the waistband of his pants then crossed over to the Laser Jet printer on top of the desk. He opened the drawer containing the paper and pulled out four sheets of A4. He crumpled them into a ball then marched back to George.

"Open wide."

"What?"

"You heard me. Open fuckin' wide."

"I don't understand."

The man withdrew his gun and placed it against George's forehead.

"Open your big fuckin' mouth and say ahhh just like you're at the dentist."

George opened his mouth.

"Wider."

When George obeyed the man shoved the ball of paper into George's mouth making him splutter and choke. Satisfied with his handiwork, the man slipped the gun back into his waistband.

"Breathe through your nose," he told George.

George sucked air in through his nostrils, his eyes flaring wide with fright.

"That's it...nice and easy," said the man.

Once his breathing started to level out the man walked behind George and grabbed one of his fingers. George thrashed about, his protestations muffled by the clump of paper blocking his esophagus.

"This little piggy went to market," said the man. "This little piggy stayed at home. This little piggy had bread and water. This little piggy had none."

Upon saying "none" the man snapped George's finger. George screamed but the sound was muted by the paper stuffed down his throat. The man walked back around in front of him.

"One down, nine to go," he said.

Tears streamed down George's face. The man watched him, indifferent to the pain he'd just caused. When George's screams receded to a whimper the man walked over to him and plucked the sodden, mangled clump out of his mouth.

"Ok, I'll ask you again George. Where are the keys to the safe?"

George was crying now and his eyes were filled with terror.

"I don't know," he said. "Please, you've got to believe - "

Before he could finish the man shoved the wet, wad of paper back into George's mouth and straightened up.

"In my line of work I don't believe anybody," he said.

Again he walked behind George and grabbed a finger. This time he didn't bother with the nursery rhyme. Instead he simply broke it in two. Once more George's body leapt with pain.

"Aggggghhhhhhh!!!" he screamed, the sound again stifled because of the glob of paper.

The man came back around and stood in front of him waiting for the sobs to ebb. When they did he bent down and extracted the paper with his fingers.

"Two down...eight to go...but because this is already boring the balls clean off me I'm just gonna shoot you next."

"I don't know...please...you've got to believe me."

"We've been through this already. I don't believe anybody. Well, maybe my mother but she's the exception to the rule."

"Please, please."

The man pointed the gun at George's knee.

"Do you like walking George?"

"Yes. I take Gerard, my sister Susan's son...to Central Park every Sunday for a walk."

"That's beautiful George, beautiful. Now, if I wasn't such a callous bastard that little story you've just told me might stop me from pulling this trigger...but unfortunately for you...I'm a heartless motherfucker...so I'm just gonna ask you the question again."

"Tell him George," Johnson shouted. "If you know where the keys are, tell him."

"But I don't know where they are, I swear to God. If I did I would tell him."

"He doesn't know," Johnson yelled.

The man shook his head.

"Usually I'd give him the benefit of the doubt and carry on snapping his fingers but with your dead buddy on the ground I'm afraid I have to hurry this along. I'm sure you understand my predicament."

"If you shoot him it might kill him," Johnson shouted.

"Maybe...maybe not. Let's find out shall we?"

"You may kill me afterwards because I won't stop until I find you."

"Oh...hide and seek. My favorite game as a child growing up."

"Don't shoot him."

"Depends on his answer."

"He doesn't know."

"George...last chance. Where are the keys to the safe?"

"Please, please, I don't know where they are."

Furious, the man stuffed the paper back into George's mouth. George's eyes bugged wide when the man pulled the gun out of his waistband. He aimed it at George's knee.

"This is your fault George, not mine."

George shook his head, tears running down his face.

"This is gonna hurt you more than it hurts me," the man said then he pulled the trigger.

George screamed as the bullet tore through his black pants and continued on through his knee. Blood, like a newly sprung well, gushed out as George squealed around the gag in his mouth.

"Fuck-sake, man up George. It's only a stupid knee," the man said.

George continued to yell with pain, the sound muted and horrible. The man waited, standing motionless and pitiless until George's sobs receded. When they did the man leant forward and pulled the paper out of George's mouth.

"Where are the keys George? Tell me and I'll phone you an ambulance."

"Please...stop...please," George gasped.

"The only thing that'll make me stop George is you telling me where the keys are? Where are they?"

"I...I...don't...know."

"Know what George? I actually believe you...but I have to say...your whining is gettin' on my fuckin' nerves. You're like a big woman....a drama queen. Should have manned the fuck up. Maybe then I'd have let you live."

The man pressed the gun against George's right eye.

"Wait! Wait!" George screamed.

"You something to tell me George?"

"My key's around my neck."

The man pulled the gun back then grabbed George's necklace and tugged it off his head. A heavy key dangled from the lace.

"Where's the other key George?"

"I swear, I really don't know."

The man placed the gun back against George's eye.

"Pity," he said. "Bye George."

The man squeezed the trigger. George's face disappeared amidst an explosion of red blood that turned the wall behind him into a piece of abstract art. As George's body slumped sidewards Johnson stared in shock, transfixed by the crimson patterns now criss-crossing the impromptu canvas. It was like some crazy painter had decided to create an original masterpiece using the human debris from the back of George's head as his medium. Outside the room the cadence of loud disco music shook the walls smothering the sound of the gunshot. The man looked across at Johnson as the smell of cordite filled the room.

"I couldn't listen to him anymore," he said. "Could you? All that squealing was giving me a headache."

Johnson didn't reply. He was still in shock at what he'd just witnessed. Meanwhile, the man strolled across to him with his arms at his sides, the revolver dangling from his fingertips. For some strange reason Johnson focused on the gun and the smoke coming out of the barrel. As it slowly filtered out it formed a hazy ethereal 'S' then drifted towards the ceiling where it elongated and dispersed. Ever so slowly, the man raised his gun and pointed it at Johnson's face.

"Where do you want it cop? Right eye? Left eye? Forehead? Cheek?" he asked as he moved the gun to each facial part that he named. As he did so the touch of the cold metal against Johnson's skin made him shiver.

"Nose? Chin? Jaw? Mouth?" the killer continued.

Johnson stayed quiet. Whilst he was frightened he didn't want the man to know it. He thought of his daughters: Rachel, Amy and Rebecca. Then he thought of his wife Jane and his heart lurched at her betrayal. Grasping at straws he decided to try and goad the man into leaving him alive.

"Thought you wanted to play hide and seek with me?" he asked.

The man's eyes locked with Johnson's as he traced the gun around the Detective's lips.

"That was a joke," he said.

"What happen? Lose your balls?" Johnson asked.

"No, I just don't like leaving witnesses," said the man then he pulled the trigger. This time, instead of a gunshot, there was an audible click as the hammer hit against an empty chamber. The man pulled the trigger two more times just to make sure. His gun was empty. He'd used up all his bullets. Four on Abramo, two on Taylor.

"Fuck!" he said then he swung around and marched over to the aquarium. Staring in at the two guns resting at the bottom it seemed for a moment he was going to dip his hand into the water to retrieve them but at the last second he changed his mind and instead walked back to Johnson.

"This is your lucky fuckin' day cop," he snarled then he turned and strode towards the door shaking his head.

When he reached the discarded socket tray he gave it an almighty kick lifting it into the air. As it somersaulted head over heel something flew out and landed on the floor forcing the man to stop and look down. At his feet was a large, sturdy key with a piece of black tape attached. Instantly the man realized it was an exact carbon copy of the one he'd just taken from George. Bending down he picked it up, his face breaking into a grin the size of New Jersey.

"Jesus wept, would you believe it?" he said, holding the key up for Johnson to see.

"Look at that," he said. "The second key. Taped to the drawer."

Johnson stayed mute, disgusted that the gunman had found what he'd been looking for. Instead, he watched in angry silence as the killer danced a happy jig through Sal and George's blood over to the safe and placed the keys in the locks. When he turned them the safe door yawned opened.

"Praise to the lord," the killer shouted, sticking his hands in.

When they re-emerged he was clutching bundles of money. The man placed them on top of the desk then pulled a black bin liner out of his pocket.

"Always come prepared, that's my motto," he said over his shoulder then he turned back and emptied the safe. When he was finished and the bin liner was bulging with money he walked over to Johnson with the bag in his hand.

"I love it when a plan comes together," he said. "Who said it?"

Johnson refused to answer.

"George Peppard...from the A Team," said the man. "Loved that show.   B.A...the   big   black   dude...I   ain't   gettin'   on   no plane...Murdoch...the   crazy   one...Face...the   ladies   man...then Hannibal...the brains of the operation...Hannibal's on the jazz!"

Johnson didn't respond.

"What's wrong?" the man asked. "You still pining over that big ape? Godsake Detective, he's yesterday's news...fuck him. More bananas for the rest of us."

Johnson refused to reply.

"The strong silent type. I like that Detective. Pity I don't bat for the other side or I'd be kissing you right now, you're very attractive...sexy."

Johnson remained silent.

"Okay Detective, you're not a big conversationalist, I understand, you're in mourning. Unfortunately, I can't stay to comfort you, I have to go. Not that your company hasn't been scintillating...because it has. You're a sparkling wit...life and soul of the party...but you have to understand...I've other pressing engagements. So without further ado...I'll bid you a fond farewell...and remind you...that you're "It"! Au revoir Detective...until we meet again."

After saying this, the murderer turned and strode to the door. When he opened it he walked out without a backward glance, closed it behind him and disappeared.

Chapter 22

Johnson was momentarily stunned. He'd expected the man to try and retrieve one of the guns from the fish tank to kill him. After a few seconds he recovered his senses. In an effort to buckle the pipe he leant back with all his weight but it refused to budge. Switching tactics he brought up his right foot then shot it forward slamming it into the pipe but it didn't break. Gritting his teeth he launched a third attack. This time the pipe bent inwards but remained intact. But Johnson wasn't for giving up. Breathing deeply, he marshaled his strength then continued kicking the pipe until eventually it broke. When it did he slid his hands free then scrambled to his feet and sprinted to the door with his hands still cuffed. When he grabbed the door handle he glanced back over his shoulder at Sal and then George. A liquid blanket of red sprawled across the floor, George's blood now intermingling with Sal's. Johnson vowed there and then that the bastard that did this was going to pay. Come hell or high water he was going to find him and bring him to justice. Johnson pulled the door open and sprinted along the hallway. A redhead wearing a mask stopped in her tracks as he raced towards her.

"Phone the police," Johnson shouted.

"What? Why?"

"Two men are lying dead in that office."

"Oh...oh..." the woman said.

In a panic she fumbled with the catch of her purse. When she managed to get it open
she pulled out her phone and held it out to Johnson.

"Here," she said.

Johnson snatched it out of her hand and dialed 911. Twenty minutes later the hotel was swarming with cops and cordoned off from the public. Inside, Johnson sat outside Richard's office thinking about his dead partner, his wife Gabriella and their young son, Angelo. Tom Adams, a big bear of a man with a penchant for kebabs, had been assigned as the lead detective. After offering his condolences he sat on the seat next to Johnson and asked him what had happened. Johnson told him from start to finish without interruption. Throughout, Big Tom nodded sympathetically. At the story's conclusion Big Tom scratched his head with a callused hand.

"Sounds like a pro Joe. Taking the letter opener with him was a smart move."

"I agree. This wasn't the first time he's killed. Too damn calm."

"I'll put an alert out to the hospitals in case he's stupid enough to go to one of them to get that arm stitched but I doubt it not if his previous behavior is anything to go by."

After saying this Tom got up and walked into the office. Johnson stayed where he was, not wanting to see Sal's dead face again. When he leaned his head back against the wall he caught Lieutenant Olivia Walker marching towards him out of the side of his eye. A striking woman in her early thirties she had the lean body of an athlete. As always her blonde hair was tied back in a severe ponytail. Rumored to be having an affair with Captain Cochrane from the 10th, half the men in the precinct were in lust with her. Nicknamed "Calam" because of her proficiency with a weapon, she was the holder of a bronze medal for shooting from the 2008 Beijing Olympics. Forthright and honest Johnson liked and respected her. She stopped in front of him and it was obvious she was torn up about Abramo's death.

"What happened Joe?" she asked.

Johnson quickly explained. When he got to the part about Sal undoing his cuffs and attacking the man Walker shook her head in annoyance.

"Always bull-headed," she said.

"I tried to stop him Lieutenant but you know what he was like."

The Lieutenant nodded.

"He'd have tackled a tiger with his bare hands," she said.

"I'll find out who did this," Johnson said. "I won't rest until I do."

"Sure you never do."

Johnson stood up.

"I want to be the one to tell Gabriella."

"You sure?"

"Sal would have done it for me."

"Then go. We'll finish up here."

"Tell Tom I want a copy of everything."

"That won't be a problem."

Johnson left immediately. By the time he reached Abramo's apartment in Little Italy he realized that he'd been crying silently as he drove. When he pulled up, the apartment was shrouded in darkness because of the late hour. Johnson checked his watch. 3.15am. He rolled his neck, took a deep breath and got out of the car. As he walked towards the path his legs felt numb, like they were made out of lead. He stopped momentarily, took another breath then opened the gate and walked down to the front door. The thought of telling Gabriella that her husband was dead terrified him but he knew it was something he had to do. He composed himself then rapped the door. A minute later the hall light came on and a silhouette appeared behind the scrolled glass.

"Who is it?" Gabriella shouted out, a hint of fear in her voice.

"It's me Gabriella...Joe."

Gabriella hurriedly opened the door. When she pulled it back Johnson realized she had a gun in her hand. She noticed him staring at it.

"Sorry," she said. "I didn't know it was you."

"Can I come in?"

Gabriella looked confused then fear began to blossom in her eyes.

"Where's Salvatore Joe?" she asked.

Johnson looked at her then, the expression on his face alerting her that something was wrong. Desperation and fear crept into her voice.

"Where's Salvatore Joe?" she repeated.

Johnson shook his head then couldn't look at her anymore. The pain developing across her face was too much for him to bear. He dropped his eyes. Gabriella clutched his shoulder.

"No Joe, please...no."

Johnson looked up again, his chin trembling.

"I'm sorry Gabriella. Sal's dead."

Gabriella squealed involuntarily then raised the gun and pointed it at Johnson's face.

"You're a liar! He's not dead!" she screamed. "You're a liar!"

Johnson reached up and gently wrapped his hand around the gun.

"I'm telling you the truth," he said.

When Gabriella didn't resist Johnson took the gun from her then stepped forward and wrapped his arms around her. She sank into them collapsing against his chest.

"I'm sorry Joe, I'm sorry."

"It's okay Gabriella," Johnson soothed. "It's okay."

As he stood there little Angelo appeared at the top of the stairs, the adult voices having woken him from his sleep.

"What's wrong Mom?" he shouted down.

"Oh my baby," Gabriella wailed then she ran up the stairs and grabbed him into her arms. When she came back down she had him clasped to her chest. A lifeline in a sea of sadness. Johnson dropped his eyes and stared at the ground as Gabriella clung to her five year old like he was the most precious thing on earth. Angelo, in tune with his mother, cried aloud, subconsciously aware that something catastrophic had just happened. After a few minutes the initial shock wore off and Gabriella's loud, heart wrenching sobs subsided to a steady stream of silent tears. Placing her son on the ground she kept him at her side holding onto his hand.

"What happened Joe?" she asked.

Johnson looked at Angelo, afraid to speak in front of him. Gabriella, noticing his reticence, released her son's hand then pushed him up the stairs.

"Go back up to bed Angelo," she said.

"No Mom, I want to stay with you."

"Please Angelo, go up to bed."

Reluctantly, Angelo did as he was told. Before he started his ascent he stared up at Johnson, his young eyes already red. If it was possible, Johnson felt his heart break all over again.

Johnson stayed for an hour. By the end he was so emotionally drained he felt like he could sleep for a week but Gabriella's departing words rejuvenated him:

"Find who killed my husband Joe," she said. "For Sal, for me, for little Angelo. For Teresa."

Galvanized by her request Johnson drove back to Vanity Hotel. When he walked into the lobby Lieutenant Walker was in deep conversation with Donato, Firth and Hank Halbrook. Donato stepped forward when he saw Johnson approach.

"Jesus Joe, I'm sorry," he said.

"It's not me you should be sorry for Francis, it's Sal's family."

"Yeah, how'd that go?"

Johnson shook his head at the memory of Gabriella's crumpled, heartbroken face.

"Bad," he said.

"You look tired Joe. Why don't you go on home," said the Lieutenant.

"No, I'm grand. I'll be okay."

"You sure?"

"Positive."

Halbrook stepped up to him.

"If there's anything I can do Joe just let me know."

"Just make sure no one gets out of here Hank before they've been questioned."

"Okay, I'll get that sorted now," said Halbrook then he turned and walked away.

"We found something upstairs Joe...top floor," said Donato.

"Let me guess? A brothel?"

"Yeah, how'd you know?"

"A little birdie told me."

"Did your little birdie tell you about the body?"

"No."

"There's a dead girl upstairs."

Five minutes later Johnson, Donato and the Lieutenant stepped out of the elevator onto the tenth floor. The corridors leading to the rooms were standard. Cream walls with red carpet thick enough to withstand hundreds of tramping feet. Donato led them to Room 1019. Before they entered they stopped outside and snapped on their latex gloves. Donato turned the handle then held the door ajar.

"Age before beauty Lieutenant," he said.

Ignoring him Walker stepped across the threshold with Johnson behind her. Inside, the room was dominated by a large king size bed with a pink duvet and matching pillows. Its central feature however was the dead woman lying spread eagled on top. Strapped to the bed by her hands and feet it looked like the woman had been involved in some type of bondage before she'd been killed. Kinky sex. Completely naked she lay with her head tilted sideways, her glazed eyes staring fixedly at some unknown point. A thin, caul like membrane covered her eyes giving them a milky translucence. Three bullet holes were in her right breast. All in close proximity around the nipple. A burst of three in compact formation.

"Do we know who she is?" Johnson asked.

Donato shook his head.

"No I.D."

"She's gotta be a hooker," Johnson said. "One of Yerzov's girls."

"Is that Yerzov, the Russian gangster?" the Lieutenant asked.

Johnson groaned inwardly at his faux pas. He'd been hoping to keep Yerzov's involvement a secret. Reluctantly he nodded his head.

"Yes," he said.

"If he's involved we'll have to tell OCCB," said the Lieutenant, a crease of annoyance crinkling her brow.

OCCB was the acronym for the "Organized Crime Control Bureau" which was responsible for investigating and preventing organized crime in New York City. Whilst they had over 2,000 men and women seconded to them they also worked in tandem with the Federal Bureau of Investigation's New York field division. Based out of One Police Plaza they'd had numerous successes over the years thanks to RICO, the "Racketeer Influenced and Corrupt Organizations Act". To date they'd badly damaged the Italian, Chinese, Russian and German mafia as well as the Westies, the Irish gangsters from Hell's Kitchen. Yet despite this fearsome reputation Johnson hated the thought of them steam rolling in and "bigfooting" his case.

"Yerzov's on the periphery Lieutenant. I don't think we need the OCCB," he said.

The Lieutenant wasn't fooled for a second.

"I'll be the judge of that Detective," she said using his formal title because she was annoyed. "I want a full report on my desk tomorrow morning at 10am detailing everything to do with Yerzov. Understood?"

"Yes Lieutenant."

Johnson cursed inwardly but because the Lieutenant was looking suspiciously at him he forced himself to appear outwardly calm.

"Was there any security up here?" he asked the Lieutenant.

"Yes, two...beside the elevator," she said.

"They say anything?"

"Not a word."

"Russian?"

"That's what their firearms certificates say. Roman Karev and Vlad Oborin."

"Two of Yerzov's heavies."

"Looks that way," said Walker. "Now that you've been so kind as to let me know he was involved."

Johnson shrugged good naturedly.

"I'd have got around to it," he said.

"Somehow I doubt that Joe."

"You still have the two goons?" Johnson asked.

The Lieutenant nodded.

"We're holding them at the Precinct," she said, "but we've nothing on them. The guns they were carrying were legally held. We'll have to let them go."

"Okay, that's fine."

"Fine? How?" she asked, confused.

Johnson explained.

"I've a C.I. in Yerzov's organization. I'll check with him later. Ask him if he's heard anything."

The Lieutenant nodded, a little dubious. Not wanting to get questioned further Johnson walked to the foot of the bed deep in thought. Turning slowly he scanned the room from floor to ceiling. As he was about to complete a full rotation he spotted something. He crossed the room to a small screw protruding from the wall. It was exactly in the middle at head height. Donato came up behind him.

"What is it?" he asked.

"A screw."

"So?"

"I've a hunch."

"You want to enlighten us?" the Lieutenant asked.

"Not yet, I could be wrong."

Johnson left and checked the other rooms. Donato and the Lieutenant followed after him like lost puppies, perplexed looks on their faces. In each hotel room on the tenth floor there was an identical screw in the centre of the wall. Johnson turned to the Lieutenant.

"Have the other call girls been questioned yet?"

"At the minute everyone's down on the bottom floor waiting to get interviewed. No one's been allowed to leave."

"I'm going down to get one of them...bring her back up."

"Why?" the Lieutenant asked.

"Just a hunch Lieutenant. If it pans out you'll be the first to know plus she'll be able to I.D the girl."

Chapter 23

Five minutes later Johnson was back downstairs. The bottom floor was thronged with clubbers. At least two hundred of them were men dressed in black tuxedos. Johnson scanned the room looking for call girls. He spotted three women with heavily applied make-up whispering frantically in the corner of the room. Johnson walked over to them. The first was an attractive Japanese woman in a tight fitting red kimono with a slash up the left leg. Standing beside two other women, one in a green gown revealing an abundance of cleavage, the other wearing a black pencil skirt and a yellow blouse, they all looked worried. Johnson flashed his shield.

"You work here?" he asked the Japanese girl.

"No," she said.

"So you're here with friends?"

"Yes."

"Would you step over here please so that I can talk to you in private?"

"Do I have to?"

"Yes, you do."

Reluctantly, the Japanese girl followed him.

"How did you get here tonight?" Johnson asked.

This threw her but she recovered quickly.

"A taxi."

"Private or public?"

"Private."

"On your own?"

She hesitated.

"On your own?" Johnson asked again.

"Yes, on my own," she said.

"Where did you get the taxi?"

"It came to my apartment."

"Which is where?"

"West 43rd Street."

"What about your friends? How did they get here?"

"I don't know."

"You met them here?"

"Yes," she said after a second's pause.

"What are their names?"

She hesitated and Johnson knew what was going through her head. If she gave her friend's real names and he ran a check then it was a guaranteed certainty they'd have form for soliciting. If she gave false names and he went back and asked her friends to verify the information then the names they gave wouldn't match. A classic pincer

141

movement. The young Japanese woman stood there helplessly unable to answer, her mouth opening and closing like a fish landed on the deck of a ship.

"Do you want to stop playing games?" Johnson asked.

She nodded dejectedly.

"Ok," said Johnson. "Let's start again. Do you work here?"

"Yes."

"As what?"

"An escort."

"What about your two friends?"

"Yes."

"Yes what?"

"Yes they're also escorts."

"Where do you work?"

"Upstairs on the top floor."

"Tell me how it operates."

"We work the disco in the basement then if a customer wants a little extra we take them up to the top floor to one of the bedrooms."

"How much is a little extra?"

"Five hundred."

"You're worth that much?"

A glimmer appeared in her eyes and she went into trick mode.

"Every cent," she said, her eyes now oozing sex.

"Don't be playing me," Johnson said.

The fake sparkle evaporated, replaced immediately by a hard stare.

"What's wrong? You gay?" she asked.

"No but I am married."

"Since when did that stop anyone?"

"Well, it stops me."

"Then you're a dying breed," she said and for the first time since they'd started talking, her face relaxed and lost its hardness.

"What's your name?" Johnson asked.

"Asako Kato."

"Child born in the morning."

This surprised her.

"You speak Japanese?"

"No, but I'd a friend whose daughter was also called Asako. He told me the meaning of it."

"Small world."

"I need you to come upstairs with me to the bedrooms."

"Thought you were married?"

"I told you not to play me."

"Now?"

"Yes, now."

"Can I tell my friends?"

Johnson looked across at the other two call girls. When they noticed him glancing over they quickly turned away.

"Okay," he said, "but make it snappy."

On the way up in the elevator Johnson prepared Asako for what lay ahead. The last thing he needed was her getting hysterical once they got into the hotel room. When he finished explaining about the dead girl strapped to the bed Asako's face was ashen.

"Can you not get one of the other girls to come up?" she asked.

Johnson shook his head.

"I'm sorry Asako," he said. "We need an I.D asap."

"I've never seen a dead body before," she said, a hint of panic entering her voice.

Johnson envied her innocence and regretted that he was about to rip it away but under the circumstances he'd no other option.

"You'll be okay," he said. "I'll be right beside you."

When they got out of the elevator Asako was surprised at the amount of police personnel milling around.

"Are there always this many?" she asked.

"Sometimes more," Johnson said. "This is a light crew."

"Who are they all?"

"Crime Scene Unit...Medical Examiner...his assistants......Patrol cops...Detectives."

She nodded as Johnson spoke, taking it all in. When they reached the bedroom the Lieutenant was waiting outside talking to Donato.

"Lieutenant, this is Asako." Johnson said. "She's kindly agreed to help us with our investigation."

The Lieutenant shook Asako's hand and smiled warmly.

"Did Detective Johnson make you aware of what's in the room?"

"Yes, he did."

"Then let's proceed," said the Lieutenant then she opened the door and entered with Donato behind her.

Next into the room was Johnson but when he looked back he realized Asako had stopped at the entrance so he walked back to her.

"It's gonna be okay," he said noticing how badly she was shaking.

Asako, her face sheet white, smiled and tried to be brave.

"If I faint will you catch me?" she asked, her eyes unable to hide the panic.

"You'll be fine," said Johnson.

"Okay," she said nodding so he gently took her hand and led her into the room.

When he reached the bed he stepped aside to let her get a full view of the corpse. Seeing the body her hand lifted to her mouth.

"Oh my god," she said, her legs instantly starting to wobble.

For a second Johnson thought she was about to collapse so he reached out and grabbed her arm.

"Take a deep breath"," he said. "In through the nose and out the mouth."

Nodding, Asako did as she was told. After inhaling and expelling a few times she grew more steady on her feet so Johnson released his grip.

"Sorry," she said.

"No need to apologize," he said.

"Do you know who it is Asako?" the Lieutenant asked.

Asako nodded.

"It's Jennifer," she said.

"Second name?"

"Jones."

"Is that her real name?"

"I don't know. That's what she told me her name was. We just used to call her JJ."

"And just for confirmation purposes, was JJ a call girl?" Johnson asked.

"Yes," said Asako nodding.

"For Yerzov?"

Asako stiffened at the mention of the Russian gangster's name.

"Relax," Johnson said. "We know all about Yerzov supplying the girls from Flawless."

Asako's eyes lit up like glaring lamps. Petrified. Johnson rested his hand on her shoulder.

"Take it easy, it's okay," he said.

Asako pulled away from him.

"It's not okay, you don't know what he's like."

"He can't harm you Asako."

"Not me, my family...my little sister...my mother...that's who he'll harm."

"He'll not know you were talking to us," said Johnson. "This stays between these four walls."

"No, I can't help you," she said shaking her head vigorously.

"At least tell me about JJ. Who was the last customer she came up here with last night?"

"Richard, the owner."

"You're sure?"

"I'm positive. Richard won a big bet yesterday so he was celebrating...at least that's what he told us."

"How big a bet?"

"I don't know but he was throwing money around like it was confetti."

"Okay, explain to me why JJ has been lying here from the early hours of this morning and we've only discovered her now? Does nobody else use this room?"

"No, we all have a room each."

"What about cleaners?"

"They only come up here once a week...usually on a Tuesday."

"That's good Asako. You're really helping us here."

"Can I go now?"

"No, just one more thing. What's missing in this room?"

Asako stared at him, her eyes frightened.

"What's missing Asako?"

Asako stalled, debating whether to answer him. Eventually she came to a decision. She nodded slowly then glanced around the room.

"There's nothing missing," she said.

"You're sure about that?" Johnson asked.

"Yes, positive."

"This is a murder investigation Asako so be very careful with your answers."

Asako's face developed a piqued, worried expression.

"There's nothing missing," she said again but this time the conviction in her voice had lessened considerably. Johnson recognized the change and shook his head in annoyance.

"You're lying Asako," he said.

"I'm not," she said, her voice high pitched and defensive.

Johnson decided it was time to push a little harder.

"If I find out you're deliberately being untruthful Asako I'll make sure you get the full five years for hampering a police investigation, do you understand?"

Asako stayed silent, her eyes terrified. Johnson raised his voice, angry now.

"My partner was murdered tonight with another man," he said. "Do you want me to take you down there Asako, show you their bodies, their blood, their brains? It's not pretty...but some bastard did that tonight so I need you to stop telling me lies...because I am not in the fuckin' mood!"

Asako shrank back from him and started shaking. The Lieutenant crossed over to her taking Asako's hands in her own.

"Please Asako," she said. "Take a last look around. Maybe there's something that you didn't notice the first time."

Asako shook her head.

"No, I can't," she said.

Johnson stood in front of her. When he spoke his voice was lowered but there was still a hard timbre in his tone.

"If you co-operate Asako," he said. "You walk away scot-free, nobody none the wiser that you helped us."

"Please," she begged. "I don't know anything."

"Okay Asako, we'll play it your way," he said. "The stupid way. The way where you get five years for being un-co-operative in a murder investigation but remember this. Your two friends are down there in the big hall. I'm sure they're not going to be so stupid when I bring them up here. They'll jump at the chance to get off with doing five years."

"Is he serious?" Asako asked the Lieutenant. "Will I really go to jail for five years?"

"Yes, I'm afraid so. It's the law," the Lieutenant replied.

Asako swung back to Johnson.

"Let me look again," she said. "I might have missed something."

Johnson nodded, his face impassive. Asako turned and again scanned the room. Johnson played along knowing it was all just an act. She knew fine rightly what was missing. She let out a fake gasp then pointed at the screw sticking out of the wall.

"The clock," she said, twisting her neck so that she could look at him. "That's what's missing...the clock."

"What type of clock?" Johnson asked.

"A round white one."

"Okay Asako, you're doing well," said Johnson then he stepped over to her and turned her by the shoulder. Now she was right in front of him. He stared down into her eyes.

"Tell me about the clock," he said.

"W...w...what about it?"

"No Asako, we're not going back to you lying again and playing the innocent. Tell me the truth because we already know about it. We just need you to confirm it."

She glanced at the Lieutenant who nodded encouragingly. Asako dropped her eyes and stared at the floor in deep thought, her face contorted with worry. When she reached a decision she lifted her head.

"You've got to promise me that you won't let Yerzov kill my family."

"No one's going to kill anybody," said Johnson. "Especially not your family."

"No, I want your word. Promise me."

"I promise you, no one is going to kill you or anyone in your family."

The fear in Asako's eyes lessened a little but it didn't disappear completely. Johnson nodded to encourage her.

"Tell me about the clock Asako."

"There's a secret camera in it," she said. "It records everything that happens in here."

"How long's this been going on for?"

"Since the hotel re-opened. Three months ago."

"Okay, run me through it from the start."

"I work in Flawless...the strip club...all of us do."

"How many of you work here?"

"Nine of us but only three at a time."

"Okay, go on."

"Yerzov called a meeting three months ago...told us to meet him here at the hotel. When we did he took us downstairs to the disco in the basement...explained the whole lay out and how much we had to charge the customers."

"And he told you about the hidden cameras in the clocks?"

"No. One of the girls...Daisy...realized there was a hidden camera in the clocks. She got suspicious...lifted one of the clocks off and checked it...but she forgot that the camera recorded her lifting it off the wall. She told the rest of us that night but the next day she disappeared, hasn't been seen since. That's why we just pretend we don't know about the hidden cameras...we want to stay alive."

"When was it that Daisy disappeared?"

"About four weeks ago."

"Any idea what happened to her?"

"I think Yerzov had her killed."

"But you don't know for certain?"

"I haven't seen a body if that's what you mean but Daisy hasn't answered her cell phone or been in her apartment. Nobody's seen her."

Johnson exchanged a look with the Lieutenant. She understood as well he did. Without a body or eyewitness testimony Asako's concerns were just hearsay. Inadmissible in a court of law.

"How many times were you up here tonight?" he asked her.

"Three."

"Which room?"

"210...it's two doors down."

"Is there a clock on the wall in 210?"

"Yes. I always look at it to make sure the customers don't go over time."

"What time were you last here then tonight?"

"Up until nine o' clock then Andrei came down and told us we all had to get out."

"The Manager?"

"Yes."

Johnson stood for a second deep in thought. It had been nine o' clock when he and Sal had arrived at the club. After the bouncer radioed up to the Manager, Kosomo must have cleared the bedrooms then lifted off the clocks and disappeared with them. As Johnson stood there with his head bowed he noticed a tiny, red droplet of what looked like blood on the wooden floor. He hunkered down to get a closer look.

"What is it Joe?" the Lieutenant asked.

"Blood, I think."

The Lieutenant and Donato squatted down beside him.

"There's more," said Donato pointing.

Johnson followed his finger. The trail of blood disappeared underneath the bed. Johnson leant in closer.

"These blood splatters have nothing to do with the girl," he said then he looked under the bed.

When he did something caught his eye so he turned his head to see what it was. Nestled against the side wall underneath the bed was a small, black metallic ball.

"You see that?" he asked Donato.

"Yeah, stand back."

When they did Donato stood up and took two yellow markers out of his briefcase. The first he placed beside the droplets of blood, the second underneath the bed beside the black ball. When he was finished he stood up.

"Stand you over by the door Joe," he said. "I'm gonna take a few photos."

When they retreated Donato lifted his camera and started snapping. After taking about twenty different pictures of the corpse and the room he knelt down and photographed the metal ball underneath the bed. Photography over, he stopped shooting and opened his brief case and took out an unused plastic container and a clean syringe. This time when he squatted down he sucked up a sample of blood. When he straightened up he squeezed the syringe's contents into the container. Next he selected a pair of tweezers, slid underneath the bed and lifted the ball. When he was back on his feet he dropped it into a see-through plastic bag that he'd taken out of his briefcase. He dangled it in front of his face so that he and Johnson could examine it. The underside of it had an opening in it with screw treads.

"This has come off something," said Donato.

"And I think I know what," said Johnson.

"What?"

"It's the metal ball that screws onto the top of a flick stick."

Donato studied the ball again then nodded his head in agreement.

"You're right Joe," he said. "It is."

"That's why Richard had the small circular indents on his face. The killer beat him with the flick stick. That part must have flown off when he was hitting him with it but what our killer doesn't know is that he was filmed."

Johnson took out his cell and phoned Adams.

"Where are you?" he asked when he answered.

"Bottom floor at the main bar. Why?"

"Stay there. I'm coming down."

When he hung up Johnson stepped over to Asako and took her by the elbow.

"What are you doing?" she asked, a little panicked.

"Take it easy. That's you finished."

"I can go?"

"Yes," said Johnson then he steered her out through the doorway and into the hall. After escorting her along the corridor he stopped at the elevator and pressed the button. When it opened he stepped in beside her and they descended together. At the bottom Asako walked back to find her friends whilst Johnson went in search of Adams. He found him in the bottom bar nursing an Espresso and talking to the barman. Johnson immediately brought him up to speed about the hidden camera.

"What about the normal CCTV?" said Adams. "That might give us something."

Johnson nodded.

"Worth a try," he said.

Adams turned to the barman.

"Where's the Control Room?"

"Out at the entrance. Small room with a red door."

"Thanks," said Adams.

Together they walked out into the foyer in search of the red door, Adams taking his Espresso with him. At the Control Room Johnson expected it to be manned so he rapped the door. When there was no answer he tried the handle. The door was open.

"That's not very secure," said Adams.

Johnson stepped into the room with Adams behind him. The room was small and square with white walls and a bank of ten CCTV screens sitting on a broad table. In two rows of five they were boxed into a wooden frame. Johnson checked the DVD slot to make sure it was recording. The slot was empty.

"Nothing in it," he said to Adams.

Next, he checked the leads running to the DVD player. Severed. Shaking his head in frustration he held the leads up for Adams to see.

"Cut," he said.

"Which narrows the focus," said Adams. "Inside job."

"Not necessarily. If they leave this unmanned anyone could have walked in."

"Suppose," said Adams. "Now what we do?"

"Now we get Kosomo's address and go pay him a visit."

"Why?"

"He took the hidden cameras...one from the room where that girl was killed. With a bit of luck if we watch the recording we'll see who killed the call girl and took Richard."

"Surely, the killer would have worn a mask."

"No, think about it," said Johnson. "If you're in a hotel room with a prostitute what's the first thing you do?"

"Make sure I've money."

"No, besides that?"

"Hide my wallet."

149

"No."

"Make sure I'm wearing a Johnny, two even to be extra safe."

"Before that."

Exasperated, Adams threw up his hands.

"I don't know, what?"

"The door? Would it be locked or unlocked?"

"Locked."

"Precisely," said Johnson. "Which means for our killer to get into the room he'd have had to rap the door and be let in."

"Oh right," said Adams. "I'm with you now. There's a spy hole in the door. So, if someone knocks you look through –"

"- and if it's a guy wearing a mask do you think you'd let him in?"

"Definitely not," said Adams.

"Which also means it's someone that Richard knew. You'd hardly let a stranger into the room."

Adams nodded seeing it now in his mind's eye.

"Okay," he said. "The killer raps the door and he's no mask on. Richard hears it, gets up off the hooker that's strapped to the bed and looks through the spy hole. Outside is a friendly face...Hiya Richard, I need to talk to you. Richard...trusting soul that he is...opens the door and lets the killer walk right in."

Johnson intervened taking over the scenario.

"Once he's in, the killer sees the hooker strapped to the bed...realizes she's seen his face...so what does he do? He puts three slugs in her chest."

"All close proximity," said Adams. "Expert marksmanship."

"Which could point to a cop, a soldier...maybe someone in a gun club. But then there's the flick stick."

Adams looked confused.

"What flick stick?"

"We found a metal ball that fits on the top of one up the stairs...blood on the floor as well...Richard's."

"What's the point of a flick stick if you've got a gun?" Adams asked.

"Because to subdue Richard with a gun the killer would have had to shoot him. He didn't want to do that."

"Why not? Sure didn't he kill him anyway."

"That I don't know...but he kept him alive for some reason."

When they emerged from the Control Room loud voices made Johnson turn around. Hank Halbrook was at the basement doors wrestling with Asako.

"Let me go," she yelled but Hank ignored her and continued dragging her into the foyer.

Johnson wondered what was going on.

"You need a hand Hank?" he asked.

"It's you I'm bloody looking," he said.

"Why? What's up?"

"This one here...Blabbermouth. That's what's up."

"Why? What she do?"

Hank stopped in front of Johnson, his hand clamped around Asako's wrist. She continued struggling trying to break free but it was useless. Hank was a twenty year veteran with hands like glue.

"She's been telling everybody that the killer's been caught on a secret camera," said Hank.

For a moment Johnson was stunned.

"I didn't know it was meant to be a secret," said Asako.

"Did you mention who took the clocks off the walls?" Johnson asked.

"Yes," she said sheepishly. "But sure where's the harm in that?"

Johnson ignored her and pulled out his phone. He scrolled through his contacts to Garin as fast as he could. Garin answered on the fourth ring.

"What?" Garin asked.

"Less of the attitude Garin."

Garin didn't reply.

"You still there?" Johnson asked.

"Yes, what do you want?"

"Andrei Kosomo."

"What about him?"

"His address. What is it?"

"How the hell should I know?"

"Don't fuck me about Garin, this is important."

"Okay, okay, I'm only shitting you. He lives beside the Port Authority Bus Terminal at West 42nd Street...number 22."

Johnson hung up then started running towards the doors with Adams on his heels. Outside they jumped into their car and sped off. As they drove across the city Adams checked his Glock.

"Can't be too careful," he explained when Johnson glanced sideways at him.

"You got that right," Johnson replied.

Adams re-holstered his weapon underneath his armpit.

"So what way are we handling this Joe?" he asked.

"We'll park down the street then walk up and simply rap the door."

"Do you know anything about this guy?" Adams asked.

"Not much. He's Yerzov's cousin, does the rota for the call girls and he has the clocks."

"You think he's the killer?"

Johnson thought about this for a second.

"Let's hope not because if he is then he'll have destroyed the film already but if he's not say a prayer we get to him first before the killer does."

Chapter 24

Ten minutes later the two Detectives parked three doors down from Kosomo's house then got out and walked up to his front gate. After opening it they walked up the path and stopped with Adams raising one of his large hands to rap the door but before he could Johnson rested a hand on his forearm.

"Easy," he said. "We don't want him to realize we're the police."

Adams nodded in agreement then gave the door a gentle tap.

"Like that?" he asked.

"Perfect."

As they waited on the doorstep Johnson examined the hallway through the glass at the top of the door. The walls were a nondescript cream leading down to a black tiled floor. At the top of the hallway against the back wall was a polished phone table above which hung a gilded mirror. After thirty seconds an impatient Adams rapped the door again. When there was still no answer or a sign of anyone being in both detectives exchanged glances.

"I don't think he's in," said Adams.

Johnson shook his head angrily.

"I bet you he's lying upstairs with the lights out thinking he's a smart guy."

Annoyed, Johnson stepped across and looked through the front window. The living room blinds were drawn but there was a small gap between the slats of the venetian blinds. Johnson pressed his eye up to the window and peered in. The room was shrouded in darkness but after a couple of seconds Johnson's eyes re-adjusted to the lack of light and he was able to see into the gloom. Andrei Kosomo was standing in the middle of the living room, a masked man's black gloved hand across his mouth and a gun to his head. Johnson jerked his head back, his mind reeling as he tried to figure out what the hell was going on. Instinctively, he withdrew his Glock and moved back to the front door.

"What's wrong?" Adams asked pulling his own weapon.

Johnson held a finger to his lips to silence him.

"There's a masked man with a gun to Kosomo's head in the living room," he whispered.

"Did he see you?"

"No, I don't think so."

"What'll we do?"

Johnson's mind raced going over the alternatives. After five seconds of deliberation, he accepted they'd really only one option. He shook his head in disgust as he reached his decision.

"I don't like it but we've no choice," he said. "We have to back out of here...pretend to leave then call for assistance."

"You sure Joe? I could go round the back...you take the front."

"No, he's got a gun to Kosomo's head...we can't risk it."

Reluctantly, Adams nodded in agreement.

"Put your weapon away," Johnson said. I don't want him looking out the window and realizing we're onto him."

Adams didn't like this idea. He frowned in frustration but after Johnson holstered his own weapon Adams did the same. Turning simultaneously they began to walk down the path but as they did so the living room door burst open behind them. Kosomo, his eyes wide with fright, charged down the hallway.

"Help," he shouted, running towards the front door.

Alerted, both Detectives turned. A second later, the gunman lurched into view behind the fleeing Manager and raised his gun.

"No!" Johnson yelled but his desperate plea had no effect.

The masked gunman pulled the trigger. The sound of the gunshot was deafening. Kosomo's body flew forward against the door, his face pressed up tight against the glass. As he slid down Johnson stepped back and freed his gun waiting to get a clear shot. When it came Johnson tensed and prepared to fire down the hallway but already it was empty. The gunman had disappeared.

"Step back!" he shouted.

Immediately, Adams moved to the side. Stepping back, Johnson raised his foot and booted the door underneath the lock as hard as he could. The wood crumpled inwards but didn't break completely.

"Again Joe," Adams encouraged.

Lifting his foot again Johnson kicked the door three more times. On the third attempt the lock finally snapped. He pushed the door to get in forgetting about Kosomo's body slumped against the bottom. The door didn't budge.

"Shit," said Johnson. "Cover me."

Adams nodded. As Johnson shouldered the door to shift the body forward Adams stood double fisted aiming down the hallway. Johnson hit the door with his shoulder a second time.

"Keep going, he's moving," said Adams.

Johnson shouldered the door three more times in quick succession. Eventually there was a gap wide enough to get in.

"That's us," he said over his shoulder.

"Go you in first then cover me and I'll come in," said Adams.

Johnson nodded then turned sideways and edged himself into the house stepping over one of Kosomo's outstretched arms. When he was fully in he hunkered down at the bottom of the stairs, his gun now aimed down the hallway.

"That's you Tom, come on."

Not needing to be told twice, Adams tried to squeeze through the same gap but as his girth was a lot wider than Johnson's he got stuck in the breach.

"I need to go on a diet," he said through clenched teeth.

"Give it a shove," Johnson encouraged.

Bracing his back against the doorjamb Adams placed his hands on the broken door and pushed. He gained a couple of valuable inches and slid through.

"Check to see if he's still alive," said Johnson.

Adams knelt beside Kosomo and checked his pulse, his two fingers held against the manager's carotid artery underneath his jaw. Throughout, Johnson kept his Glock trained down the hallway.

"He's got a faint pulse," said Adams grabbing out his cell phone. As quick as he could he punched in 911. The dispatch operator answered immediately.

"This is Detective Thomas Adams from the Midtown North Precinct. I've got a 10-71 here. Send an ambulance and back up to 10th Avenue. We're chasing the perp," he said

"Follow me," Johnson said when Adams hung up.

Stepping down the hallway, every sense in his body was attuned to his surroundings. Knowing that corners and doorways were the most dangerous areas within a house his awareness tightened when he came to the living room door. Adams, who was right behind him, spoke into his ear.

"I don't think he went in there Joe."

Johnson spun around.

"Stay quiet," he said in a harsh whisper.

Immediately contrite Adams mumbled an apology.

"Sorry," he said.

"And will you move back," said Johnson. "I can feel your breath on my neck."

Adams nodded an apology then took a step backwards. Swinging back round Johnson edged round the open doorway from as far back as possible to give himself an early field of vision into the room. Once he was sure it was empty he stepped back out.

"Clear," he said quietly.

Adams nodded to show he understood. When Johnson turned to the next door Adams kept a wary eye on the doors opposite in case the murderer suddenly appeared. Swinging his gun from side to side he licked his lips in anticipation.

"I've got your back Joe," he said.

Johnson waved a hand over his shoulder then gripped the handle of the second door. Turning it as quietly as he could he pushed the door forward. Inside was the kitchen. He looked back over his shoulder at Adams.

"Stay you here," he said motioning with his finger and pointing downwards.

Adams gave him a quick thumbs up then went back to standing guard in the hallway. With every sense in his body on high alert Johnson stepped onto the black and white checkered linoleum into the kitchen. The room appeared empty but there was a door at the top right hand side that was closed. Johnson approached it with full concentration, his eyes wide as the adrenalin pumped through his veins. As he needed a free hand to open the door he switched from a double handed grip to a single. In his mind's eye he could see the gunman behind the door, his gun aimed and ready. Wary of this Johnson stayed at the side of the doorway then reached out and grabbed the handle as silently as he could. Sweat beaded on his forehead and his breathing quickened. After counting silently to three in his head he wrenched the door open. Simultaneously, he pulled his hand back to avoid a possible bullet. Nothing happened. He stood silently, his heart hammering inside his chest. Was the gunman waiting, his gun trained on the open doorway? Or was the room empty? Johnson stepped back traversing the door in a wide circle, both his hands gripping the gun again. As he slowly stepped round in a semi-circular motion it became apparent that the space behind the door was used as a small utility room. A white washing machine squatted on the floor with a shelf and a big cupboard above it. On top of the shelf sat a large box of washing up powder beside an upright iron whose cord hung down over the edge. An ironing board sat at the side of the cupboard on top of the shelf leaning up against the wall. Johnson continued edging round until he could see the right side of the tiny room. A wash basket with dirty laundry spilling out sat below a row of coat hangers upon which hung various coats and jackets. Fearing the gunman might be squatting down behind the basket Johnson stepped in quickly with his gun pointed downwards and kicked the basket over. There was nothing behind it but an open kitbag with a towel protruding. Johnson let out a breath he hadn't realized he was holding then turned and walked back out into the hallway. Adams looked askance at him when he emerged. In reply Johnson shook his head then pointed at the four doors ahead of them.

"Which one?" Adams asked, his voice barely audible.

"The closest one," Johnson said pointing at the white door on the right hand side.

Adams nodded then waited on Johnson to take point and approach the door first. Johnson did. Again he opened the door as gently as he could. This time it swung open into an empty bathroom. Johnson breathed a sigh of relief. When he came back out Adams's face was as white as the porcelain bath Johnson had just looked at.

"You okay Tom?" he asked.

"Not really."

Johnson gave him a reassuring pat on the shoulder.

"Just stay cool big man."

"I'm trying."

The next two doors also proved to be empty. Behind one was a bedroom, the other a hallway cupboard. Adams pointed his gun at the only door that was left.

"He must have gone that way," he said.

"Just keep your eyes peeled," said Johnson, "and make sure you don't shoot me in the back."

"Don't worry, I won't."

Johnson gripped the handle of the glass paneled door. Through the small window frames he could see a wooden dining table surrounded by six matching chairs. Johnson opened the door slowly and stepped in, the hairs on the back of his neck standing on end. He ducked down and glanced under the table. Nobody there. He straightened up.

"Clear," he said then he continued through the room, every sinew in his body stretched taut.

Even his skin felt tight like it was about to rip and his jaw ached because he'd been clenching his teeth. Forcing himself to open his mouth and breathe he sucked in five consecutive breaths. Gradually, he started to relax. Now he was approaching another glass paneled door at the opposite end of the dining room that led deeper into the house. Edging up to it slowly he was extremely wary as he knew he could be seen through the glass. Ever so slowly he reached out to grab the door handle but as soon as his fingers touched it a bullet smashed through the window, narrowly missing his head. Instinctively, he dived to his left as more bullets followed the first.

"Back! Back!" he screamed when he landed but already Adams had launched himself sideways. Together, they rolled in the glass then scuttled backwards to sit up against the wall. Panting wildly, Johnson turned and looked at Adams and was surprised to see a massive smile on his face.

"What has you so happy?" he asked.

"All that waiting Joe...murders me. At least now we know where he is."

"You're a weird man Tom."

"It's not the first time I've been told that and I'm hoping it won't be the last."

From below in the bottom room the killer shouted up to them, his voice again extremely deep.

"So you found me Detective...well done...I'm impressed...gold star buddy."

Johnson didn't reply. Instead, he dropped forward onto his elbows and crawled up to the back wall in an effort to take as wide a berth as possible around the doorway. As he edged forward glass stuck in his elbows making him wince so he slowed his pace and concentrated on avoiding getting cut.

"Where are you going?" Adams asked, his voice a worried whisper.

"Getting a better position," said Johnson without looking back.

When he got to the back of the room he flipped over then sat up against the wall. Feeling a piece of glass cutting into his thigh he pried it loose then flicked it away. As it skidded across the floor the killer's voice sailed up through the house again.

"You not feeling talkative Detective? Cat got your tongue?" he shouted.

Johnson dropped his head sidewards, his Glock extended in front of him. The man was leaning around the bottom doorway, his gun ready. Johnson saw him a millisecond before the man saw him. It was enough. Johnson opened up, firing a burst of three. The man ducked back out of view.

"You get him Joe?" Adams shouted, hope high in his voice.

"No, don't think so."

The man's voice boomed from below again.

"Close but no cigar Detective," he yelled.

"Is that right," said Adams, getting annoyed at the man's disdain. "Then take this."

"No, not from...," Johnson started to shout but already Adams had his head and arm stuck around the doorway. Luckily, the man hadn't popped back out. Adams emptied his magazine then pulled back around the corner of the wall. A huge grin split his face as he pulled a fresh clip from his ammo carrier.

"Jesus, it's great to be alive, isn't it Joe," he said.

"Not for long if you keep firing from there. Get up here to me."

"Why?"

"Just do it."

Adams crawled up to him on his hands and knees and sat beside him. Johnson glared at him.

"From now on you do what I say, understood?"

"Why, what I do wrong?"

"Everything. You were just lucky that time."

After saying this Johnson scrambled to his feet. Adams looked up at him.

"What are you doing?"

"Mixing it up. Different height. Closer proximity."

Johnson stepped into the middle of the room. When he looked back at Adams the big man gave him a thumbs up. Johnson nodded then without saying another word he stuck his head around the corner. This time the man was waiting and started shooting. Bullets cut through the door sending glass and splinters everywhere. Johnson pulled his head back to safety behind the wall.

"Jesus, that was close," he said sucking in a huge breath.

"You want me to go?" Tom asked.

"No, just relax, sit there."

The killer shouted up to them again.

"This game of hide and seek is brilliant Detective...I'm really loving it. Glad I decided to play...brings back memories of my childhood."

Neither of the Detectives replied. For a full thirty seconds no more shots came. Then, suddenly, there was a single gunshot followed by a large pane of glass breaking. It shattered on the ground.

"Sounded like a window breaking," said Adams.

"I'll find out," said Johnson. "You stay there."

Johnson poked his head round to get a quick look. Shots immediately peppered the glass paneled door mixing the sound of gunfire with broken glass and flying splinters. Johnson pulled back.

"He's shot the bottom window out," he explained to Tom.

"Want me to go?" Tom asked.

"No, wait."

As Johnson said this the sound of running feet and crunching glass could be heard. Johnson risked a quick glance round the doorway. The man was hurtling across the bottom room in full sprint, his arms and legs pumping wildly.

"He's making a run for it," Johnson shouted.

Together he and Adams stepped in front of the broken door and opened up. The man returned fire in mid sprint forcing them to take cover. When they did the man hurdled a flowery couch then launched himself out the shattered back window. Johnson popped his head out again.

"He's getting away," he shouted.

Together, they ran to the bullet riddled door and dragged it open. Johnson, the first one through, raced across the room and jumped up onto the window ledge. The man, who was now in the back garden, spun and fired at him. Instinctively, Johnson threw himself backwards into the room. Landing heavily on his right shoulder he rolled onto his back as Adams hurried over to him.

"You okay Joe?"

"Don't mind me, get him."

Unable to jump up onto the ledge Adams grabbed both sides of the window frame as leverage. Whilst the wood attached to the wall was strong enough to hold him the batten up the middle snapped in half when he tried to haul himself up. Falling backwards onto the floor, he blinked in confusion at the wood now clutched in his hand.

"I need to go on a diet," he said.

Beside him, Johnson struggled to his feet and jumped up onto the ledge. Outside in the garden the man was scrambling over the back fence. Johnson raised his gun and took aim.

"Police!" he yelled but the gunman ignored him and dropped to the other side.

Cursing under his breath Johnson jumped down into the back garden, his feet slipping momentarily on the shattered glass. Immediately he re-adjusted his stance to keep his balance then sprinted across the garden and gripped the top of the fence but when he hauled himself up to get a look, the gunman, who'd spun and waited for just such an opportunity, opened fire. Johnson instantly let go and dropped to the ground as the fence was shot to pieces above him. Scuttling backwards away from the line of fire he covered his head with his hands as bullets riddled the middle and lower parts of the planks. Behind him, Adams was back on his feet and looking through the window.

"You okay Joe?" he asked.

"I'm fine," said Johnson then because the shooting had stopped he inched back up to the bottom of the fence using his elbows and feet. Behind him, Adams clambered up onto the ledge and at last jumped into the back.

Johnson, his eye pressed up against the gap in the fence, stared through at the gunman. Now, he was running towards a white minivan with a New York Knicks bumper sticker on the back.

"Fuck!" he shouted then he pressed himself upwards and scrambled back to his feet.

"Back," he screamed. "He's getting away."

"Back?!! I'm only fuckin' through!" cried Adams.

"Go! Go!" Johnson shouted pushing him backwards.

Totally confused, Adams turned and once more tried to get up onto the ledge but again he couldn't lift his heavy bulk. Frustrated, Johnson pushed him out of the way then jumped up and spun around.

"Come on," he shouted. "Grab my hand!"

When Adams took it he hauled him up then together they jumped into the bottom living room. When Johnson landed he immediately burst into a sprint. Behind him, Adams yelled for him to wait but Johnson ignored him and kept running through the house. When he reached the front door Kosomo's prone figure was still slumped on the floor so he quickly stepped over it then slid through the gap in the door. As he did so he glanced back to check on Adams. Thankfully, he'd made some progress and was now lumbering up the hallway.

"Hurry up!" Johnson yelled.

Adams, his face red with exertion, shouted back.

"I'm doing the fuckin' best that I can!"

Chapter 25

Johnson raced down the pathway. When he reached his car the gunman's white minivan slewed round the corner at the side of the house and hurtled down the street.

"Fuck!" Johnson cursed sticking the car key into the door lock but with the avalanche of adrenaline surging through his body he almost snapped it in half.

At the last moment he felt the key twisting so he eased back and forced himself to turn it gently. When the car door opened he dived in and quickly started the engine. For a second he deliberated driving off without Adams but when he glanced up the pathway the overweight Detective was already through the door and shambling towards him. Five valuable seconds later, he climbed in beside Johnson, gasping wildly.

"Jesus, I need to go on a diet," he said.

Ignoring him Johnson pressed down hard on the accelerator. A cloud of fumes exploded from the exhaust and the car leapt forward. Simultaneously, ear-splitting revs ripped the air like a thunder clap. Both Detectives flew backwards against the headrests. When the car leveled out their heads unglued.

"Take it easy Joe, you near broke my neck," Adams yelled.

Johnson shot him a look.

"Take more than that Tom to break that fat neck," he said.

"I could sue you Joe."

"Sue away big man."

"I fuckin' will."

Johnson flashed a grin at him then gripped the steering wheel and gritted his teeth. Pent up anger and frustration coursed through his system.

"I've got you now you bastard," he said.

Beside him in the passenger seat Adams unhooked the radio from underneath the dashboard and pressed in the button.

"Dispatch, this is Detective Adams. We're in hot pursuit of a white minivan along 11th Avenue heading towards 53rd. Make of vehicle, a Renault, license plate, Charlie, November, November, 3, 6, 2, 9. I want an All Points Bulletin for this vehicle. Occupant is a 417, suspected of a 187 of a police officer. Over."

"Roger that Detective, vehicles will be dispatched."

"10-4."

Adams kept the mike in his hand and glanced at Johnson.

"Back up's on the way," he said.

Johnson nodded but didn't look at him. At the corner leading out of the street he braked late. To compensate he gave the wheel a mighty wrench. When he did the back of the car veered dangerously threatening to tipple over. Two wheels came off the ground and for a couple of seconds it seemed their pursuit was about to end but in desperation Johnson twisted the steering wheel again. This time it worked and the minivan tilted sideways with two wheels slamming back onto the tarmac. Immediately, Johnson accelerated.

"What are you doing Joe? Are you crazy?! Slow down!!" Adams yelled.

"And lose him? No fuckin' way Tom."

Johnson gunned the engine, his eyes narrowed into slits, his knuckles white. Next to him, Adams began to bless himself.

"Mary mother of God, help me," he said after making the sign of cross.

At the second corner out of the street onto the hill Johnson was just as wild. Again he screeched round on two wheels.

"Stop Joe!! Stop!" Adams screamed.

Johnson twisted the steering wheel as hard as he could and again the car dropped back onto four wheels. Bug-eyed, Adams gripped Johnson's arm.

"Please Joe, for the love of God slow down!!! You're goin' to kill us!!"

Johnson shook him off.

"Get off me!!" he said.

Adams sat back and clasped his hands in prayer.

"God, if you're up there I just want you to know that I'm sorry for every sin I've ever committed!"

Johnson paid him no heed and pumped the accelerator. In response, the car shot forward like a racehorse on steroids. A hundred yards ahead the minivan hammered down the hill. Johnson stamped hard on the pedal forcing the needle on the speedometer to spin from sixty up to a hundred. Adams watched its arc with fearful eyes.

"I knew I should have made a will," he said.

Johnson's lips peeled back in a savage snarl.

"There's an intersection at the bottom," he yelled. "If I get there at the same time I'm gonna ram straight into him."

Adams wasn't sure if he'd heard right.

"What?" he asked.

"Brace yourself," Johnson shouted.

"No way Joe. You can't!!"

"Who can't?! Fuckin' watch me!"

Johnson stomped down hard on the accelerator, his face a grim, determined mask. The gap between them started to close.

"I've got you now," Johnson said.

Adams pointed through the window.

"There's a car at the intersection."

Johnson sat up straighter in his seat.

"I don't think he's going to stop!" he shouted.

And he was right. Instead of slowing the gunman raced into the middle of the intersection then at the last possible moment he tried to brake.

"He's going to crash!" Adams yelled.

But he was wrong. Somehow, by sheer good luck or divine inspiration, the gunman managed to miss the green car by a hair's breadth. To do so however he had to change direction. Now, he hurtled towards a brick wall on the opposite side. Johnson was jubilant.

"He's gonna crash," he shouted.

But he too was wrong. At the last possible second the gunman again managed to get control of the minivan. It slewed wildly then straightened away from the wall and gained purchase.

"No way!!" Johnson yelled. "How did he do that?"

"Look out!!" Adams shouted.

Ahead of them, an old woman had got out of her car. Unaware that two ton of metal was hurtling towards her she stood in the middle of the road shaking her fist at the departing minivan.

"Get out of the way," Johnson screamed.

The woman turned. Transfixed, a deer in the headlights, her mouth opened in a silent, horrified circle.

"Turn!! Turn!!!" Adams roared.

In a last act of desperation, Johnson wrenched the steering wheel sideways but it was too little too late. He misjudged and the car started to tipple over in mid spin.

"No!!!" Adams screamed.

Johnson realized he'd lost control and braced for impact but as the car spun in a vicious circle the back end clipped the side of the green car. Miraculously the Fusion righted itself, bounced backwards then stopped dead beside the old woman. It had missed her by a matter of inches. Smoke billowed from underneath the Fusion shrouding the intersection in a grey cloud.

"Is she alive?" Adams asked.

Johnson, numb and disbelieving, turned his head and looked out the window. The old woman was still standing.

"Yes," he said, his voice flooding with relief.

From underneath the car smoke continued to waft upwards. When it started to clear Johnson rolled the window down to shout out an apology to the old woman.

"Are you okay? I'm really sorry," he yelled.

The old woman stared back at him in a state of shock. Frozen in place she was like an ice statue with bulging eyes. After a couple of seconds she began to thaw and once more was able to move. Able to function again her focus narrowed to the two Detectives in the Fusion.

Johnson watched as a rigid fury swept across her wrinkled features and she advanced towards them.

"Oh shit!" he said pressing the button to roll the window up.

When it reached the top he gunned the engine.

"What are you doing Joe? Let me out!" Adams yelled at him.

"I can't. You're my lucky charm," he shouted then he plunged the accelerator as a frantic Adams tried desperately to open the door.

"Too late for that buddy!" shouted Johnson. "The central locking is on."

As the wheels spun the smell of burning rubber filled the air as the old woman reached the car. Amidst the clouds of smoke that now enveloped the Fusion she pounded on the window.

"Come out here you cowards!" she shrieked then because she was wrapped in smoke she began to cough as tire fumes clogged her mouth and nostrils.

"Sorry!" Johnson again shouted out to her then again he pressed hard on the accelerator. This time the Fusion shot forwards leaving the old woman in their wake.

"Let me out Joe! Let me out!" Adams continued shouting.

"No can do buddy, sorry," said Johnson as he sped down the road.

As he did so he glanced in the rear view mirror to make sure the old woman was all right. When he did he was surprised to find her running after them but after a couple of seconds she stopped in the middle of the road and raised both fists.

"Motherfuckers!" she shouted then simultaneously she flicked up her two middle fingers before pumping them up and down with an energy Johnson found it hard to believe an old woman could possess.

"Here, you see that Tom?" he shouted across to Adams. "That old woman is giving us the double bird!"

In response, Adams raised his own middle finger and stuck it up against the side of Johnson's face.

"Not us. You! You fuckin' prick!" he screamed.

Johnson shook his head and laughed out loud.

"Well, at least there's nothing wrong with her."

"Yeah and what about me? I'm trapped in a fuckin' car with a lunatic."

"I'm only a lunatic because I'm chasing a murderer...a cop killer."

Ahead of them, the white minivan was still in sight. Now, it was speeding towards another intersection. When it flew round it the two Detectives watched it disappear up a slip road.

"We'll catch him soon," said Johnson. "He's on the highway."

Five seconds later they reached the intersection.

"There's a car!" Adams shouted, afraid of a repeat performance.

This time however Johnson slowed down and allowed a young man in a blue Taurus to drive around ahead of them.

"Satisfied?" he asked. "I'm being sensible."

"The only time I'll be satisfied is when I'm out of this fuckin' car."

Johnson accelerated then turned the corner to go onto the highway but when he did he was surprised to find the white minivan sitting parked. Instinctively, Johnson braked but the minivan, which had been sitting idling, shot backwards.

"Look out!" Adams shouted but it was too late.

The minivan ploughed straight into them buckling the hood of their vehicle as it pushed them backwards. Amidst the screeches of folding metal and hissing steam the front and side windows crumpled then imploded sending glass flying everywhere. As the car slid backwards, the airbags automatically inflated with a loud hiss followed by a thunderous smash when the Fusion slammed into the wall at the side of the intersection. On impact the two Detectives jerked spasmodically but the airbags did their job saving them from serious injury. Instantly, the driver of the minivan accelerated forward to break free from the mangled Fusion. As he did so the metal squealed in protest but the vehicles managed to separate. On Johnson's side the steering wheel had been shunted forward. Now, it was pressed up against his chest trapping him underneath against the seat.

On the opposite side Adams had been lucky. He'd only the airbag to contend with which already had begun to deflate. Johnson sat for a couple of seconds, stunned, trying to get his bearings. When he did and his brain was once more thinking clearly he looked through the shattered front windscreen only to jerk back in surprise. The gunman was in the middle of the road with his legs splayed and a gun in his hand. When Johnson made eye contact the man opened fire. Trapped behind the steering wheel Johnson tried to slide down but it was hopeless. He was a sitting duck.

"Get down!" he screamed trying to warn Adams.

Alerted, Adams slid beneath the dashboard as bullets smashed into the front of the Fusion. Across from him Johnson worked his hand down to his Glock. After a few frantic seconds he was able to free it and bring it up. On the opposite side Adams was peering over the dashboard, his own gun in his hand. Together, the two Detectives returned fire. When they did the gunman turned and sprinted back to the minivan. Johnson kept firing until his magazine emptied. As he reloaded the spent airbag rested on top of him like a giant, used condom.

"He's back in the minivan," Johnson shouted.

Hearing this, Adams rose from below the dashboard, a new magazine loaded and ready. Twenty feet ahead of them the minivan started to drive off. In a last desperate act Johnson started shooting through the front windshield of the Fusion. Adams joined in. Together, the both of them discharged their weapons until their magazines were once again empty but it had no effect for the minivan kept driving and soon disappeared over a crest in the road.

"Ring Dispatch!" Johnson shouted.

Adams took out his phone and made the call. After he explained the whereabouts of the minivan and the direction it was going he hung up.

"Don't worry Joe, they'll get him."

"They better."

"He was a determined son-of-a-bitch, wasn't he? Really wanted to kill us," said Adams.

"But he didn't which is his mistake," said Johnson. "Because I'll not rest until I get him."

"You look stuck Joe," said Adams. "Can you get out from under that?"

"No, I can't move. You?"

"I think I'm all right. I'll try and open the door."

Adams grabbed the door handle and pulled. Only then did he remember that the door was locked.

"Where's the switch for the central locking Joe?"

"It's down at my left. I think I can get to it," said Johnson then he straightened his arm to reach the switch. When he pressed it in the passenger door clicked open. Freed, Adams climbed out and walked round to Johnson's side of the car. He spoke to him through the broken window.

"Are you okay Joe?"

"I'm fine. Just get on the phone to the Fire Department so I can get out of here."

Adams nodded, took out his cell and called the emergency services. After he hung up he came back to the window.

"They're on the way," he said.

"Good."

"But while I have you here Joe...as a captive audience so to speak...I'd just like to tell you that you nearly fuckin' killed us."

Despite the stern expression on Adams' face all Johnson could do was laugh.

"What's so fuckin' funny Joe? I'm goddamned serious."

Johnson laughed even harder and because the steering wheel was on top of his chest it hurt like hell but he couldn't help himself. Not finding it funny, Adams turned away in disgust. Stifling his laughter, Johnson called after him.

"Tom, come back."

"Fuck off."

"I want to phone the Precinct and I can't reach my cell."

Reluctantly, Adams did an about turn and trudged back. He handed Johnson his phone.

"I should just shoot you and blame it on that other guy," he said.

"Ballistics Tom."

"Yeah, I know. That's why I'm not."

Johnson phoned the Precinct and asked to be put through to Lieutenant Walker. She came on the line after a minute.

"Yes Joe. What's up?" she asked.

Johnson explained their predicament. Once he'd finished his story the Lieutenant told him she was on her way. For a fleeting moment Johnson considered phoning his wife but he dismissed the notion and handed the phone back to Adams. As he did so the old woman that he'd almost knocked down arrived at the side of the car. When she peered through the Fusion's broken window and realized it was Johnson that was trapped underneath the steering wheel her face lit up like a Christmas tree. Elated, she tapped a bony finger against the side of Johnson's head.

"God did this," she said.

"Ma'am, stop that. I'm a Police Officer."

She cackled then, a sound so hideous that Johnson recoiled sidewards.

"My son is a cop," she said. "And he's nothing like you. Courtesy, professionalism and respect. Remember those words?"

Johnson nodded. She was quoting the words written on the back doors of the NYPD squad cars.

"I was chasing a felon Ma'am...in hot pursuit."

"You nearly killed me at that intersection," said the old woman.

"I'm sorry Ma'am, I truly am."

She held an arm up into the air, pointing a bony, wrinkled finger at the New York sky.

"God is watching," she said. "You remember that. Everything you do is being monitored. Everything."

Then with that she turned and walked away. When she passed Adams she slapped him hard across the face in mid stride but didn't stop. Again, Johnson burst out laughing. Adams, half his face inflamed, came over rubbing his cheek.

"I should run her in for assault," he said.

Hearing this, Johnson laughed even harder.

Chapter 26

Three minutes later Johnson heard the sirens. The Fire Department were the first to arrive. When two fire fighters approached the car and looked in Johnson recognized one of the faces. It was his old school friend Gerard 'Gerdy' Byrne. They'd attended St. Teresa's Elementary School together on West 52nd Street. Gerdy was as equally surprised.

"Joe? Is that you?"

"It is Gerdy."

"Don't worry buddy, we'll have you out in no time."

True to his word Gerdy and his co-workers had Johnson free inside fifteen minutes. Gerdy, a stocky man with steel grey hair and an unflinching stare had previously been a bus driver before entering the Fire Department. Now, he looked Johnson up and down.

"You don't look too bad for being forty one Joe."

"I could say the same for you Gerdy. You look as fit as a fiddle."

"Training to do a triathlon in a couple of months. How are you feeling? Is your chest all right?"

Johnson rubbed it.

"Yeah, it's fine," he said.

"You sure? You might have cracked something."

"No, my chest's grand but my side feels a bit stiff."

Johnson winced as he touched it.

"You still remember the prayer Joe?" Gerdy asked.

It took Johnson a second to realize what Gerdy was referring to but then he remembered. He broke into a smile.

"The prayer of the Sacred Heart of Jesus?" he asked.

"From the depth of my nothingness...," Gerdy began.

Johnson joined in.

"...I prostrate myself before thee, O most sacred, divine and adorable heart of Jesus, to pay thee all the homage of love, praise and adoration in my power. Amen."

The two of them laughed when they finished.

"Catholic education, learn your prayers and everything will be okay," said Gerdy.

"Well, that's what I tell my kids," said Johnson.

"Many have you?"

"Three girls. You?"

"Four sons," said Gerdy. "The eldest is eighteen. He's in Afghanistan...21st Infantry Regiment."

"You must be proud of him."

"I am."

At that moment two paramedics, a male and a female, marched towards Johnson. The female, a robust looking redhead with muscles and braided hair, carried a medical bag.

"Can we check you out?" she asked.

"No. I'm okay," Johnson replied.

"It'll only take a few minutes."

Johnson tried to make light of things.

"It's okay," he said. "I'm a tough old bird."

Suddenly a voice spoke from behind him.

"Tough or not, you're getting checked out Joe."

Johnson swung round. It was the Lieutenant.

"Look, I'm fine."

"Let the professionals be the judge of that."

Realizing he was fighting a losing battle Johnson held his hands up in acquiescence.

"Okay," he said.

"Over this way," said the redhead.

When Johnson followed her across to the ambulance she stopped at the back doors and opened her medical bag.

"So what happened?" she asked.

"A minivan reversed into me...sorry, into us."

"That's not very nice."

"No, neither was the person driving it."

"Then make sure to catch him."

"Don't worry, we will."

"Do you wanna take a seat?" the paramedic asked.

Johnson shook his head.

"No, I'm fine."

"Do you have any pre-existing medical conditions?"

"I've a dodgy knee but other than that...no," said Johnson but when he spoke there was a hitch in his breathing.

The paramedic noticed him wincing.

"Are you having difficulty inhaling?" she asked.

Johnson wanted to lie but he decided against it.

"Yes," he said.

"Okay, I'm just going to check your ribs, see if any of them are fractured."

"Look, I'm fine."

"Listen Detective...the muscles used for breathing pull on the ribs so if you're feeling pain it's most likely because you've fractured a rib."

"You don't understand...I've a killer to catch."

"I do understand but if you're running about with a fractured rib there's a good chance you'll puncture a lung...cause yourself serious damage."

"Caught between the devil and the deep blue sea."

"This isn't a joke Detective."

"Do you see me laughing?"

"You're being frivolous."

"It's my care-free nature."

"I'm not here to verbally spar with you."

"Just when I was beginning to like you too."

"The feeling's mutual."

"I'm honored," said Johnson.

"Now may I examine you?"

"Of course, feel free."

"Thank you."

The paramedic prodded Johnson's ribs gently with her fingers. As she did so she kept a close eye on his face watching for a reaction. In return, Johnson tried to look impassive, pain free but when she switched to his left side he couldn't help but react. Involuntarily he pulled away. The paramedic stepped back, her assessment finished.

"You'll have to go to the hospital," she said.

"Sorry, no can do."

"You don't strike me as a stupid man."

Johnson laughed then instantly regretted it as a flash of searing pain raced up his side.

"Know what," he said. "I really like you."

"Don't try and butter me up...you're going to the hospital."

"Look, I'll do a deal with you. As soon as I catch the killer the first thing I'll do is go to the hospital."

"No."

"Then I'm sorry."

The paramedic folded her arms.

"Have you ever heard of a thing called Flail Chest?" she asked.

"No, can't say I have."

"It's a serious problem that happens when three or more ribs are broken in more than one place. That's what I think you have Detective."

"Look, I appreciate the concern...truly...I do...but I've got a job to do."

"You need to go to the hospital to get an X-ray."

"Later," Johnson said and he stepped around her.

When he did the Lieutenant was standing waiting with a stern look in her eye.

"Get into the ambulance Joe," she said.

"Look, I'm fine, there's nothing wrong with me."

"It's an order Joe not a request."

Adams came over then, his large bulk appearing over the Lieutenant's shoulders.

"Kosomo's alive," he said.

"What hospital?" Johnson asked.

"St. Luke's."

Johnson turned and looked at the Paramedic.

"Can you take me to St. Luke's?"

"Sure."

"Okay then, let's go."

"What about me?" Adams asked.

"Get you in the back with me. You can hold my hand."

St. Luke's was on Tenth Avenue, number 1000. When they got to it Johnson sent Adams in search of Kosomo. Once he was gone the Paramedic guided him through the white corridors to the Accident and Emergency Department. After giving his details to a receptionist behind a glass partition Johnson took a seat and waited. The Paramedic came over and shook his hand.

"Thanks," Johnson said and meant it. She'd proved genuine which in a cynical city like New York was rare.

"I hope you catch him," she said.

Johnson's good mood evaporated.

"Don't worry, I will," he said.

Nodding curtly she turned and left. As she disappeared up the corridor Johnson took his cell phone out and rang Adams.

"Well?" he asked.

"He's stabilized...heavily sedated."

"When do they think he'll come round?"

"I asked a nurse...a friend of my sister's. She's gonna ring me when Kosomo wakes up."

"Okay, get down here. We're going."

"Joe, you can't. It's too dangerous. You need to get seen."

"No. What I need to do is catch Sal's killer."

Five minutes later Adams came up the corridor with his phone to his ear. When he reached Johnson he passed it across.

"Who is it?" Johnson asked.

"The Lieutenant."

Johnson shook his head in disgust then put the cell to his ear.

"Hello Lieutenant."

For the next two minutes the Lieutenant laid down the law over the phone. If Johnson so much as moved Adams was to place him under arrest and cuff him until he was seen by a Doctor. When Johnson hung up Adams took the phone back off him.

"Sorry Joe but it's for your own good," he said.

It took an hour for Johnson to get examined. After a multitude of x-rays they gave him the all clear. No broken ribs but bad bruising. A female doctor wrapped bandages round his body then prescribed him some painkillers. Back outside they ordered a taxi and went back to the Precinct.

When they walked through the doors into the foyer Gums told them the Lieutenant wanted to see them so they got the elevator up to the Bullpen and walked into her office.

"Well?" she asked Johnson when they entered.

"All good...slight bruising...nothing serious."

"Is he telling the truth Tom?"

"Yes Lieutenant. I was there when the Doctor gave him the results of the X-rays."

"Okay, then I've news for you both. They've found the minivan."

Instantly, Johnson was alert, a hound on the scent.

"The driver?" he asked.

"No. He got away but they're looking for him."

"Where's the minivan?"

"Bottom of West 70th Street. The shooter escaped into Central Park."

Johnson gritted his teeth, annoyed at hearing this.

"Did they run the license plate?" he asked.

"False."

"Anybody searched it yet?"

"No. I thought I'd leave that to you two."

"We've no car," said Johnson.

Smiling, the Lieutenant took a set of keys out of her pocket and dangled them in front of Johnson's face.

"I've signed you out a new ride," she said.

Johnson accepted the keys when she passed them across.

"What is it?" he asked.

"A black Ford Escape SUV. Brand new."

"Thanks Lieutenant," he said.

The drive over to West 70th Street took twenty minutes. When they reached the cordon and drove under, the scene was crawling with uniforms and parked squad cars. When they got out Hank Halbrook strode over to meet them.

"Nobody's touched it Joe," he said.

Johnson looked across at the white minivan. It was parked haphazardly, the rear end jutting out into the middle of the road with the driver's door wide open. Walking towards it they both started to slow as a putrid stench reached their nostrils.

"You smell that?" Johnson asked.

Adams nodded.

"Yeah," he said.

From experience they both knew what was causing the smell. Johnson circled around the minivan to see if they'd scored any hits during the gun battle. The back doors were crumpled from the impact and pockmarked with bullet holes, one dead centre of the basketball on the Knick's bumper sticker. Johnson pulled his latex gloves out of his inside pocket and tugged them on. Adams did the same then walked round to the passenger side and opened the door. Johnson stepped over to the driver's side. The smell emanating from inside the van was overpowering now. Johnson pulled himself into the driver's side using the steering wheel then turned round and knelt on the seat to look into the back. Stuck between the seats was the body of the missing girl, her blonde hair clotted with caked blood. On the opposite side Tom was also staring down.

"We better get this bastard," he said. "I want him so bad I can taste it."

"Don't worry, we'll get him. He's not getting away," said Johnson.

As he turned to get out he felt something wet seeping through his pants. He clambered out and looked at his knees. There was blood on them. Wet blood. Fresh blood. The killer's blood. A surge of euphoria flooded through Johnson's system. With a bit of luck DNA analysis would identify the killer.

"Looks like we hit him Tom," he said pointing at the blood pooled in the crease of the seat.

"Good," said Adams. "I hope he's bleeding to death at this very minute."

Seeing the key still in the ignition Johnson took his phone out and snapped a quick photograph making sure to capture the New York Knicks key ring that was attached. Next, he searched the door pocket. It contained a map of New York and a half empty bottle of water along with a discarded Snickers wrapper. Across from him Adams opened the glove compartment then stuck one of his huge hands inside and rifled around.

"Bulls eye Joe," he said pulling his hand out.

When Johnson looked across at him a vehicle registration booklet was clamped in his fist. After opening it and looking at the address Adams phoned the Precinct to see if the minivan had been reported stolen. It hadn't.

"Our killer can't be that stupid to use his own minivan," Johnson said.

"It's either that or the person that owns the van doesn't know it's been stolen."

"Only one way to find out," said Johnson. "Who's it registered to?"

"Hell's Kitchen Warriors Basketball Club," Adams said.

"Address?"

"12 West 51st Street."

"Let's go," said Johnson.

Chapter 27

Within minutes they were on 8th Avenue. The sun was large in the sky and a slight breeze was meandering through the city. Up high it slipped around the skyscrapers then dropped to street level to ruffle the hair of pedestrians. Johnson thought of Sal and a wave of sadness washed over him. His heart lurched so he clamped his jaw shut and fought back the tears. It worked and the dam held. Gripping the steering wheel he vowed to himself that he'd catch his friend's killer.

At the Chipotle Mexican Grill Johnson took a right onto West 51st. The Hell's Kitchen Basketball Club was ten feet away on the right. Driving through the gates he parked the SUV and again his thoughts flashed to Sal. He'd have loved this new ride he knew and so would he but without him it was a pyrrhic victory. Like him Sal had hated the Fusion. It had been one of the few things they'd actually agreed upon. Shaking his head he got out of the vehicle and walked into the club. It was a modern one storey building with lots of glass and white painted walls. Inside, they'd two options. Left or right. They took the right and ended up in a large lounge. Already, a few early birds were propping up the bar, taking the edge off in the only way they knew how. Johnson called the barman over.

"Yes, what would you like?" he asked.

Johnson flashed his shield.

"I'm here about the club minivan. Who's responsible for it?" he asked.

"Leo," said the bartender. "He's the chairman."

"Is he around?" Johnson asked.

"He's in the office. Do you want me to get him for you?"

"Yes."

Two minutes later a thin man in his late forties with a bald head and sad eyes walked up to them. Dressed in jeans and a t-shirt his eyes were red-rimmed from either crying or a hangover.

"You looking me?" he asked Johnson.

"Are you Leo?"

"Yes."

"We're here about the club minivan. Do you have any idea of where it is at the minute?"

"James has it."

"James who?"

"James Davis. He coaches the under sixteen team."

"Do you have an address for this James?" Johnson asked.

"Yes, of course."

Five minutes later they were back in the SUV armed with the address. Another ten after that they reached 112 11th Avenue. When they got out and walked up the pathway Johnson was the one that rapped the door. When no one answered he lifted the letterbox and peered in. There was a light shining underneath the door at the far end of the hallway. Music was also playing so Johnson cocked his ear and tried to make it out: "Spanish Train" by Chris de Burgh. If he remembered rightly it was about God and the Devil playing poker for the souls of the dead.

"There's somebody definitely in," he said. "I can hear music."

"That's why he's not answering then," said Adams. "He can't hear us."

Johnson rapped the door again, harder this time but nothing changed. Frustrated, he lifted the letterbox and shouted through.

"Open the door! Police!"

Still no one answered. Annoyed, he tried the handle on the front door. It rattled in his hand but wouldn't open.

"Fuck this," he said. "I'm going round the back. You stay here Tom and keep rapping the door."

When he stepped down from the porch there was a wooden gate at the side of the house so he stuck his hand over the top hoping to find the latch. When he did it was cold to the touch and a little slippery but he managed to find the release and unlock it. When he pushed the gate open it emitted a loud squeaking noise like something out of a horror movie. Stepping through Johnson walked down the side of the house, his feet splashing through the puddles of water that had pooled after the rain. On his way he passed a garden shed and a green oil tank raised up from the ground on breeze blocks. There was also an old mattress that stank so badly Johnson had to cover his nose. When he turned into the back the kitchen window was directly facing him. A red roller blind covered it so he stuck his face up tight against the window searching for a gap that he could peer through. There was none. Whoever had fitted the blind had done a perfect job. Impatient, Johnson moved up to the patio doors. This time there were venetian blinds on the inside, long slats that hung down covering the door. On this occasion he was luckier. Two of the slats had twisted together leaving a small opening halfway down. Johnson stuck his eye up to the gap and peered through. Inside, a man and woman were sitting drinking at a table, both of them clearly inebriated. To get their attention Johnson rapped the window with his knuckles. It worked and their heads swivelled around searching for the source of the noise. Knowing they hadn't seen him yet Johnson rapped the glass again. This time they spotted him, both their bodies stiffening at the sight.

"Police," Johnson yelled. "Open up."

Nonplussed and still extremely wary the man stood up.

"Show me some ID," he shouted out, lifting a bottle up by the neck.

Stepping back Johnson withdrew his wallet then pressed it up against the glass. The man scrutinized Johnson's ID glancing from the photograph then up to Johnson's face and back again.

"It's okay," he said over his shoulder to the woman.

"Are you sure?" she asked. "They can fake those things on the internet."

The man stopped, his faith in the legitimacy of the Identity card and Shield suddenly shaken.

"How do I know it's real?" he shouted out to Johnson.

Johnson withdrew his Glock and held it up to the window beside the ID.

"Okay," the man said then he turned the key in the door and Johnson entered.

Ignoring the man Johnson opened the kitchen door then strode down the hallway and let Adams in. When they returned to the kitchen the woman was sitting on the man's knee with a glass of vodka in her hand.

"What's your name?" Johnson asked the man.

"James Davis, why?"

"Do you drive a minivan?"

"Yes, it's sitting out front."

"Are you sure about that?"

"Watch honey," the man said then when the woman got up from his lap he walked outside and checked the driveway. When he came back in there was a perplexed look on his face.

"It was there last night," he said. "Someone must have stolen it."

Johnson studied the man's face as he spoke watching for a lie but there was none. The man was telling the truth. Either that or he was an accomplished actor.

"When was the last time you used the minivan?" Johnson asked.

"Thursday night...I manage a kid's basketball team...my little brother plays. I took them to a game up in Harlem."

"What happened after the game?"

"I dropped all the kids home then I came back here, parked the van in the driveway. The next day I got a lift to work."

"What do you work at?" Johnson asked.

"I'm an English Teacher."

"What time did you park in the driveway on Thursday night?"

"Roughly around nine."

"And your name please?" Johnson asked the woman.

"Mary Roberts."

"When did you arrive?"

"I got here last night at about quarter past eleven. I'm a residential care worker in a children's home. My shift finished there at eleven then I got dropped here afterwards."

"Was the minivan in the driveway when you arrived?"

"Yes, I think so."

"You think so?"

"No, I mean yes. It was definitely here."

"Is your key to the minivan here?" Johnson asked.

James nodded then slipped Mary off his knee before crossing to a wall cupboard. When he opened it he lifted out a black bowl and sifted through it, his face growing darker by the second.

"My key's not here," he said.

"Can you describe the key?" Johnson asked taking out his phone.

"It's just an ordinary key with a New York Knicks key ring."

Johnson held his phone up showing James the photograph he'd taken of the key ring back at the minivan.

"Is that the key?" he asked.

"Yes, that looks like it," said James.

"Okay, so you park in the driveway on Thursday, go into the house and put your keys in that bowl, is that correct?"

"Yes," said James.

"Was anyone else in here on Thursday night or Friday?"

"No, definitely not."

"Okay, did the two of you go out on Thursday or Friday night?"

"Yes, we went out for a drink last night," said Mary.

"So this place was empty?"

"Yes," said James.

"Then that's when somebody broke in and took the keys."

"No, we'd have known if someone had broken in," said James. "There'd have been a broken window or something."

"Maybe somebody had a key to this house."

"No one has a key to this house except me," said James.

"Well, someone got your key without breaking a window. We just got to figure out who," said Johnson then he took out his phone and rang the Precinct.

Gums, who was on the desk, answered immediately.

"Gums, do me a favor and send over two uniforms to canvass a street for me. There was a possible burglary last night so I want the neighbors questioned to see if they seen anything."

After giving Gums the address Johnson hung up, thanked James and Mary for their co-operation and then left the house.

"Now what do we do?" Adams asked.

"I want to go back to Kosomo's house. See if the clocks are there."

"But sure the killer would have got them."

"He never had them when he was getting away."

"Maybe he took the memory cards out of them."

"Possible...which means the clocks will be there. If they are and the memory cards aren't in them then we know the killer has them."

Chapter 28

When they got to Kosomo's house it was cordoned off. As Johnson walked up the pathway he spotted Kelly talking to Halbrook in the garden. Kelly turned and stared at him as he passed but he didn't say anything. Either did Johnson. Inside, it took twenty minutes to search the house from top to bottom. There was no sign of the clocks.

"Phone your nurse friend," Johnson said to Adams.

"Her name's Dorothy. And she's not my friend. She's my sister's friend."

"Okay, then phone Dorothy your sister's friend."

"She said she'd phone me."

"Doesn't matter. Phone her. We need to talk to Kosomo. Find out where the clocks are."

"Know what Joe, sometimes you're a real ball breaker."

"And I love you too. Now phone her."

Adams took out his phone and rang Dorothy. After a short conversation he hung up.

"Well?" Johnson asked.

"Kosomo's awake but he's not supposed to have any visitors. He's only out of surgery half an hour."

"Tough, he's getting visitors."

"He'll not speak to us Joe."

Johnson took out his cell, switched it to loudspeaker so that Adams could hear then phoned Garin.

"Where are you?" he asked when the bouncer answered.

"Flawless. Why?"

"I'm picking you up in ten minutes."

"What for?"

"I'll explain when I get there."

"But I'm working."

"I don't care. You're coming with us."

Before Garin could object Johnson hung up.

"Who was that?" Adams asked.

"Someone that Kosomo will speak to."

When Garin got into the SUV ten minutes later he wasn't happy.

"Lose the face," said Johnson.

"I'm not your whipping boy," said Garin, anger stamped all over his face.

"I didn't say you were."

"You can't just snap your fingers and expect me to come running. I have a job."

"Stop your complaining. This'll only take half an hour."

"What is it?"

"We need you to talk to Kosomo."

"But sure he's in hospital...half dead. At least that's what I heard."

"He's awake. We need you to speak to him. Ask him what he did with the clocks."

"What clocks?"

"There were clocks in the hotel with hidden cameras in them. Kosomo took them before he was shot but the killer never got them which means Kosomo gave them to somebody or stashed them somewhere."

Half an hour later they were back at St. Luke's Hospital. Dorothy, the ward nurse, met them outside Kosomo's room. A stout woman with a blonde bob and an apprehensive face it was obvious she wasn't happy with their presence.

"He's not supposed to have visitors," she said. "I told you that Tom."

"Look I'm sorry Dorothy but this is important."

"I don't care. You have to wait."

Johnson intervened. Waiting was not an option.

"Dorothy," he said. "This'll only take a minute."

She swung round to him, her face an anxious mask.

"But I could lose my job," she said.

"I understand that...but that man in there has information that could help us find a killer...a cop killer...a cop that was our friend...my partner...murdered tonight in cold blood along with another man."

Dorothy's eyes filled with compassion. Johnson knew then she was going to relent.

"One minute," she said, "That's all?"

"Maybe even less."

"Okay," she said. "But make sure you're quick."

Johnson turned to Garin.

"Right, you know what to do?"

"Find out where the clocks are and if Kosomo told the killer where they are."

"Exactly. Go."

Garin disappeared into the room. Outside, Dorothy paced up and down checking her watch.

"Relax," Johnson said. "He'll be out shortly."

When Garin still hadn't returned after five minutes Dorothy began to get increasingly agitated.

"He's taking too long," she said.

"Relax Dorothy. They're friends," Adams said. "Kosomo's probably glad to see a friendly face."

Dorothy shook her head as she glanced up and down the ward.

"He has to come out. Please Tom, make him come out."

At that moment Garin opened the door and stepped into the corridor.

"Well?" Johnson asked.

"He gave the clocks to Yerzov."

"Where?"

"At Annabelle's house."

"The woman that collects the money at the strip club?"

"Yes. Kosomo dropped them off at her house then went home."

"What about the killer?" Johnson asked. "Did Kosomo tell him where he dropped the clocks off to?"

"Yes."

"Okay then, we need to hurry. What's Annabelle's address?"

"55B Ninth Avenue, it's an apartment."

"Do you have a number for her?"

"No."

"Phone Yerzov."

"For what?"

"To warn him," said Johnson. "The killer doesn't want anyone that's been near them tapes staying alive."

Garin took out his phone and rang Yerzov. The phone rang eight times then switched to answering machine. Garin hung up rather than leave a message.

"No joy," he said.

"Then we've no choice," said Johnson. "We have to get over there."

"But they mightn't even be in," said Garin.

"There's only one way to find out."

When they got into the SUV Johnson stuck the strobe light on the roof. They couldn't afford to waste a second. But even with the siren blaring it was difficult getting through New York's notorious traffic. Now Johnson appreciated what Sal had been saying about the taxis clogging the roads. They were everywhere. A solid mass of yellow metal choking the arteries of the city. An infestation. A plague. Johnson did his best, racing at parts then slowing at others to grind his way through the congestion. Eventually, they made it to Ninth Avenue. The apartment block was half way up the street. Johnson pulled up outside it.

"You stay in the car and keep ringing Yerzov," Johnson told Garin.

Garin nodded and took out his phone as Johnson and Adams got out of the car and hurried into the building. 55B was on the ground floor. It had an egg box door. Cheap plywood with compressed cardboard inside. Johnson pushed the doorbell. No one answered. Bereft of patience he tried again but this time he kept his finger on the button. Still nothing. Adams turned to walk away but Johnson grabbed him back by the shoulder.

"Did you just hear someone scream?" he asked.

Adams stared back, his face screwed up in confusion. After a couple of seconds the penny dropped.

"We need probable cause to enter a premises without a warrant," he said. "Is that what you're getting at?"

"Yes Einstein but you still haven't given me an answer," said Johnson. "Did you hear that scream?"

Adams nodded slowly.

"I heard it," he said.

Johnson lifted his foot and booted the door underneath the lock. His foot went straight through so he extracted it carefully, wary of the splinters he'd just created. Next, he leant forward and shoved his hand through the hole. Reaching upwards he searched for the button on the door lock. When he found it he pulled it down and the door yawned open. After he retracted his hand he straightened up and took out his gun with Adams doing likewise. Together they entered the apartment, their guns held out in front of them.

Yerzov and Annabelle were in the kitchen. Both dead. Yerzov was slumped backwards over the table with his neck in tatters whilst Annabelle's head dropped forward onto her chest. Vivid purple bruising was visible on her neck with two noticeable thumb prints at the back. Johnson looked at her from the side. Her tongue was protruding. This left him in no doubt that she'd been strangled. Her arms hung limp at her side. On the floor, over against the kitchen counter, was the tiny derringer she'd pulled on Johnson. This time she hadn't succeeded in getting the drop. Blood was everywhere, on the kitchen table, on the floor, on the walls. Everywhere. And because it was everywhere the stench, that coppery smell that Johnson had come to hate, pervaded every inch of the room. Spilt coffee was also splattered on the floor.

The two Detectives checked the rest of the apartment, opening closets and checking underneath beds. The place was empty. Johnson holstered his weapon and walked back into the kitchen whilst Adams remained in the hallway and called it in. Johnson stepped over to Annabelle. Not wanting to contaminate the crime scene he took a pair of latex gloves out of his pants' pocket and slipped them on. He pressed two fingers against Annabelle's carotid artery. There was no pulse but even through the thin rubber of his gloves he could feel the warmth of her body. From experience he knew they hadn't been too far behind the killer. Minutes possibly. Up close he could smell Annabelle's perfume. Roses. A natural scent that disappeared when he straightened up. He lifted up the clocks that were sitting on the table then examined them individually, one after the other. The memory cards were missing from each of them. Adams entered the kitchen.

"The Lieutenant's on her way," he said.

"Okay."

"Are the memory cards still in the clocks?" Adams asked.

Johnson shook his head.

"No," he said.

"So now what?" Adams asked.

Johnson felt deflated. Like he'd just went twelve rounds with a heavyweight boxer and been knocked out in the last round.

"No idea," he said. Without the memory cards I don't know where to go."

"We've still got the blood from the minivan. That might give us our killer."

"Yeah, hopefully," said Johnson slipping his hand into his pocket. Pulling out his phone he rang Donato. The Crime Scene analyst answered on the second ring.

"What's up Joe?" he asked.

"Are you doing the blood on the minivan?"

"Yes, why?"

"Is there any chance you could rush it through...make it a priority?"

"I'll get right on it now?"

"How long?"

"Three hours."

"That's great Francis. Thanks."

"Not a problem."

They both hung up.

Outside, a car screeched to a halt. Johnson instantly became alert. He pulled out his Glock and stepped into the hallway with Adams behind him. Dispatch had only been informed so whoever it was, it certainly wasn't back up. Way too quick. Together, the two Detectives leveled their guns at the open doorway and waited. Car doors opened and slammed then heavy footsteps rushed up the pathway. Johnson braced himself. Two big men in grey suits kicked their way past the broken door with guns in their hands. One of the men was black, the other white.

"Police! Lower your weapons!" Johnson shouted.

The two men stopped but neither of them lowered their guns. Mexican standoff.

"Police!" the black man roared back. "Show us your ID!"

Johnson studied the man's eyes. There was a ferocity there. A rage. An intensity. Johnson's gut told him the man was close to pulling the trigger.

"Easy," he yelled to calm the man.

"I.D!" the man shouted.

Johnson switched his grip to one hand then pulled out his wallet and flipped it open.

"Now show us yours," he said.

The two men quickly pulled out their shields. Satisfied, Johnson and Adams lowered their weapons. When they did the two men ran past them into the kitchen.

"No!" Johnson heard one of them shout.

"Jesus!" the other said.

Johnson and Adams followed them in. The black man had his hands on his head whilst the white guy was shaking his head over and over again in disbelief. Both their faces were filled with anguish. The black man took his hands down.

"We better tell the Boss," he said.

The white guy nodded. His face was sallow, drained of blood. Pain and sorrow were etched into every contour of his face. The black man took out his cell then walked into the hall to make his call.

"What's going on?" Johnson asked.

The white guy looked at him. There was a shocked, glazed expression on his face. Johnson recognized it because he'd seen it so many times over the course of his career. Twice within the last two days. It was the thousand yard stare. The blank countenance of someone that had just lost someone close to them.

"The woman is one of ours," the man said.

"What?"

"The woman...Annabelle...she's an undercover cop."

Johnson stood there stunned. Jolted. After a couple of seconds he found his voice.

"What Bureau are you from?" he asked.

"The OCCB. I'm Detective Donald Harris," he said. "That other man is my partner Detective Kenneth Lewis."

"Stationed where?"

"One Police Plaza."

Lewis came back into the kitchen.

"The Boss is on the way in," he said.

"What's her real name?" Johnson asked, nodding at the woman he'd thought was Annabelle.

"Jennifer Carter," said Harris. "Seven years with the Department. The last eight months undercover."

"Jesus Christ," said Adams. "We better catch this bastard. That's two dead cops now and four civilians."

When back up did arrive and the apartment block was cordoned off it was like a three ring circus inside the apartment. As well as tons of uniforms and an abundance of Detectives the Police Commissioner had arrived. Johnson was surprised that a dead undercover agent warranted such a display of brass. It made him wonder what was really going on. When the Lieutenant arrived she quickly brought him up to speed.

"Do you know who that is?" she asked.

"Yeah, she's a cop...Jennifer Carter."

"Do you know who's daughter she is?"

"No idea. Who?"

"The Chief of Department's daughter."

"You're shitting me!"

"I shit you not."

Johnson checked inside the apartment looking for Adams so as to fill him in about the Chief. When he couldn't find him he went outside. Adams was standing at the police cordon having a smoke. Johnson walked up to him.

"Filthy habit," he said.

Adams took a last draw then dropped the butt on the ground before grinding it out with his shoe.

"I'll give them up tomorrow," he said.

"Tomorrow never comes," Johnson replied.

"Reformed smoker Joe?"

"How'd you guess?"

"I'm a Detective remember."

"Did you hear?" Johnson asked him.

"Hear what?"

"About who Jennifer Carter's father is?"

"No, who is he?"

"The Chief."

"Shit. Really?"

"Yeah," said Johnson then a screech of tires made him turn around.

Behind them was a red news van that had just bumped up onto the curb on the opposite side of the police tape. When the passenger door flew open an energetic TV reporter with an excited face and Charlie's Angel's hair jumped out and flounced up to them with a cameraman in her wake. Stopping in front of them with a microphone clamped in her fist she thrust her mike into Johnson's face.

"Is it true that the Chief of the Police Department's only daughter is one of the victims?" she asked.

Instead of answering both policemen gave her a disdainful look then turned on their heel and walked away.

"Now the shit's really going to hit the fan," said Adams.

Johnson nodded in agreement.

"That's one secret wasn't kept too long," he said.

Behind them more tires screeched as additional media vans pulled to a stop. Soon a whole horde of anchormen and women from different networks were vying for position at the police lines. Johnson looked back as they crowded the tape. Hounds on the scent with glossy hair, expensive suits and lipstick.

Chapter 29

Back in the kitchen Johnson stood at the fridge with Adams and watched the Police Commissioner Harry Boyd. Dressed immaculately in a black suit complete with matching waistcoat and a blue silk tie Boyd was an elemental force of nature. Big and raw boned his head resembled a breeze block on top of a thick neck with intelligent blue eyes that never sat still. A Vietnam Vet that had served with the Marine Corps he was a renowned fitness fanatic that at the age of sixty three still spent an hour each day in the gym doing weights and aerobics. A former cop himself he was now serving his second term as Police Commissioner. In the kitchen he stood with his arms folded staring down at the dead face of Jennifer Carter. Captain Edward Mannard was at his side, also taking in the grisly scene.

"Does the Chief know yet?" Mannard asked.

The Commissioner nodded.

"I stopped on my way here," he said. "Told him personally."

"How'd that go?"

"Terrible," said the Commissioner. "He broke down. Near collapsed. I had to sit him on a chair."

"The worst fear as a parent...losing a child."

The Commissioner gave a solemn nod.

"Yeah," he said, the single word filled with empathy.

"So where is he?" Mannard asked.

"Waiting on his wife to get home. She's an Official for the NEA."

The NEA was 'The National Education Association', the largest labor union in the US. The Police Commissioner turned towards Johnson.

"You're Johnson, isn't that right?" he said.

Johnson was surprised the Police Commissioner knew him.

"Yes Sir," he said.

"Explain to me what's going on here Detective," the Commissioner asked.

"There's a killer on the loose and at the minute he's trying to clean house, get rid of anyone that might have seen the film of him killing a prostitute and taking Richard Wright who he also later killed. Yerzov had the film hidden in those clocks. That's why he and Jennifer were killed."

The Commissioner turned towards Captain Mannard.

"I want a meeting tomorrow," he said, "with everyone involved. Nine o' clock sharp at One Police Plaza...in the Conference Room."

"Yes Commissioner," said Mannard.

Having seen enough the Police Commissioner exited. As he did so Donato arrived with his Crime Scene team and asked them to leave the kitchen.

The next morning Johnson arrived at One Police Plaza half an hour early. The building itself was located on Park Row in downtown Manhattan near City Hall and the Brooklyn Bridge. Rectangular in plan it was an inverted pyramid in elevation with thirteen levels. As Johnson was early he got the elevator up to the eighth floor to see the Real Time Crime Center, an anti-crime computer network that consisted of a powerful search engine as well as a huge data warehouse. After taking a stroll around for fifteen minutes he got on the elevator again and rode up to the 'fourteenth floor' containing the conference room and the Commissioner's office. When Johnson got out of the elevator he turned left and walked along a corridor to an open plan reception area. An intelligent looking red head with cute freckles on her face sat behind a desk typing on a computer. She looked up and smiled when Johnson stopped in front of her.

"I'm here for the meeting at 9am," he said.

"Yes," said the receptionist lifting up a sheet of paper with names printed on it. "Your name please?"

"Detective Joseph Johnson."

The receptionist lifted a pen and ticked his name off.

"The meeting is in the Conference Room Detective but the Commissioner wants to speak to you first before the meeting starts," she said.

After saying this she buzzed through to the Commissioner on the intercom system.

"Yes Kirsty?" came the Commissioner's voice.

"Detective Johnson is here Sir."

"Thank you Kirsty, send him in please."

Kirsty released the buzzer then pointed at a glass paneled mahogany door that had the NYPD Shield engraved on the glass.

"That's his office there Detective."

"Thank you," said Johnson then he stepped over and politely knocked the door.

"Come in," the Commissioner shouted out. "It's open."

When Johnson entered the Commissioner began to get up but as he pushed his chair back the phone rang on his desk. Holding a hand up in apology he pointed for Johnson to take a seat in front of him. As the Commissioner lifted the handset Johnson crossed the room and sat down. The Commissioner's desk was a large oak affair littered with family photographs. Also on the desk was a closed laptop and a miniature bronze statue of an NYPD Officer with his arm around a young boy. In his other hand the Patrolman carried the NYPD flag. It was a replica of the large memorial statue that Johnson had passed in the lobby on the way in. There was also a 9/11 memorial candle sitting at the corner of the table. With the window open and a slight breeze blowing in it guttered valiantly, it's delicate aroma, cinnamon, permeating around the room. Behind the Commissioner on the wall was another homage to the 9/11 catastrophe: A huge oil painting showing the NYPD and the New York Fire Department during the horror of the Twin Towers attack. Above the towers which dominated the centre of the painting a guardian angel ascended from the flames into heaven carrying both a Firefighter and a Police Officer in her arms. "Fidelis ad Mortem" the NYPD's motto was embossed on a gold nameplate attached to the pine frame of the painting. Translated from the Latin it meant "Faithful until death." Alongside this was the NYFD's motto: "New York's Bravest." The Commissioner covered the mouthpiece with his hand and looked across at Johnson.

"I'll only be a minute Detective," he said.

Johnson nodded, content to continue studying his surroundings. It was an impressive office filled with the history of the NYPD. In one corner were two flags attached to long black poles. They criss-crossed each other at the mid-point, the red, white and blue furls of the stars and stripes opposite the green and white bars of the NYPD's flag. The Commissioner finished his phone call then stood up and came around the desk towards Johnson. When he reached him Johnson stood up and they both shook hands.

"You've never been in my office before, have you Detective?" the Commissioner asked.

"No Sir," Johnson replied.

"All these men on the wall are previous holders of this office."

Johnson stared at the framed photographs adorning the walls. The only face he recognized was that of a young Theodore Roosevelt. The Commissioner noticed Johnson's gaze stopping on the man that had later become the youngest President in American history.

"You can feel his determination, can't you?" he said.

Johnson nodded in agreement. Across the years Teddy's strength of will emanated through his unflinching gaze and set jaw. The Commissioner turned towards Johnson. Like Roosevelt he too radiated a raw power, a potency of such depth you could feel it coming off him in waves.

"How close are we to catching the killer?" he asked.

"We're working on some leads Sir but at the minute we've no clear suspect."

"That's not what I want to hear Detective."

"I'm sorry Sir."

"Sorry's not good enough Detective. I want results."

"I know that Sir. I'll do my best."

The Commissioner nodded then checked his watch.

"Six minutes to nine," he said. "We should go into the Conference Room. I abhor lateness."

The Commissioner led the way back out into the reception area then over to another mahogany door with the words 'Conference Room' embossed on a gold nameplate. The Commissioner opened the door and they both walked in. The room was large and spacious with a large window allowing plenty of light to flood in. A huge rectangular table dominated the centre of the room. The Commissioner, as was his right, sat at the head of the table. Johnson took the third seat on the right. Within minutes the room started to fill. Adams was the first to arrive after Johnson. When Adams sat down the door kept opening for the next five minutes until the seats around the table were all taken except one. Besides Johnson and Adams, Donato the crime scene analyst was there as too was Lieutenant Walker and Charles B Firth the Medical Examiner. From the OCCB side of the case were Detectives Harris and Lewis and the OCCB Chief Gregory White but there were also three people that Johnson didn't know. Two women and a man. Johnson wondered if they'd reached their quota and the meeting was about to start when the door opened unannounced and the Chief of the Department, John Grey, entered. All of them stood as one then waited until he'd taken a seat before they sat down again.

"Gentlemen," the Chief said. "I don't mean to intrude but under the circumstances I'd like to be personally kept up to date on this case as it concerns my daughter Jennifer."

Johnson watched the Chief closely as he spoke. Although he tried to fight it his bottom lip trembled when he said his daughter's name. Johnson's heart went out to the man. As a parent Johnson couldn't even begin to imagine what he was going through at this time. An elegant man with a full head of grey hair he was well liked by the patrons of New York for his implementation of the 'Stop and Frisk' policy. Now however he was a shell of a man running on fumes. When the Chief sat back the Commissioner took over proceedings.

"Okay gentlemen, we all know why we're here this morning. Yesterday, the Chief's daughter, police officer Jennifer Carter, was murdered alongside the Russian gangster Vitaly Yerzov. Now the reason she was with a thug like Yerzov in the first place is that she was working undercover for the OCCB building a case that I am told was only days away from fruition. On a personal level, I knew Jennifer Carter extremely well and was very fond of her. Admired her, not only for her dedication and commitment to the job but for the fact that as a person...as a human being...as a lady....she had that rare commodity called belief. Belief in herself...belief in her job but first and foremost a belief that she was making a difference out there. Somehow turning back the tide, making New York City a better and safer place to live. Therefore, I appeal to you gentlemen...find Jennifer Carter's killer...make it your number one priority...because I promise you...you will have my heartfelt thanks and gratitude when you do."

The Commissioner paused to let his words sink in then started speaking again.

"Okay, the first thing I want to do is make sure everybody knows each other then establish a chain of command. So if we start from this side could everyone please introduce themselves for the others benefit."

After the introductions were made Johnson now knew who the strange man and two women were. The three of them were FBI agents from the New York Field Division that worked in tandem with the OCCB's Joint Organized Crime Task Force: Agents Bailey, Cook and Weiss, the latter two being the females. The three of them looked intelligent and capable. Once the introductions were over the Commissioner informed them that Gregory White, the OCCB Chief, would lead the investigation. After this was established White took up the reins.

"Okay, from now on," he said, "The two investigations that are currently going on are from this moment onwards amalgamated into one investigation under my command. Everyone, including the agents from the FBI will report directly to Lieutenant Walker who in turn will then report directly to me. I in turn will then report to the Commissioner. Any questions?"

Nobody spoke.

"Okay, good. Now that that's sorted we can get down to brass tacks. Detective Johnson, you first. Bring us up to date on your investigation at the minute."

"So far we're chasing a ghost...a lethal ghost Sir. A man..."

Agent Cook intervened.

"You're sure it's a man?" she asked.

"Yes certain," said Johnson. "I've met the killer face to face. It's definitely a man."

"Okay," she said and sat back.

Johnson paused for a second. The interruption had thrown him. Momentarily off-track he re-gathered his train of thought then began to speak again.

"The person we're dealing with," he said, "has in my opinion killed before. Possibly a few times. The reason I'm saying this is because of how comfortable he was in shooting Detective Abramo, my partner and then George Taylor the joint owner of Vanity Hotel. On both occasions he was ruthless, calm and efficient."

"Are you sure it's the same person that killed Officer Carter and Yerzov?" asked Bailey.

"No, I can't say that for certain. I can surmise...make a logical guess...but as to concrete evidence...no."

"What about forensics?" White asked looking across at Donato.

Donato straightened up in his seat.

"To date," he said, "we have a footprint from the first murder scene. From a Nike trainer, size nine, with a slice across the left foot. If we can find the person that's wearing that trainer then we have our killer. As well as that we have the bullets from Abramo's murder...38. Special rounds from a 38. Smith and Wesson Special. Therefore if we can get the gun then we can match that to the bullets. Lastly, there's the blood found inside the minivan on the driver's seat," said Donato. "After analysis it was identified as Type B blood but when it was run through the National DNA Database there was no match."

"A dead end?" White asked.

"Yes Sir...until we catch the killer then we can match him to the blood."

White switched his attention to the opposite side of the table.

"Detective Harris?"

"As you know Sir, the OCCB, under your command, has been carrying out a lengthy undercover operation into Vitaly Yerzov and his criminal empire. On the day that Detective Carter was killed she had a hidden button camera sown into the lining of her jacket."

"Has the film from it been watched yet?" White asked.

"No Sir."

"Is the film here?"

"Yes Sir," said Harris glancing nervously at the Chief.

White, noticing Harris's reticence, looked askance at the Commissioner.

"Sir, should we play the recording?"

In turn the Commissioner looked across at the Chief.

"You don't have to stay for this John," he said.

The Chief, tears standing in his eyes, looked around the table at everyone present. Johnson felt uncomfortable under his gaze but he met his eye as did everyone else in the room. This wasn't the time for shrinking violets.

"No, I'll stay," said the Chief.

"You're sure?" the Commissioner asked.

"Yes, positive."

"Okay, back to you Harris."

Chapter 30

Harris nodded then stood up with a computer case in his hand. After he extracted the laptop he connected it to the interactive white board and pressed play. On screen a close up of Jennifer Carter's face appeared. The memory of her wiping his scraped chin raced through Johnson's mind. A pang of regret that he hadn't got to know her better tweaked his heart but one glance at the Chief's distraught features and he realized his grief was nothing compared to his. Johnson stared up at the screen as Jennifer maneuvered her coat to capture the best angle. Then, on screen, a forceful knock could be heard. Jennifer stood up then disappeared as she opened the front door to her apartment. Someone walked in but the camera only captured whoever it was from the waist down.

"What are you doing here?" Jennifer asked, a hint of fear clearly evident in her voice.

"What's wrong? You're my employee. I can't call round to see you?"

"I didn't even know you had my address."

"I got it out of the duty register. Why, is there a problem?"

"No, of course not."

"Good."

"I'm just about to go out though," said Jennifer.

"Really?"

"It's my friend's birthday tomorrow. I want to buy her a card and a present."

"It was my birthday last week. You never got me anything."

"I didn't know."

"So if you did you'd have got me something, is that what you're saying?"

"I'd have bought you a card."

"No present?"

"I don't really know you that well."

"And whose fault is that? How many times have I asked you to sit behind for a drink after work?"

"But I drive, I wouldn't risk my license."

"But sure I've told you I'd pay for a cab."

"I know but I'm not that type of person."

"What type of person?"

"The type that sits behind for a drink."

"But sure we're friends...work colleagues...I don't see why not."

"Maybe when I get to know you better."

"Sure we'll get to know each other better now, eh."

After saying this, the previously unidentified person sat down at the table. The camera now had a perfect shot of him. It was Vitaly Yerzov, the head of the Russian mob. Dressed in a loose fitting blue suit with a white shirt open at the neck he oozed menace.

"What happened at the club after I left?" he asked.

"That cop arrested Garin."

"For what?"

"For punching him on the back of the head so as you could get away."

"Sure, it's what he gets paid for. Where's Garin now?"

"The cops had to release him. They'd no evidence against him."

"What about the CCTV?"

"Garin pulled the tapes as soon as he knocked the cop out."

"Smart thinking...not like him."

On screen Yerzov's phone rang. He took it out of his jacket pocket and answered it.

"Calm down Andrei, speak slowly...okay...right...and you've left the club with the clocks? ....Good, bring them to me. I'm at Annabelle's apartment...55B Ninth Avenue. Yes, now Andrei, right this minute."

Yerzov hung up.

"What is it?" Jennifer asked.

"The cops are at the hotel."

"Why's Andrei bringing clocks here?"

"You're forever asking questions Annabelle."

"This is my apartment Vitaly. I don't want anything illegal going on in here. I'll not stand for it."

"Relax. Once Andrei gets here and gives me the clocks I'll leave. It won't be a problem."

"What are they for? Tell me. I'm not having them brought in here if they're illegal."

Instead of answering, Yerzov dipped his hand into his jacket and languidly pulled out a gun. It was a revolver. Yerzov rested it on the table with his hand curled around the butt. On screen the barrel, which was aimed directly at the camera, looked like the mouth of the Lincoln tunnel.

"Do you know anything about guns Annabelle?" Yerzov asked.

"A little," she said, fear laced through her voice.

"You still carry that pea shooter...the derringer?"

"No."

"You're lying. I was told you had it today. Pulled it out on that cop."

"It's back at the club. I leave it behind the ticket counter."

"Are you lying to me Annabelle?"

"No, why would I lie?"

Yerzov paused, deliberating whether she was telling him the truth or not. Finally, he continued speaking.

"You like this gun Annabelle?" he asked holding up the revolver.

"No."

"What about history Annabelle? You like history?"

"No."

"This gun dates back to the Russian Imperial Army...an army that my great grandfather was in. He owned this gun...an M1895 Revolver. Sturdy...reliable...but do you know what's unique about this gun Annabelle?"

Jennifer shook her head.

"No," she said.

"A sound suppressor can be fitted to it."

After saying this Yerzov took a silencer out of his jacket pocket and slid it over the barrel.

"With this attached," he said, "This gun becomes the perfect assassination weapon."

"You're scaring me Vitaly."

"Why? Have you a guilty conscience Annabelle? Something you want to tell me?"

Again she shook her head.

"No."

"Then relax. You've got nothing to worry about."

"Then put the gun away."

Yerzov didn't reply. Instead he started a different thread of conversation.

"Do you not like me Annabelle?"

"Of course I do."

"You do?"

"Yes."

"Do you find me attractive?"

"Yes, you're a handsome man."

"Then sit beside me."

"What for?"

"To talk...to get to know each other."

"I can talk to you from here."

Yerzov smiled then twisted his hand so that the gun was now pointed across the table.

"I'm not asking Annabelle. I'm telling," he said.

Jennifer slowly came around the table. Yerzov patted the chair beside him. When Jennifer sat down she clasped her hands together on her lap. On screen her eyes bulged with fright and her breathing grew shallow. Yerzov wrapped one of his brawny arms around her shoulders then lifted the gun and pressed it up underneath her chin.

"There now, isn't this cozy," he said.

"Please Vitaly, don't hurt me."

Yerzov grinned then slowly opened his mouth allowing his tongue to loll out. Seizing Jennifer by the back of the neck he leant forward then gave her cheek a long, lascivious lick.

"Ummm," he said. "You taste lovely...like vanilla ice cream."

Jennifer tried to recoil backwards but Yerzov pulled her in tight.

Johnson cast a quick glance across at the Chief. Whereas beforehand his face had been deathly white now it was an ashen grey with silent tears streaming down his cheeks. Johnson switched his focus to Harris hoping to catch his eye and signal for him to cut the feed. But like everyone else in the room he too was fixated on what was taking place on the screen. Johnson returned his gaze to the interactive whiteboard. Now Yerzov had his hand inside Jennifer's blouse as he sucked on her neck. Throughout he kept his eyes open staring up at her.

"Please...stop," Jennifer begged.

"Oh, what have we here?" said Yerzov pulling his hand out of her bra.

Clasped in his fist was Jennifer's derringer. He snapped it open then tapped it on the tabletop until the two bullets fell out. Next, he lifted the gun and threw it across the room.

"Thought you left that in the club?" he said.

"I thought I did."

"What? You didn't know it was in there?"

"No, I forgot."

Yerzov grinned, a wide, feral slash filled with malice.

"I like you Annabelle," he said, "and do you know why? Because you've got balls....big brass ones swinging between your legs."

After saying this Yerzov stuck his hand between Jennifer's thighs.

"Sorry, my mistake," he said as he felt around. "You're all woman."

Again Johnson risked a glance at the Chief. This time his jaw was jutting out and his fists were clenched. Johnson looked up at the screen again feeling utterly helpless.

"You hungry Annabelle?" Yerzov asked.

"No," she said.

"I think you are."

"I'm not."

"You fuckin' are," he said. "Now lift up one of the bullets."

"What?"

"You heard me. Lift up one of the fuckin' bullets."

"Please Vitaly."

"You shouldn't have lied Annabelle. I don't like being lied to."

"I'm sorry."

"Too late. Now lift up a fuckin' bullet before I pull the trigger on this gun and blow your pretty head off."

Jennifer picked up one of the bullets. On screen it looked like a tiny golden rocket between her fingers.

"Put it in your mouth," Yerzov said.

After a moment's hesitation Jennifer did as she was told.

"Swallow it," said Yerzov.

When Jennifer failed to comply Yerzov forced her head back by shoving the gun up hard underneath her chin. At the same time he pinched her nostrils closed with his other hand. As Johnson watched it he was reminded of what he'd done on Grant when he'd forced him to swallow his own mucus. On screen Jennifer's eyes watered as she ingested the bullet. Yerzov removed his hand and sat back. The gun he kept pressed against Jennifer's throat.

"I'm really enjoying this," he said.

"Please Vitaly, I've never did anything to you," said Jennifer. "I've always been your friend."

"Then why do you refuse me? That's not being my friend."

"I don't really know you."

Before Yerzov could reply there was a loud knock on the door. Yerzov stood up with the gun in his hand.

"Stay seated," he said but now on screen the men in the Commissioner's office could only see him from the waist down. Yerzov disappeared from view then a few seconds later he entered again along with a second person. Now all that could be seen on screen was Jennifer's frightened face and two sets of legs: One with dark blue jeans which was Yerzov and the other wearing black pants with a white shirt tucked into them. Johnson took this to be Kosomo. This was confirmed when Yerzov spoke to him.

"Set them over there Andrei," he said.

A second later a New York Jets kitbag was deposited on the kitchen table.

"Did the cops say what they wanted?" Yerzov asked.

"No and I didn't wait around to find out."

"A wise decision. When the police arrive at your house tell them you felt sick and had to go home."

"Okay."

"Andrei, don't leave me here with him," Jennifer suddenly shouted.

On screen Kosomo faltered.

"Go," said Yerzov waving his gun at him. "Me and Annabelle are about to get acquainted."

Johnson watched the screen with a leaden heart as he already knew the outcome. Kosomo's footsteps came next followed by a slamming door. Seconds later Yerzov sat back down beside Jennifer clearly visible to the people watching. This time he stuck the gun against Jennifer's left breast.

"Now where were we?" he said.

"You were going to behave like a gentleman and leave my apartment," said Jennifer.

"No, that's not what's going to happen," said Yerzov raising his free hand and extending his index finger.

He touched Jennifer's lips then ever so gently he began to draw circles around the contours of her mouth.

"You've such a beautiful mouth Annabelle," he said. "Has anyone ever told you that?"

"No."

"Well, trust me...you have."

"Please Vitaly...this isn't you. You're a gentleman."

He stopped, his finger paused on the bow of her top lip.

"No, sorry, I can't," he said beginning to trace the curve of her mouth again. "You're much too beautiful to resist."

"No Vitaly, please."

Again Yerzov ignored her pleas.

"Open your mouth," he said.

Immediately Jennifer clamped her lips shut. Yerzov shoved the gun in hard between her breasts.

"I said open your fuckin' mouth."

Jennifer refused to obey him. Instead, she clenched her teeth together as hard as she could. Yerzov cocked the hammer of the revolver with his thumb.

"If you haven't opened your mouth and started sucking my finger by the count of three then I'm going to pull this trigger and blow your beautiful head off. Do you understand?"

Jennifer refused to answer. Instead, she gazed back at Yerzov with terrified eyes. Yerzov began to count with his finger pressed up against Jennifer's mouth awaiting entry.

"One...two..."

Jennifer opened her mouth and Yerzov slid his finger in. He pushed it in and out simulating the movements of fellatio as Jennifer sucked his finger.

"Now that is heaven," said Yerzov. A perfect starter before the main course."

Johnson once more looked at the Chief. Now, he was no longer trying to fight his feelings. Tears flowed freely down his face and it was obvious he was in a huge amount of emotional pain. Johnson stood up.

"Turn it off," he said.

Everyone in the room turned and stared at him.

"I said turn it off," he repeated.

Harris, unsure of what to do, looked at White then at the Commissioner. The Commissioner nodded.

"He's right," he said. "Turn it off."

Harris's face filled with relief as he happily carried out the order. Johnson stayed standing.

"May I talk you outside Sir," he said to the Chief.

Chapter 31

The Chief nodded then slowly got to his feet.

"Keep me updated," he said to the Commissioner then he crossed to the door and exited with Johnson behind him. Outside in the reception area, the Chief kept walking so Johnson followed him out into the corridor. Again, the Chief didn't stop. Instead, he marched over to the four elevators that ferried people up and down the building and pressed the button. Turning around he looked at Johnson, his face wet with tears.

"Thank you," he said.

"No need Sir," said Johnson. "No parent should have to endure that."

"I thought I had the strength to watch it," the Chief said with a weak smile. "But evidently not."

"You have my solemn promise Sir that I'll do everything within my power to bring your daughter's killer to justice."

"I know that Detective and I appreciate it," the Chief said then he pulled a handkerchief out of his pants' pocket and wiped his face.

"She wouldn't listen to me," he said. "I begged her...pleaded with her to leave the police force...especially after I became Chief...but she wouldn't listen. Headstrong, like me...bull-headed. I can look after myself she said."

Johnson nodded not knowing what else to do. As they stood there, an uncomfortable silence ensued, only broken when one of the elevator doors opened. The Chief stepped in then turned around and pressed the button for the ground floor. As he waited for the doors to close his cheeks glistened with tears.

"Find my daughter's killer," he said.

"I will Sir," Johnson replied and then the doors slid shut.

As the elevator descended Johnson's respect for the Chief grew exponentially. Before he'd only ever seen him from a distance, at funerals or on TV. But now, after having met him face to face he felt he'd gotten a good sense of the man. Underneath the cool exterior and the public facade the Chief was as susceptible to heartache and pain as the next man. Vulnerable and sensitive. Flesh and bone. And like every other parent in the world he had the same fears and insecurities that came with that obligation. Now, the worst fear that all parents harbored had become a reality. Johnson turned and walked back to the Commissioner's office. When he re-entered and took his seat the Commissioner nodded at Harris and the film re-started. On screen Yerzov removed his finger from Jennifer's mouth then wiped it dry on his shoulder.

"Stand up and undress," he told Jennifer.

"Please Vitaly, no," she begged.

Yerzov slapped her hard across the face. Jennifer's right cheek was instantly inflamed, a stinging bright red.

"When I speak you obey," said Yerzov. "Do you understand?"

Jennifer was crying now, her tears making her mascara run in dark streaks down her cheeks. Yerzov slapped her again.

"Answer me slut. Do you understand?"

"Yes," said Jennifer, sniffling now as her tears intermingled with the mucus bubbling out of her nose.

When Jennifer stood up and started to undress Johnson found himself digging his fingers into the fabric on the underside of his chair. It felt coarse, like hessian. He kept pressing until his fingers punched through the material. On screen Jennifer was now standing in her underwear.

"Don't be shy Annabelle," said Yerzov. "Take everything off."

When she hesitated Yerzov got up and placed the gun against her navel. On screen, although they could no longer see her face the people present in the Commissioner's office could hear Jennifer sobbing as she stripped in front of her tormentor.

"Good girl," said Yerzov when she'd discarded the last of her clothes.

Next, he pushed her back onto the table so that her head was in front of the camera. Now, the only thing the people in the room could see was a close up of Jennifer's brown hair. Yerzov raped her then on top of the table. When it was over the sounds of Yerzov's apish grunts and Jennifer's sobbing would haunt those that had watched the secret recording forever. Afterwards, Yerzov pulled up his jeans then sat on the chair and watched Jennifer as she slowly got dressed. When she was fully clothed he made her sit beside him. Once more they were both visible on the screen.

"Do you know what I love after sex?" said Yerzov.

Jennifer didn't reply. Instead, she looked at him with a blank face totally devoid of emotion.

"Coffee," said Yerzov. "Along with a cigarette. Has to be the best combination in the world...besides me and you of course. We make a great team, don't we?"

When she continued staring at him with vacant eyes Yerzov got annoyed and slapped her again. But it had no effect. Yerzov grabbed her by the shoulder and started shaking her.

"Earth to Annabelle...come in Annabelle," he shouted.

But she was gone. Withdrawn into herself. An age-old self defense mechanism to help people escape from trauma. Over the years Johnson had seen the same dulled expression on countless occasions. On screen Yerzov grabbed a fistful of Jennifer's hair and yanked it repeatedly.

"Coffee!" he shouted. "I want coffee!"

Eventually, Yerzov's yelling penetrated Jennifer's skull. She stood up and Yerzov released her.

"About fuckin' time," he said.

Jennifer walked over to the counter, lifted the kettle and filled it with water. After it was on the boil she opened a wall cupboard, lifted out a cup then retrieved milk from the fridge.

"Two sugars," Yerzov said holding up the same number of fingers.

Jennifer opened the cutlery drawer and withdrew a teaspoon.

"That's my girl," said Yerzov.

When the kettle boiled Jennifer poured the hot water into the cup, added the milk and two sugars then walked towards Yerzov with the cup in her right hand.

"This better be nice," said Yerzov. "If it's not Daddy's gonna have to spank you Annabelle."

When Jennifer got to Yerzov, the gangster reached up to take the cup from her grasp. When he did Jennifer lifted the cup up above his head then poured the hot, scalding liquid into his upturned face. Yerzov screamed and jumped to his feet with the gun still in his hand. Blinded by the boiling coffee that had seared his eyes he fired wildly as Jennifer returned to the cupboard drawer and withdrew a ten inch bread knife. With the silencer covering the barrel the gunshots sounded like an angry cat spitting. Yerzov fired all six rounds in quick succession, every bullet missing its intended target. When the gun clicked on an empty chamber he snarled in frustration then flung the pistol across the kitchen.

"You fuckin' bitch! I will choke the life out of you," he screamed then he stumbled forward, blindly flailing his arms trying to find her.

But Jennifer wasn't trying to escape. Instead of running for the door she walked straight into Yerzov's outflung arms then as he yelped with joy at the prospect of strangling her she plunged the pointed bread knife repeatedly into his neck. Bright red arterial blood sprayed from his throat dappling Annabelle in a fountain of fine mist that made her face, neck and hands look like they were covered with thousands of tiny, red freckles. After ten seconds Yerzov fell back onto the seat with his head almost severed from his body.

Johnson sat stunned. Mesmerized. When he'd been watching Jennifer take her revenge he'd been silently cheering her on but now with Yerzov dead Johnson knew there was worse to come.

"Pause it," said the Commissioner.

On screen Jennifer was now frozen sitting next to Yerzov staring at his dead face with the knife still in her hand.

"We can't let this get out," said the Commissioner.

"Why not?" Johnson asked. "She was perfectly within her rights to do what she did."

"Maybe morally...yes Detective...but under the law there is no vigilante justice."

"He fired a gun at her six times. It was a miracle he didn't kill her. So if that's not self defense I don't know what is."

The Commissioner nodded slowly as he considered this.

"Okay, that's a fair point," he conceded. "That's the angle we'll take because this'll be impossible to keep a lid on.

"Will we play the rest of the video?" White asked.

The Commissioner looked across at him.

"We don't have a choice," he said.

Harris pressed play and again they were all glued to the film. After a couple of minutes Jennifer slowly came out of her comatose state and withdrew her cell phone. Her face was an agonized mask as she held the phone to her ear.

"Donald, it's me Jennifer. I've just killed Vitally Yerzov," she said then after Donald replied she spoke again. "I'm in the apartment."

When she hung up she slumped back in the chair then sat staring into space. A few minutes later someone could be heard knocking on the front door. Jennifer got up and disappeared for twenty seconds. When she re-entered the kitchen someone was with her. Only visible from the waist down it looked to be a man. In his right fist was a Smith and Wesson revolver.

"The clocks are in that bag," said Jennifer then she sat down again beside the dead mobster.

On screen the man lifted the bag off the ground and set it on the table. He unzipped it then started lifting the clocks out. One by one he withdrew the memory cards and stuck them into his pants' pocket. Johnson cursed under his breath. He'd been hoping that Forensics might have been able to pull some fingerprints from the clocks but on screen the man was wearing black leather gloves. As soon as he had the last memory card in his pocket the man walked behind Jennifer and wrapped his hands around her throat. Jennifer, still traumatized from what had just happened, sat still, staring inwardly into her own private hell. Unaware of what was really going on she only started struggling when the man tightened his hands around her neck. The gloves, like molasses, had a liquid life of their own. Like coiling black snakes the man's fingers formed a ghastly halter-neck as he squeezed the life from her body. On screen the man could be seen from the waist down as he slowly and methodically choked Jennifer to death. She struggled in his arms for perhaps thirty seconds but it was too little too late. Finally, her tongue protruded and she was motionless, a frozen gargoyle with a purple death mask as her final epitaph. But still the man maintained his Lucifer grip on what was now a limp doll, a flaccid effigy of what had once been a vibrant young woman. After another minute the man's hands slipped from around Jennifer's crushed windpipe and he disappeared off screen.

Although Johnson hadn't realized it he'd been holding his breath throughout the strangling. Now, an explosive gust of air escaped from his body. The others in the room were also affected but nobody asked for a time out and so the film kept rolling. Three minutes later Johnson and Adams made their illegal entrance followed by Harris and Lewis. When the film was over the Commissioner started the ball rolling.

"Okay gentlemen, I hope we didn't just put ourselves through that for nothing. Please, for the love of God, somebody tell me they got something from that."

"I did Sir," said Johnson.

"Good, tell me then Detective."

"When the killer was strangling Jennifer I think he had a scar on his left wrist."

The Commissioner jerked his head around to Harris.

"Harris, put it on again," he said, "and rewind it back to the strangling. Pause when Johnson says so."

"Yes Sir."

Harris did as he was asked then paused the feed when Johnson said stop. On screen there was a definite gap between the top of the man's gloves and the cuff of his jacket. A narrow band of skin was clearly visible with what appeared to be a centimeter long scar on the top of the left wrist.

"Can we zoom in?" Johnson asked.

Harris duly obliged but when he magnified the image on screen it started to pixelate turning into a spread of colored dots.

"Sorry," said Harris. "The pixels are really low on this because it was a button cam."

"Okay, it's a start," said the Commissioner. "But that doesn't mean we discount people that don't have a scar on their left wrist because that was not conclusive...you'd agree with that Detective Johnson?"

"Yes Sir, could have been a marker or anything."

"Precisely so let's not get complacent gentlemen. Okay, anybody get anything else from the tape?"

Everyone present shook their heads.

"Well, if that's the case, then get out there and find this son of a bitch."

Chapter 32

Johnson got up from the table and exited with Adams walking beside him.

"Jesus, I never want to see that again," said Adams as they made their way over to the elevators.

Johnson nodded in agreement. It had been grim viewing. Thoroughly depressing and soul destroying. As they stepped onto the elevator Adams' cell phone rang. When he answered it Johnson could tell by the way his face lit up that something had happened.

"What is it?" he asked as soon as Adams had hung up.

"That was Dorothy from St. Luke's, my sisters' friend. She just told me that a man has just walked into St. Luke's to get his upper left arm stitched."

"Did she say who it was?"

"No."

"Phone her back. Tell her to keep an eye on this guy, make sure he doesn't leave."

Adams nodded, seeing the wisdom in this and made the call.

"Sorted," he said when he disconnected.

Back in the SUV Johnson put the siren on top of the roof then stuck the 4x4 into gear and raced through the city streets. As usual heavy traffic blighted their journey but after a stilted ride they eventually pulled up in front of St. Luke's. After parking in a space reserved for Doctors they climbed out and walked quickly towards the entrance only for gunshots to ring out. Johnson and Adams drew their weapons simultaneously then crouched low and started running. When they reached the hospital's revolving doors and peered into the reception area they saw a man with bright ginger hair lying on the floor inside. A gun was in his hand and he was lying face down with his arms and legs flung out. From where they were standing it looked like the man on the ground was dead. A large pool of thick blood was spreading around his body. Adams took out his cell, called for back-up and then hung up. Johnson tightened his grip on his Glock, the sweat of his hand making the butt feel sticky. More gunshots echoed from inside.

"I'm not waiting," Johnson said. "I'm going in."

"No Joe, you can't. Wait on back up."

"Sorry Tom. I need to get in there. See what's going on."

"I'll tell you what's going on. There's people shooting at each other and we don't know who."

"Then it's about time I found out, isn't it," he said pressing his hand against the revolving door. It was cold to the touch. He pushed it and it started to slide round. When the gap was big enough he slid in then walked round in a circle on his haunches. When the doors completed their revolution back to the inside of the hospital Johnson raced out expecting to be shot at. But no shots came and he reached cover behind a pine counter. As he sat with his back pressed against the wood the revolving doors slid round again, this time disgorging a red faced Adams who rushed across to him. Like him, Adams too was lucky and no shots rang out.

"Thought you were waiting for back up?" Johnson whispered.

"And have you talking about me. Don't think so Joe."

Johnson turned around then slowly raised his head over the top of the counter. Besides the man lying splayed on the floor a doctor and two nurses were also lying prone with their hands over their heads. Johnson ducked back down.

"Still no sign of the shooters," he said then more gunfire echoed up from the left corridor.

"Now we know where they are," Johnson said.

"Then let's go," said Adams.

Johnson nodded remembering the gun battle in the house. Adams hated waiting. Johnson stood up then edged up to the mouth of the corridor with Adams beside him. He popped his head around the corner. A man was halfway down the corridor crouching behind an upturned stretcher with his back to them. Oblivious of their presence all his efforts were concentrated on whoever he was shooting at. Johnson turned back to Adams.

"I'm going to sneak down," Johnson said keeping his voice low. "You stay here and cover me."

"Okay, be careful Joe."

"It's my middle name."

Johnson edged into the corridor down on his haunches, his gun out in front of him. All the way down he kept expecting the man to turn, see him and then to start shooting but he never did. Eventually, Johnson got right up behind him and pressed his gun in tight against the back of the man's neck.

"Police," Johnson said. "Lower the gun."

The man stiffened and for a second Johnson knew he was contemplating swinging round. Johnson dug the gun in harder.

"Drop it," he said.

After a couple of seconds the man's body relaxed and he placed the gun on the floor beside him.

"Okay, turn round," Johnson said.

The man obeyed and slowly turned. When he did Johnson realized it was Danny Riley, his lifelong friend from Hell's Kitchen.

"Joe," said Danny, just as surprised as he was.

"What's going on?" Johnson asked.

"Bit of an argument."

"Don't mess me about Danny. Who are you shooting at?"

"Dimitry Garin," Danny said.

And as the name escaped Danny's mouth it suddenly all made sense to Johnson.

"Crawl back up the corridor," Johnson said. "There's another Detective at the top. He'll arrest you."

"Arrest me?"

"Detain you. Keep you safe."

"Garin fired first Joe. Killed my friend."

"But what were you and your friend doing here?"

"I wasn't feeling the best so I came in to get a checkup and Garin started shooting."

"Don't bullshit a bullshitter Danny. Go back up the corridor and stay low."

"Don't worry, I'll be like a limpet mine stuck to the floor."

As Danny made his way up the corridor Johnson risked a glance over the top of the stretcher. Immediately, a bullet ricocheted of the iron frame forcing Johnson to duck back down.

"Garin, it's me Johnson," Johnson shouted over the top. "We've arrested Riley."

"Fuck you cop, think I'm stupid," came the reply.

"I'm going to look over the stretcher. When I do don't be shooting. I just want to talk to you."

When Garin didn't reply Johnson took this as a good sign and risked a second glance over the top of the stretcher. This time Garin didn't fire. Johnson could see half of Garin's head peering round the corner of a wall, only one eye showing. Johnson stood up with his gun in his hand but he made sure to keep it down by his side so as Garin understood he wasn't a threat.

"I only want to talk Garin...that's all."

"Go ahead then...talk."

"There's no way out of this...you must know that. Back up's already here and all the exits are blocked."

"Those Micks were here to murder me."

"Well, they said you fired first."

"Yeah, to stop them killing me."

"Look, we can talk about this back at the station."

"No, I've a better idea."

Garin disappeared behind the wall. There was a shrill scream then a second later he stepped into the hallway with a nurse in front of him. It was Adam's sister's friend. Dorothy. Garin had one of his thick forearms wrapped around her neck with his gun stuck to her head.

"I'm walking out of here cop...now step the fuck back or I'll put a hole in her head."

"You're only making things worse for yourself Garin."

"I'm already going down for the Mick, a dead nurse won't make any difference...now step the fuck back."

Johnson held up both his hands to show he was complying. As he did so Dorothy stomped down hard on Garin's foot and slipped free from his grasp. With her face contorted into a rigid mask of fear resembling Munch's famous painting she ran down the corridor. Behind her, Garin, who had recovered his balance, started to raise his gun. As Johnson's hands were already up he simply had to straighten his arm and pull the trigger. The gunshot was loud, the noise magnified tenfold because of the confines of the narrow corridor hemming them in. A neat hole appeared in the centre of Garin's throat as the nine millimeter bullet cut through his neck. Clutching at the blood that started to gush out Garin tottered on shaky legs then his face slackened and he toppled backwards like a falling oak. When he hit the floor there was a loud crack as his skull smashed against the tiles. But it made no difference to Garin. He was already dead.

Dorothy ran into Johnson's arms, screaming and shaking with fear.

"It's okay, it's okay," said Johnson but her body continued to shake uncontrollably so he held her until she stopped trembling. Then, seconds later, the corridor flooded with blue uniforms. Releasing Johnson passed her over to a Patrolman then holstered his gun and walked up to Garin. Up close his still face now looked serene. Peaceful. Johnson found this a little disconcerting as in life Garin had always worn a permanent sneer on his face. Kneeling beside the brutish enforcer he rolled up Garin's sleeve. There was a neat puncture wound with four fresh stitches at the top of his right arm. Exactly where Sal had stabbed him in the hotel. Johnson rolled the sleeve back down then stood up as Adams walked up to him.

"Is it him Joe?" he asked.

"Yeah, it's him."

"But why?"

"Probably fed up being the monkey. Decided it was time to be the organ grinder."

"I'll be glad to put this one behind me Joe. Jennifer's death has really thrown me. I can't even bare to think of the torment the Chief is going through."

"Well, at least we got our killer. That'll go some way to helping the Chief and Gabriella find closure."

"Yeah, hopefully," said Adams.

"What you do with Riley?"

"I gave him to one of the Patrol guys...told him to stick him in the back of one of the squad cars."

Outside Johnson found Danny stuck in the back of an Impala. He got him out and took off his cuffs.

"If you tell me the truth I'll let you walk. If you don't and you spin me a load of bull I'm putting these cuffs back on you and you can fend for yourself. Your choice Danny."

"What do you want to know?"

"How'd you end up here and why were you here?"

"I was in Molloy's having a beer with Smithy...that's the guy with the ginger hair that's dead...then somebody phoned me."

"To the bar?"

"No, to my cell."

"Who was the phone call from?"

"It was anonymous Joe...with-held number."

"I told you not to yank my chain Danny. Who made the phone call?"

"I'm being serious...the guy never said who he was and he didn't leave a number."

"You better not be bullshitting me."

"I'm not. The guy told me that if I was looking for Garin I'd be able to find him in St. Luke's getting his arm stitched up."

"How did he know you were looking for Garin?"

"Sure, everybody knows I'm after Yerzov and his mob. That hotel Yerzov took over is in Irish territory. You know that Joe...we grew up there. Hell's Kitchen is ours."

"Not anymore Danny. You've got to get with the times. Hell's Kitchen is up market now. Gentrified. Full of actors and artists."

"Full of stuck up assholes you mean Joe."

"Yes."

"Yeah, agreed but Hell's Kitchen is still Irish territory."

"So that's what this gang war has been about?"

"Yeah. Yerzov thought he could move in and nothing would be said but we're still here Joe and we're not having the carpet whipped out from under us."

"So you went to the hospital to do what? Whack Garin?"

"More like have a word with him, try and convince him it was in everybody's best interest if Yerzov discreetly moved back to his own part of New York."

"Yerzov's dead."

Surprise showed on Danny's face.

"Really?" he asked.

"I just watched him dying an hour ago on a hidden camera."

When he heard this Danny's face lit up like the Times Square Ball.

"Now that has made my day," he said. "Now we'll just have to contend with Garin."

"Not anymore, he's dead too."

"Jesus Joe, I'm gonna do the lottery today. It's not that often I'm this lucky."

"Okay Danny, it's good seeing you. Safe home."

Danny held his right hand up like they used to do in the old days. There was a small white scar across his palm. Johnson had one in the exact same place. As thirteen year olds they'd cut their palms with a steak knife then clasped their hands together and promised to be blood brothers. Friends for life. Johnson clasped Danny's hand like he'd done a million times in the past but not for years now.

"I love you Joe," said Danny.

Johnson smiled at this but it was true because he felt the same way. They'd grown up together, served in Iraq together and now even though they were on opposite sides of the fence as far as the law was concerned they were still life-long friends that'd die for each other.

"I love you too," Johnson said.

Danny released him, gave Johnson a curt nod then turned and walked away. As Johnson watched him leave he thought of the time Danny had saved his life in Saudi Arabia. 30th January 1991. The Battle of Khafji. During a fire-fight Johnson's gun had jammed as one of Saddam's Republican Guards had been about to shoot him. At the last second Danny had arrived and shot the Iraqi Guard instead.

Three hours later Johnson paid a visit to the Chief Medical Examiner's Office to view Garin's body. Again the receptionist with the wide mouth was working. This time she recognized Johnson and pointed him down to the autopsy room. When Johnson entered Firth was stitching up a large 'Y' in Garin's chest.

"There's a gown and mask in the locker Joe," he said.

After Johnson put them on he pulled on a pair of latex gloves and walked over to the table.

"Is there a scar on his left wrist?" he asked.

"No," said Firth.

"You're sure?"

"Positive but check yourself if you don't believe me."

Johnson lifted Garin's left hand and examined his wrist. Firth was right. There was no sign of a scar either on the top, the bottom or the sides. To be sure Johnson checked the right wrist as well. It too was scar free. Niggling doubts began to creep into Johnson's mind.

"Did you test his blood?" he asked Firth.

"Yes, some alcohol and cocaine."

"What about blood type?"

"A."

"A. You're sure?"

Firth turned and lifted up a clipboard with the 'Autopsy Protocol' sheet attached to it. When he passed it across Johnson ran his finger down the checklist and stopped at number 10: Blood Type. In the designated box next to it the letter 'A' was written in black ink.

"How many blood tests did you run?" Johnson asked.

"Three. I'm very thorough."

"What about his feet? What size trainer would he have worn?"

"Ten. It's also marked on the sheet. Number fourteen."

Johnson checked the Protocol Sheet. Again Firth was right. 14. Size of feet: 10. Now, the alarm bells in Johnson's head began to ring a little louder.

He thanked Firth then exited and went back down to the underground car park. As he drove up the ramp he went over things in his mind. The blood found in the minivan had been Type B not A and the size of the Nike trainer footprint found beside Richard Wright's body had been nine not ten. Add in the fact that Garin had no scar on his wrist and there was only one conclusion: Garin wasn't their man. The puncture wound in the top of his right arm was an attempt at misdirection which meant the real culprit was still out there.

Johnson drove home and hurried into the house. In the kitchen he dragged the wash basket out of the utility room then searched through it until he found his pants underneath a wet towel. He breathed a sigh of relief. If his wife had loaded a wash then the blood on the knees would have been lost. Racing back out to the car he made a quick return to the Medical Examiners.

"He's in his office," said the secretary when he entered.

Johnson thanked her then opened the office door and entered without knocking. Firth, who had been busy writing up notes, stopped what he was doing and looked up.

"Back again Detective."

Johnson held up the pants.

"Will you run a blood test on these?" he asked.

"Why?"

"I knelt in the killer's blood in the minivan after our gun battle with him."

"You don't want it done now, do you?"

"I'm sorry but I do."

"Okay," said Firth resigning himself to the fact. "I'll take a sample and run an analysis."

"Thank you."

Half an hour later Firth handed Johnson his findings on a fresh Protocol Sheet.

"Type O," he said as he passed the sheet across.

Johnson screwed up his face in confusion. Firth noticed his facial contortions.

"Something wrong Detective?" he asked.

"This doesn't add up," said Johnson. "Donato told me the blood in the minivan was B but this is O and Garin's blood is A.

"Maybe he made a mistake, isn't as thorough as I am."

"What was the blood type of the murdered girl in the back of the minivan?"

"She was Type B," said Firth.

"You're positive?"

"Oh yee of little faith," said Firth then he turned and walked across to a steel filing cabinet.

Opening the second drawer he hunted around then came out holding Kimberly Johnson's autopsy file. Withdrawing the Protocol Sheet he handed it across to Johnson: 10. Blood Type: B it said.

Johnson handed the sheet back to Firth then took out his cell and rang Donato. There was no answer. Johnson thanked Firth for the second time that day then once more got the elevator down to the underground car park and left. As he drove up 1st Avenue he decided to call over and see Donato at the Forensics Department in One Police Plaza. Donato would figure out what the mistake had been. Unless there'd been a third person in the minivan that had also been bleeding in the driver's seat? Johnson discounted this theory immediately. Only one man had been driving. At least that's all he had seen. When Johnson reached the car park outside One Police Plaza he phoned Donato but again there was no answer. Johnson got out then entered the lobby and got the elevator up to the fourth floor. Captain Nancy Wilson, the Head of the Crime Scene Unit looked up when he entered.

"Hiya Joe," she said.

"I'm looking for Donato," Johnson explained.

"You've just missed him. He's going on holiday tonight. Just handed in his Request Form."

"He can do it that suddenly?"

"Not usually but he said he needed the time off to recover from his sister's death."

"His sister died? When was this?"

"Three days ago, Friday afternoon. Didn't you hear? She hung herself. Donato was the one that found her."

Johnson stood there stunned as the jigsaw pieces started to slot into place.

"Where's he going?" he asked.

"Thailand, where he always goes. Says he's going to retire there someday."

Instantly Johnson thought of the gunman telling him to visit Isra Anuwat in The Sapphire Lodge in Thailand.

"Okay thanks Captain," he said then he made his way back down to his car. Once he was in the SUV he checked his Glock and took off the safety. Loaded for bear he stuck the gun back into his shoulder holster then drove over to Donato's townhouse on the Upper East Side. Not wanting to give Donato a heads up Johnson parked in a side street then walked round to find Donato in his driveway loading a suitcase into the trunk of his Chevy.

Chapter 33

When Johnson opened the front gate it squeaked and Donato swung around.

"Jesus Joe," he said. "You near gave me a heart attack."

"Just came over to give you my condolences, just heard about your sister."

"Yeah, tragic," said Donato beginning to relax a little.

"So what happened?" Johnson asked entering the driveway and closing the gate behind him.

"To be honest, I don't know. I called to see her on Friday and found her hanging in the hallway. She'd hung herself from the banister of the stairs."

"No note?"

"No, nothing."

"Was she married?"

"Yeah...just had a new born son too. Only two months old. The Medical Examiner thinks she had Post Natal Depression."

Johnson walked up to him, real close so that he could see into the trunk.

"You going somewhere?" he asked nodding at Donato's suitcase.

"The Hamptons. I need to get away for a few days, clear my head."

"Fancy Nancy told me you were going to Thailand, go there all the time."

Donato's eyes narrowed when Johnson said this.

"No," he said. "She's mistaken. I'm going to the Hamptons. Do you fancy some pizza Joe? I was just about to stick one in the oven."

It was an obvious attempt at changing the subject. Johnson decided to play along.

"Yeah, sure, you know me. Never refuse food," he said.

As he followed Donato into the house Johnson opened the buttons on his suit jacket then slipped his hand underneath his armpit to open the clasp on his shoulder holster. In the hallway he noticed two more suitcases sitting side by side. When they entered the kitchen Donato opened the fridge and took out a pizza.

"Tombstone Pepperoni okay Joe?" he asked, looking over his shoulder.

"Yeah, great," Johnson replied.

As Donato ripped open the box Johnson scanned the kitchen. It was masculine with black gloss cupboards, charcoal counter tops and black appliances including the cooker and the fridge. A large oak table ran along the right hand wall surrounded by six black leather chairs. On top of the table was Donato's wallet sitting beside his passport. Johnson picked up the passport and flicked through it. Numerous stamps for Thailand were stamped on the pages. He set it down again as Donato, who had his back to him, ripped the cellophane off the pizza. Johnson lifted up the wallet and opened it. Inside in one of the pockets was Donato's Blood Donor card from the New York Blood Center. It was gold signifying that Donato had donated five to nine gallons of blood. Printed on the front was Donato's blood type: O. Johnson returned the card to the wallet and set it back on the table as Donato finished popping the pizza into the oven. When he turned around Johnson was standing with his arms folded trying to look nonchalant.

"You want a beer Joe?"

"Sure, why not."

Donato opened the fridge again and pulled out two Heineken. After he closed the door he bit off the bottle tops with his teeth and spat them into the sink.

"Old party trick," he said holding out one of the beers.

Before he took it Johnson glanced at Donato's wrist. There was a small white scar visible on top. Johnson accepted the beer then reached out with his free hand and grabbed Donato by the upper arm.

"Thanks," he said and then he squeezed.

Donato visibly winced. When Johnson released him Donato flicked his bottle upwards splashing beer into Johnson's eyes. Instinctively, Johnson brought his hand up to wipe his face. When he did Donato dropped his bottle, stepped in close and went for Johnson's gun. Johnson released his bottle just as Donato got the gun free then the two of them wrestled for possession of Johnson's Glock in the middle of the kitchen. Close enough to smell each other's breaths Donato head-butted Johnson but because Johnson had his chin tucked in Donato's forehead caught him on the top of the head rather than the nose. Now the gun was between them but ever so slowly Donato was managing to turn it towards Johnson's face. Fearing Donato would manage to get it twisted completely Johnson switched tact and pressed the magazine release so that the magazine slipped harmlessly to the floor. Now the gun was useless, a simple piece of hard plastic. Johnson shoved Donato back then bent down, scooped up the magazine and quickly stuck it into his pocket.

"Nearly," said Donato waving the empty Glock.

Then he pointed the gun at Johnson and pulled the trigger. There was an audible click but nothing else.

"Just in case you had one in the breech," he said. "Never know, I could've got lucky."

Donato set the gun on the table then spread his hands wide.

"You could let me go you know Joe."

"You killed Sal."

"He went for me...left me no choice."

"What about George Taylor then. Why'd you kill him?"

"He was my sister's friend...knew that Richard had raped her. Sooner or later he'd have said something to the police about it...would've led back to me."

"I don't understand."

"My sister was a painter...an artist. Richard Wright commissioned her to paint those portraits of dead musicians in the lobby of his hotel. He even commissioned her to paint a portrait of him...then afterwards...in his office...he slipped a roofie into her drink and raped her. She gave birth to his baby two months ago. To find out if it was his she got a DNA analysis done last week. You see, she'd just got married...wanted desperately for the baby to be her husband's...but as you know Joe, life isn't a fairy tale. The baby was Richard's so on Friday my sister left a note for her husband to find and then killed herself. Tied a rope around the banister then formed a noose and placed it over her head. But I was the one found Cynthia Joe. I was the one cut her down and found the note, read all about Richard and how he'd raped her. There was no way I was letting him live after that."

"Where did you take him?"

"Back to my sister's house. Made him look at Cynthia's dead body that I'd laid on the settee...then I got a Roofie Joe and made him swallow it. Three hours later when it had kicked in I got him to climb up on a chair then I put a noose around his neck and pushed him off. Afterwards, just to be thorough, I shot him in the head."

"You killed the Chief's daughter."

"I didn't know she was an undercover cop."

"Would it have made a difference?"

"No, she seen my face when she answered the door to me."

"Same as the prostitute in the hotel."

"Leave no witnesses Joe, you should know that."

"How did you get the keys to the minivan?"

"A lock pick. Used it to get into the house then took the keys."

"Then you tried to make Garin your patsy."

"I stabbed him in the arm as he was coming out of his apartment. What gave me away?"

"The lie you told about the blood in the minivan. You said it was 'A' but Garin's blood was 'B'. Then when I had the blood analyzed it was actually 'O', your blood type."

"So now what?"

"Now you should surrender...give yourself up."

"No thank you. I'll go for option B," said Donato then he charged at Johnson.

Having no time to move Johnson ended up tussling with him in the middle of the kitchen. Immediately, Donato sunk a hard knee into his balls forcing him to bend double and gasp for breath.

"Fuck, I felt that," said Donato now grabbing Johnson in a headlock.

Tightening his arm he slowly tightened the choke hold. Realizing he'd very little time before he went limp Johnson stamped down hard on Donato's foot. Donato squealed and for a momentary second his grip lessened. It was enough for Johnson. Using both hands he pulled Donato's forearm down, freed his head and stood up. Donato wiggled his foot to make sure it wasn't broken.

"Toe stamping Joe," he said. "You should be ashamed of yourself."

Johnson raised his hands into a boxer's stance.

"All's fair in love and war," he said.

Donato grinned.

"Ain't that the truth," he said and then he charged.

As he came in Johnson jabbed him twice in the face. Donato's nose sprayed blood but when Johnson looked at him he realized Donato was enjoying this. Donato raised his own hands now, copying Johnson's stance.

"This is the way all quarrels should be decided Joe," he said. "Mano et mano."

Johnson stayed quiet watching his eyes for a tell. Reading him perfectly, he palmed down his jab then followed through with his own jab over the top. It was a solid punch and his knuckles rapped against Donato's eyebrow splitting the skin and spraying blood onto Donato's white shirt.

"Bastard!" Donato snarled. "I only fuckin' bought this."

"Tough," said Johnson raising himself onto his toes

Screaming like a mad man Donato ducked his head and ran forward swinging wildly. Covering up Johnson took the punches on his forearms and backtracked out of range. Donato, falling into the trap, chased after him. When he did Johnson hit him a straight right down the middle snapping Donato's head back but it wasn't enough to stop him. Shaking his head Donato kept coming, spitting a glob of blood onto the kitchen floor as he advanced.

"Now that was sore," he said then lunging sidewards he scooped up a cup from the counter and launched it at Johnson's face.

"Here Joe, fancy a coffee," he shouted as the cup left his hand but Johnson's reflexes were equal to the task and he managed to get his hands up.

But it was enough for Donato to charge in again. With a loud thud their bodies slammed together and for a second time the two men swayed in a dangerous embrace.

"You're mine now fuck-face," Donato snarled as Johnson fought to break free.

But Donato's grip was like a vice. Growling like a wild dog he head butted Johnson hard in the face catching him on the cheekbone. Immediately, Johnson retaliated by head-butting Donato back but it was like a pea bouncing of a tank. Laughing, Donato head-butted Johnson a second time. This time Johnson got it in the mouth and his teeth rattled in his skull.

"How do you like them apples?" Donato snarled.

In response Johnson pressed his feet against the ground and pushed forward forcing Donato back against the fridge.

"Aaaaghhhh!!!" Donato screamed as his head rammed against the edge.

Seizing the opportunity Johnson freed his right arm and elbowed Donato in the mouth. Once, twice, three times. Donato let go of him and pushed him back. Using the lull to catch his breath Johnson stood panting, his hands raised and ready. In front of him, his face bleeding profusely, Donato licked blood from his lips then spat a glob on the floor.

"You're a tricky bastard," he said, his voice filled with hatred.

"And you talk too much," said Johnson, then, having had enough, he stepped forward and launched a five punch combination that he practiced regularly in the gym. Head, body, head, body then a brutish uppercut to finish. It caught Donato flush on the point of the chin and he dropped like a stone. Out cold.

Chapter 34

As Donato lay unconscious Johnson handcuffed him then used his own tie to truss his legs. Satisfied that he wouldn't be able to escape he walked into the hallway and checked the suitcases. As they were both filled with clothes he went out to the Chevy and opened the suitcase in the trunk. It was filled with the money taken from Richard's office. Johnson zipped it shut then lifted it out and walked round to the SUV he'd parked in the side street. After he locked the suitcase in the trunk he took out his cell and phoned Adams.

"What's up Joe?" Adams asked.

Johnson quickly explained the situation to him leaving out the part about the money. Adams told him he was on his way. When he arrived Johnson asked him to keep an eye on Donato then he went round to the SUV and drove back to his house. Carrying the suitcase upstairs he slid it under the bed then locked up the house and made his way back to Donato's. When he pulled up at the kerb the first thing he noticed was the absence of Donato's Chevy from the driveway. Johnson parked then jumped out and ran into the house. Adams was on the kitchen floor unconscious. Johnson slapped his face a couple of times to revive him. Eventually, after four or five slaps Adams began to wake up. Groggy and still a little disorientated Johnson helped him up then sat him on one of the leather seats surrounding the table. Once he was sure Adams wasn't going to keel over Johnson filled him a glass of water. After five minutes Adams was fully compos mentis.

"What happened?" Johnson asked.

"When Donato woke up he complained that the tie you'd wrapped around his legs was too tight and cutting off his circulation. Like a fool I took the tie off then agreed to let him sit at the table. To get up from the ground he used the counter as leverage then when he was on his feet he grabbed the kettle, swung round and hit me over the head with it."

As Johnson stood there wondering what to do next his phone rang in his pocket. He pulled it out and looked at the screen. It was Donato. Johnson answered and put the cell to his ear.

"This isn't over," he said.

"Shut up and listen," Donato said. "I have your wife so if you ever want to see her again go to Central Park now and bring along my money."

Johnson glanced at Adams to see how much he'd heard then walked out into the hallway out of earshot.

"If you harm her," he said. "I will scour the earth for you."

"Diana Ross playground in one hour Joe. Bring my fuckin' money."

Donato hung up. Johnson stood there immobilized for a couple of seconds then he gathered his wits and walked back into the kitchen.

"I have to go," he told Adams.

"Go where? What's up?"

"Personal business."

"What'll I do about here?"

"Call it in. Tell them about Donato."

"You sure you're okay Joe, you look a bit piqued."

"Me and Jane have been fighting...you know how it is."

"Can't live with them...can't live without them."

"Yeah, exactly."

Johnson turned and exited. Outside he phoned Jane's cell. Donato was the one that answered.

"Clock's ticking," he said before hanging up.

Frustrated, Johnson drove back to the house and retrieved the money then drove to Central Park and parked in West 81st Street. When he got out he checked his Glock but this time he put one in the breech. Satisfied, he walked into Central Park then over to the Diana Ross play park. When his cell phone rang he took it out and answered.

"Good man Joe. I like a man that's punctual," said Donato.

"I thought this was about your sister?"

"Started out that way but the lure of the lucre is too strong Joe."

"Okay, so now what?"

"Now I want to make sure you came alone Joe so walk across the park to the Metropolitan Museum of Art. If I see anything suspicious then Jane here is getting one behind the ear. Understood?"

"Put her on, I want to hear her voice."

A second later Jane's voice came through the phone.

"Don't come for me Joseph, he'll kill you. Stay away," she said.

Donato whipped the cell phone away from her.

"Don't be listening to her Joe. I simply want the money. Once I get that you and Jane can go play happy families."

"Okay, I'm walking over."

"And keep your cell on Joe, I like talking to you."

"Don't be hurting my wife Francis."

"Don't you worry about that. You give me the money and she'll be fine."

It took Johnson ten minutes to reach the Museum.

"Okay, I'm at the front doors," he said.

"Go to the Department of Arms and Armor and wait," said Donato and then he hung up.

Johnson entered the museum then walked round to "The Department of Arms and Armor". It was an awe inspiring exhibition displaying knights of old in polished armor complete with lances and swords. Most of the figures were mounted on horseback but a few armored knights stood ready for battle in glass cases. Johnson stopped beside a huge photograph of Dr. Bashford Dean, the department's founding curator. Dressed as a Samurai warrior he looked vital and alive in the aging photograph. After ten minutes when there was still no sign of Donato Johnson decided to phone his wife's phone again but as he pulled out his cell Donato materialized in front of him with a nauseating grin on his face.

"Is this for me?" he asked taking the suitcase out of Johnson's grasp.

"Where is she?" Johnson asked.

"All in good time Joe. Just have a bit of patience. Once I'm clear and I've checked that the money's all here I'll release her."

"You better," Johnson said.

Donato nodded then turned and exited. As soon as Donato was out of sight Johnson took out his cell and phoned Riley.

"He's on his way Danny. Make sure you don't lose him."

"Don't worry Joe, I'm on him."

"Just find my wife Danny."

Johnson went back out to the SUV. As Danny phoned through updates he followed his directions until Danny told him Donato had entered an apartment block just off 11th Avenue. Johnson put his foot to the pedal and hurried over.

"How long's he been inside?" he asked when he got out of the vehicle.

"Two...three minutes."

"Which apartment?"

"Third floor, number nine."

"Which one is that from here?"

"Up there. That one with the red curtains," said Danny pointing.

Johnson pulled out his Glock and clicked off the safety.

"You want me to go up with you Joe?" Danny asked.

"No buddy," Johnson said holding up his hand. "This is something I have to do alone."

Danny grasped Johnson's hand in their old grip.

"Be careful," he said.

"It's my middle name."

Johnson went up the fire escape at the back of the apartment block. Outside the window with the red curtains he stopped and tried to find a gap to peer through. Suddenly the curtains parted and there was Donato with Johnson's wife in front of him, his gun pointed at her head.

"I saw your shadow Joe," he shouted out. "Come on in."

Instinctively, Johnson had stepped back and raised his own weapon. Now he aimed it through the window at Donato's face. Donato made Jane open the window.

"You shouldn't have come Joseph," she said.

Johnson clambered through the window with his gun still up and pointed.

"Right, close the window and the curtains Joe," said Donato.

Johnson did as he was told then stood in the middle of the room with his gun pointed at Donato whilst in turn Donato pointed his weapon at Jane's head.

"Who else is with you?" Donato asked.

"The whole building is surrounded. You may give up."

Donato laughed at this.

"You're on your own Joe, aren't you? The Lone Ranger."

"No, the building is surrounded. Half the Precinct's down there."

Then Donato stiffened.

"There's somebody else at the window," he said.

Johnson turned and looked. True enough, through the curtains the outline of a shape could be seen.

"Bring whoever it is in Joe."

Johnson opened the curtains and then the window with his gun still trained on Donato. Standing outside on the fire escape with a sheepish grin on his face was Danny Riley. In his hand was a ridiculously large handgun, a Desert Eagle .50 Caliber pistol. Johnson opened the window.

"Come in Danny," he said, "but keep that cannon up."

Riley climbed through and stood beside Johnson.

"Sorry," he said.

"Don't worry, he spotted me too."

"Flimsy curtains," Donato explained.

Again Johnson closed the window and then the curtains. Now there were two of them with their guns trained on Donato.

"Okay gentlemen, this is the way it's going to work," said Donato. "I'm gonna back out of here with Jane and the suitcase whilst you two gentlemen stay right here and chew the fat. Agreed?"

"No," said Johnson stepping forward and placing his gun against Donato's forehead. "This is the way it's going to work. You're going to release my wife or I pull the trigger and blow your brains out."

"But think about that Joe. Even if your bullet did manage to enter my brain before I pulled the trigger my finger would spasm automatically. Jane here would be dead too."

"That's a risk I'm willing to take. Are you?"

"Yeah, let's play Joe, you know me. Always like to roll the dice."

Danny walked over then and placed his big monstrosity of a gun against Donato's nose.

"I want to play too," he said.

"Ok," Johnson said. "I'm gonna start counting up to three. Once we reach three we pull the triggers. Agreed?"

"Agree..." Donato started to say and Johnson pulled the trigger.

At the same time Riley yanked Jane forward and down away from the barrel of Donato's gun but Donato never got the chance to pull the trigger. Instead he flew backwards and landed in a heap on the settee, a big smoking hole in the middle of his forehead.

Chapter 35

Sal's funeral was the next day. Johnson got up at 8am and woke his children. Jane was now staying in her mother's.

"Why is Mom in Granny's Daddy?" Rebecca asked.

"She just wanted to see her own Mom," said Johnson not wanting to divulge his wife's infidelity to his children.

"Is she going to your friend's funeral?"

"Yes, we'll see her there."

Johnson dressed in his blue dress uniform. The funeral cortege was scheduled to leave Sal's apartment at eleven that morning but he wanted to get to Sal's apartment a couple of hours beforehand to spend some time with Gabriella and Angelo. Downstairs he made the children their breakfast: Cereal, tea and toast. After they'd brushed their teeth and pulled on their jackets he loaded them into the SUV and they drove over to Sal's.

When they walked up the pathway Johnson knocked the front door then waited patiently with his children clustered around him. Ten seconds later Gabriella answered with a handkerchief in her hand. She had a plain black dress on and her hair was tied back in a tight ponytail with a black ribbon. Her face was puffy and the redness around her eyes indicated she'd been crying. When she seen Johnson and his brood she burst into a fresh flood of tears so Johnson stepped into the hallway and hugged her. As he rubbed her back and tried to soothe her she dropped her head onto his shoulder and wept. After a minute she composed herself and straightened up so he let her go. Sniffing loudly, she gave him an apologetic smile then dabbed at her face with the handkerchief.

"I'm sorry Joe," she said.

"You don't have to apologize to me Gabriella," he replied.

She smiled weakly at him, all her inner strength and vitality gone.

"Come on into the kitchen," she said. "I'll make you a cup of coffee."

"No, I'm okay," he said.

"No to coffee Joe? That's a first," she said, a brave smile on her face.

"I don't want to put you out," he said.

She grabbed his arm.

"Stop being silly Joe. Come on."

As they walked towards the kitchen they passed the living room door which was wide open. Johnson glanced in at the coffin perched on the chrome stands. Angelo was at the side in a black suit staring at his father's face. Johnson stopped and watched him, his heart tightening at the sight. Gabriella appeared at his shoulder.

"I've told him his Daddy's in heaven," she said.

"And what did he say?" Johnson asked wanting to hear the answer.

"He asked me if his Dad was an angel now. I told him yes."

"God bless him," said Johnson feeling his throat contract with sorrow then before he started crying he turned away. Gabriella, who was right beside him, couldn't help but notice the grief on his face.

"Come on, I'll make you that coffee," she said.

When they entered the kitchen it was packed solid with Sal's family. His mother and father were there as too were his Aunts and Uncles, his younger brother and his three sisters that looked like they modeled for a living with their dark Italian looks and brown eyes. Bonfilia, the oldest, whose name meant 'good daughter', pushed her wheelchair over to him when he entered. When she reached him she beckoned him to bend down then hugged him fiercely before holding him at arm's length.

"Thank you for killing my brother's murderer Joseph," she said.

"I'd no choice," he said. "He was about to shoot my wife."

Bonfilia again grabbed him down to her but this time she kissed him lightly on both cheeks. When she released him she gave him a curt nod then wheeled back to her sisters. Behind her Johnson straightened up in time to accept a cup of coffee proffered by Gabriella.

For the next hour they stood in the house chatting quietly then at eleven precisely two burly funeral directors arrived wearing long black coats and solemn faces. After draping the green and white NYPD flag over the coffin they carried it out into the hearse. Once it was safely loaded one of them nipped back in and retrieved the chrome stands the coffin hand been displayed on. Slowly, the apartment disgorged the mourners until only Gabriella and Angelo along with Johnson and his daughters were left in the apartment. Gabriella took her son by the hand then opened the front door to exit but when she looked outside her breath caught and she stopped dead in her tracks. Lining the street, in fact covering it as far as the eye could see, were thousands of uniformed police officers from the NYPD, state police and upstate New York, all waiting patiently to pay their respects to their fallen comrade. Gabriella's heart swelled with pride whilst Angelo's eyes bulged in amazement at the sea of blue blanketing the street. As they walked down the pathway every officer waiting took off their hat and held it across their heart. Gabriella straightened her back and lifted her head. Clasping her young son's hand her eyes glistened with tears as she joined the front of the funeral cortege. Slowly, the hearse in front started to make its way through the streets of Little Italy. As it passed the uniformed mourners they lifted their white gloved hands and saluted Sal on his final journey. Johnson walked with his three daughters in the second row behind Sal's immediate family. Surreptitiously he glanced around looking for Jane but he couldn't see her. Behind him walked the Lieutenant and Charles B. Firth, the

Medical Examiner whilst at the front leading the mourners ahead of the hearse were the NYPD's Emerald Society Bagpipe Band playing "Amazing Grace."

After a few hundred yards the funeral directors asked people to give the coffin a lift so Johnson joined Sal's brother and father and three cousins then together they carried Sal on their shoulders towards St. Joseph's church in Babylon. After three more lifts from different groups of six the coffin was once more placed in the back of the hearse. This was the signal for everyone to go to their cars and drive to the church.

At the funeral service Johnson sat in the front pew with his daughters. As at all NYPD funerals, the Mayor got up and spoke. Staying with tradition he announced that Abramo had been posthumously promoted to Detective First Grade. Johnson thought it was a nice gesture as it increased the widow's pension that Gabriella would receive. Not that she'd be needing it as Johnson had given her the suitcase of money he'd taken from Donato.

"It's a small measure of our appreciation for the supreme sacrifice that he made," the Mayor said. "Salvatore Abramo died a hero."

When the Mayor finished his eulogy the Police Commissioner got up and spoke.

"Detective Abramo was a role model," he said. "A man people looked up to and admired. Throughout his life he firmly believed that good should prevail over evil which is why other Officers felt safe in his presence. He was experienced, tough and hugely respected but he didn't start out like that. Like all of us that are standing here in uniform today Sal too began life in the NYPD as a rookie. 1992 was the year he joined the service which as we all know was a year when the crack epidemic was on the rise and violent crime was at its peak. Back then and throughout his career Sal was on the front lines but he handled everything that came his way. Never ducked an assignment. It must also be mentioned that during his time on the force crime plummeted by ninety per cent in his precinct which is a sign of his dedication and commitment to the job. Unfortunately, this brave man has now been taken from us but he is not forgotten and either is the bravery he showed whilst doing his duty."

When the Commissioner finished Gabriella stood up and made her way up to the pulpit.

"First of all I'd like to start by saying that my husband would be so honored and so proud if he knew that all these people...fellow officers...were going to attend his funeral," she said. "It makes me proud to be the wife of an NYPD officer for Sal was a brave man, a loving husband and a dedicated father. It is said that when a hero falls, an angel rises. I believe that to be true of Salvatore Abramo, my husband. May he rest in peace for eternity."

Once the ceremony was over six uniformed officers wearing white gloves carried Sal on their shoulders out into the hearse with their arms crossed in front of them. Once the coffin was loaded into the back Johnson got into the SUV and drove to the cemetery with his three daughters. One of the first cars to arrive they had to wait ten minutes before the hearse turned up and the undertakers unloaded the coffin. The priest from the church, Father Carbone, arrived shortly after them with a black monkey hat pulled down tight on top of his head to ward off the biting wind. It was bitterly cold and Johnson was glad he'd made his children wrap up and wear coats. As the crowd filtered into the graveyard Johnson spotted Jane with her sister Dawn. Johnson turned away before she caught him looking. When everyone was present Father Carbone led them in prayer, starting off with the "Our Father" and then the "Hail Mary". When the prayers were finished he invited the immediate family to throw soil onto the top of the coffin which had been lowered into the grave by two undertakers. The first to take up the offer was Gabriella, who after throwing soil in with the trowel given to her by one of the undertakers, dropped a single red rose into Sal's grave. It was a poignant moment, one Johnson would never forget as when the flower left Gabriella's hand her knees buckled and she started to fall. Johnson, who was standing next to her, lunged forward and grabbed her by the arm. Pulling her back he held her as she sobbed uncontrollably. A heart wrenching sound made all the more terrible by Angelo's own sad chorus.

After the burial Johnson dropped his children off at his Mom's then went to Sal's wake to get drunk. It was being held in The Mulberry Street Bar, only three hundred yards from where Sal had lived. The barman, a small beefy man with only three fingers on his right hand, regaled those present with a story about Sal and how one night he'd stopped two crack heads from robbing the place by banging their heads together and knocking them unconscious. This proved to be the spark that lit the flame. For the next three hours stories abounded about Sal's heroics until eventually someone suggested in all seriousness that a statue of Sal should be erected outside One Police Plaza. Johnson, a sad, forlorn figure in the corner of the bar, raised his glass of whisky and seconded the motion.

THE END

If you would like a free sneak preview of the first chapter of the next book in this series then please email below:

newvisionbooks@hotmail.com

Fidelis ad Mortem series: Book 2 coming soon.

Printed in Great Britain
by Amazon.co.uk, Ltd.,
Marston Gate.